A PLUME BOOK

THE BUTTERFLIES OF GRAND CANYON

MARGARET ERHART is the author of five novels. Her fourth, *Crossing Bully Creek*, won the Milkweed National Fiction Prize. Her essays have appeared in *The New York Times*, *The Christian Science Monitor*, and in several anthologies, including *The Best American Spiritual Writing 2005*. Her commentaries have aired on National Public Radio. She lives in Flagstaff, Arizona, and teaches creative writing to elementary school students. She is a hiking guide in Grand Canyon.

Praise for *Crossing Bully Creek*

"Erhart's descriptions of her characters are reminiscent of Jane Austen's, in their devastating precision." —*Los Angeles Times*

"*Crossing Bully Creek* is likely to be mentioned in the same breath with Faulkner because they share some commendable commonalities." —*The Historical Novels*

"Erhart's well-crafted, comp   the Deep South from the Depression to the   gs back and forth in time." —*Booklist*

Pr

"The author of the ma   *Cotton* gives us another quiet novel that reve   ths of the soul." —*Booklist*

Praise for * sta Cotton*

"Engaging . . . Erhart movingly portrays her protagonists contending with more of life than they can grasp." —*Publishers Weekly*

Praise for *Unusual Company*

"The novel unfolds like a movie." —*The New York Times*

Queen   Old World Swallowtail

the Butterflies of

GRAND CANYON

MARGARET ERHART

Schellbach's Fritillary

Dogface

Buckeye

A PLUME BOOK

PLUME
Published by the Penguin Group
Penguin Group (USA) Inc., 375 Hudson Street, New York, New York 10014, U.S.A. •
Penguin Group (Canada), 90 Eglinton Avenue East, Suite 700, Toronto, Ontario, Canada
M4P 2Y3 (a division of Pearson Penguin Canada Inc.) • Penguin Books Ltd., 80 Strand,
London WC2R 0RL, England • Penguin Ireland, 25 St. Stephen's Green, Dublin 2, Ireland
(a division of Penguin Books Ltd.) • Penguin Group (Australia), 250 Camberwell Road,
Camberwell, Victoria 3124, Australia (a division of Pearson Australia Group Pty. Ltd.) •
Penguin Books India Pvt. Ltd., 11 Community Centre, Panchsheel Park, New Delhi – 110
017, India • Penguin Group (NZ), 67 Apollo Drive, Rosedale, North Shore 0632, New
Zealand (a division of Pearson New Zealand Ltd.) • Penguin Books (South Africa) (Pty.)
Ltd., 24 Sturdee Avenue, Rosebank, Johannesburg 2196, South Africa

Penguin Books Ltd., Registered Offices: 80 Strand, London WC2R 0RL, England

First published by Plume, a member of Penguin Group (USA) Inc.

First Printing, January 2010
10 9 8 7 6 5 4 3 2 1

 REGISTERED TRADEMARK—MARCA REGISTRADA

LIBRARY OF CONGRESS CATALOGING-IN-PUBLICATION DATA

Erhart, Margaret.
  The butterflies of Grand Canyon / Margaret Erhart.
    p.   cm.
  ISBN 978-0-452-29549-0 (pbk. : alk. paper) 1. Married people—Fiction. 2. Flagstaff
(Ariz.)—Fiction. 3. Domestic fiction. 4. Nineteen fifties—Fiction. I. Title.
  PS3555.R426B88   2010
  813'.54—dc22   2009034102

Printed in the United States of America
Set in Horley Old Style
Designed by Eve L. Kirch

For my father, who loved the river
that runs through Grand Canyon

By now, it is well known that the picture of the scientist as the eccentric personality without human feeling, pursuing truth by the numbers, wearing sterile gloves at all times, is false. But the particular way that a person trained in logical thinking must negotiate his or her way through the illogical world of human passions—that is a subject worthy of art.

Alan Lightman, *Nature* magazine, March 17, 2005

ACKNOWLEDGMENTS

As a fiction writer, I am more apt to foray into the realm of motive than I am into a world of scientific data. But this book called for facts, and in this area my guides were many, past and present. Dr. Larry Stevens shared his prodigious knowledge and curiosity about every bit of flora and fauna in the Grand Canyon region, and especially the butterflies. Glenn Rink, a modern-day Elzada Clover, helped out with cacti. Christa Sadler made the rocks come alive, and Northern Arizona University's Cline Library provided me with an excellent collection of photographs and correspondence that breathed life into the historical characters who populate this novel. I am especially indebted to Louise Hinchliffe, Preston Schellbach, and Steve Verkamp, who shared their memories of the South Rim and the people who lived there in the 1950s. Kim Besom and Colleen Hyde made the Grand Canyon Museum Collection available to me. Jim Babbitt generously offered historical information about Flagstaff. For critical readings of the manuscript in all its many incarnations I would like to thank Ann Baker, Stephany Brown, Stephen Erhart, Victoria Erhart, Rose Houk, Warren Perkins, and Ann Walka. Tony Hoagland, poet and friend, provided H. C. Bryant with the title *What Narcissism Means to Me*. Ann Hadley drew the butterflies. Countless others, with whom I've hiked or run the river, have contributed to this book by their contagious passion for a place—this place—Grand Canyon. To them I say thank you and read on.

Prologue

The trail to the river is steep, the footing unreliable. An animal track is what it is. Bighorn sheep, mule deer. Water is life and takes life, as he well knows.

His traveling companion has the pale, fleshy look of an indoorsman. Last night they camped at Cottonwood Creek, and the city man complained of the food while above them the stars spread thin and bright across a blue-black bucket of sky. The man likes it here where the canyon opens and the sky is broad, but the city man took no interest in what hung above them. Instead, he opined on the scarcity of flavor in his tinned stew.

The man showered this morning at the pourover down canyon and air-dried in the shade of a cottonwood—it was shade hot already. The city man scarcely wet his head. He'd brought a comb and stood over a pool, grooming his reflection. It was then the conversation turned muddy. He asked about the gun, and the man in the shade said it was nothing; he carried it out of habit and duty. The city man let on he didn't believe that, but he wasn't a coward either. Maybe there were dangers—lion or bear? The man in the shade nodded without saying yes.

Now they've hiked out a few miles to the west and come to the cairn that marks the vertical trail. The ground is soft and clouds of dust rise behind their boots as they descend. The city man pants with the effort of holding back. He can see the river below him, the liquid tongue of a rapid. He can feel it wanting him, drawing him downward. His thighs burn and his legs shake. He's afraid of falling and certain of it. He calls ahead to the other and says, "I'm going back." He turns, but in turning dislodges a rock that starts the earth around him sinking and sliding, and he slides with it, grabbing with his good arm at roots and rocks and a flat green cactus. The sky above him is dressed for a storm and he sees it. All the while he hears the sound below, the rapid's deep exhalation, like the openmouthed breathing of a heavy sleeper.

Later, on the way up, the man removes his pistol and thinks to throw it in the river from above. But he buries it in his pocket again and climbs with the agility of an unburdened traveler. His lungs fill and empty, and he can feel their rhythm and that of his heart. Briefly, he thinks of Gracia, though he does not allow himself to feel victorious. It has not gone as he wished. There was no suitable ending. The rain is behind him. He can feel it, a light spray borne by the wind. The air is cool, almost cold, the noise of thunder sharp and increasing. An urgency compels him as he gains the flat ground and hurries eastward, stopping at the creek only to eat and fill his canteen with water.

GRAND CANYON

1951

A Silver Ringing

The surprise to her is not how large the mountain looms but that it is, on the twenty-ninth of June, entirely covered with snow. The light is failing as Mr. and Mrs. Morris Merkle arrive at last at the little station in Flagstaff, Arizona. They see what appears to be a grubby town, but behind it stands a most awe-inspiring sight, an eloquent chapter in prehuman history: the San Francisco Peaks. It is not a chapter they have ever read before, or even conceived of, living in St. Louis.

Relieved to escape the train, they stumble across the platform, searching for their luggage and the Hedquists. Morris Merkle is experiencing some trouble breathing. Jane, his young wife, has a headache but hardly notices. It is cool, almost cold. Only a handful of people have gotten off the train, some of them just to stretch their legs. The station building is lit up inside. In the distance, high up against the darkening sky, a few gaudy neon signs advertise hotels—the DuBeau, the Downtowner, the Monte Vista. Fleabags, surely, thinks Mrs. Merkle.

Suddenly Morris calls out, "Dotty! Dotty, darling! Over here!" and walks quickly in the direction of a long-legged woman wearing a pair of dark slacks and a short canvas coat. Her face resembles his; her long graying hair is rolled in a bun in a way that nevertheless fails to make her look school-marmish. Jane Merkle has no recollection of this particular Dotty Hedquist. It has been two years since they last saw each other, and her memory of her sister-in-law is less complimen-tary, less womanly. In fact, in a shallow recess of her mind she wonders if there has been some change, some rearrangement in relationship perhaps, some affection or appreciation coming to Dotty from a quarter not connected to her marriage. These things have been known to make a dour woman glow.

"Jane, dear," says Dotty, and with great effort gives her sister-in-law a stiff hug, followed by a peck on the cheek. Jane feels almost as if she has been bitten. Dotty holds her at arm's length. "What a lovely dress you have on. It suits your youth. Quite the fashion, I imagine, though out here nobody pays much attention to any of that. You look so fresh!"

Oliver Hedquist heartily shakes Jane's hand, as he always does, and suggests they round up the luggage. The train whistle sounds, and the trainmen beam their lanterns under the wheels while the conductors hop aboard and in slow motion pull up the metal steps. The cars rumble by, gaining speed, shaking the ground, until the last one passes and there across the tracks lies the other half of town.

There are three bags on the platform. One of them is a large leather suitcase belonging to Morris Merkle, who, though he is not prone to thoughts like these, finds it almost an act of magic that he can pack shirts and shoes and trousers and socks and underwear and a good jacket or two into a defined rectangular space in St. Louis, Missouri, and without much attention to the process on his part, the whole lot arrives in Flagstaff, Arizona, and awaits him on the platform. He begins to walk away with his retrieved belongings. His brother-in-law points him toward the car. But Jane is not so caught up in the magic as her husband, for she has discovered that, of the three items on the platform, one belongs to her husband and the two others to a couple of mismatched ladies who rode the train from Chicago. One wears trousers, the other an orange dress. They are obviously old friends, traveling lightly. Yet she who packed a footlocker full of her favorite dresses and skirts and fancy blouses, and her good hairbrush with real sow bristles and a monogrammed silver back, is left in this new land with what she's wearing and the contents of her purse. This is the sum of it, and it will have to do until she finds a shop, which will surely not be this evening, or perhaps anytime soon. And as for borrowing clothes from Dotty, she quickly decides she would rather throw herself beneath a train. Jane Merkle has never believed in slacks beyond the confines of the home, except in winter when she has to shovel snow, and she strongly suspects, from earlier comments, that slacks are all poor Dotty's got. And yes, her sister-in-law cuts an impressive figure in them these days, but Jane does not, she's certain she does not, and she won't look a fool for the sake of conformity. When in Rome remember you're from St. Louis—that's her motto.

After much apologizing on the part of Oliver Hedquist for the loss of Jane Merkle's wardrobe, though in what way he might be responsible even he can't figure out, they pile into the Chevrolet and head off to find, in his words, "something to chew on." Jane Merkle hopes it won't be anything too old or tough or spicy. There are a few Chinese restaurants along the main road, which is the famous Route 66, Oliver informs them. Jane wills the car not to stop at these places, which are dimly lit and steamy, each with an old Oriental woman sitting by the window, gazing out. The car goes on, and finally they come to a Howard Johnson's. Oliver Hedquist pulls into the empty parking lot and Dotty says, "It's too cold for ice cream, Oliver." To which he responds, "I'm afraid I've got my heart set on fried clams."

They hurry inside and Jane, who hasn't had one in years, orders a chocolate milk shake. Dotty has a chicken sandwich and iced tea. The men order clams, followed by pie and coffee. Finally Oliver says, "Well, you two must be tuckered out, and we've got a drive ahead of us. Shall we?"

Jane dozes in the backseat and wakes to the swerving motion of the car and the dreamlike sight of two deer caught in the headlights, leaping across the road. Morris sleeps upright with his head against the window. She takes his hand, and he snuffles like a piglet and gently begins to snore. Later, in the Hedquists' home, in the bed she must share with her husband, Jane lies awake and considers the strangeness of having arrived at last at the Grand Canyon and found, to her great surprise, there was nothing to see, nothing but darkness. Despite the hour, Oliver had not driven them straight home but to the lodge on the rim, where he and Jane walked the few steps out to the edge of the canyon, which might have been the edge of the world. And behold! A great nothing! She must have expressed her disappointment, to which he replied, "Well, of course. There's no moon. You can't expect to *see* much. But there's no wind tonight, so you can hear it."

"Hear what?" asked Jane.

"Listen."

She listened. She struggled and strained to listen, and heard nothing. "I'm afraid I don't hear a thing."

"But you do," he encouraged her. "You've never thought of it as sound. You've thought of it as the absence of sound. It's that ringing."

She prayed to hear something ring. She wanted to please the old man. And just as she had given up and was about to lie—a little white lie—by saying, "Yes, of course. That ringing," she *did* hear it. How extraordinary. As loud as a swarm of mosquitoes, but set in a higher octave, and continuous. One continuous, clear, high-pitched silver ringing. The sound of the Grand Canyon. She laughed, and he did too. He placed his hand on her elbow, turning her in the dark, and without another word they walked back to the car.

The next morning her husband is not in the bed. She walks through the house and finds him in the kitchen, trying his hand at coffee.

"Morris?" She tries not to sound incredulous.

"Ah, dearest, good morning. I'm just . . . creating something here."

"A mess," she says. "I can see that."

"Well, yes," he laughs self-consciously. "I'm a few over par in the *cocina*, I must admit, but you, my lovely wife, were asleep, and the Hedquists seem to have gone out, and—"

"*Cocina*?" she asks.

"It means kitchen."

"It means kitchen?"

"Yes, it does," he says firmly. "In Spanish."

"You've taken up Spanish?"

"I have. I mean, I haven't, but Dotty has. She keeps the book right here by the sink so she can . . . let's see. So she can *lavar* and," he searches the page, "so she can *lavar* and *aprender* at the same time. There!"

Jane is beyond astonishment, but she keeps it to herself. She gives her husband the task of making toast while she organizes the coffee. She looks for eggs but finds none. There is almost nothing in the icebox and little to eat in the cupboards. Oliver's recent retirement seems to have taken its toll. She finds some old jam and a tub of margarine and places them on the table. Morris burns the toast but remains optimistic and cheerful. "Nothing a bit of scraping won't take care of," he announces. She covers her ears. She can't bear the sound of scraping.

"*Lavar, lavar, lavar*," says Morris to himself as he washes up the plates. Repetition is the only way he can learn anything. He is feeling different this morning, full of energy, alive and feisty, like a somewhat younger man. No wonder Dotty's having a go at another language. It's the air, perhaps. He's never been in air so thin, so unoppressive. It melts, that's what it does. Unlike Missouri air, which thickens as it touches the skin, this Arizona air seems to vanish as one passes through it.

Upon their return the Hedquists seem surprised to see him at the sink. "I've sent Jane off to get dressed," he explains. "She has nothing to wear."

"Well, she must borrow some of my clothes," says his sister, brushing past him, charging down the hall. "And Moose," she calls back, "for heaven's sake leave those dishes."

"All done!" he announces brightly, looking around for a towel on which to wipe his hands. And there it is, towel rack and towel located conveniently at hip level, close enough to the sink to be useful, yet not so close as to obstruct movement or catch one in the groin. The logic of domesticity suddenly overwhelms him. How is it that he's never noticed it before, never surrendered himself to its calming influence? The pair of plates clean and drying upside down, the washed utensils, glasses, coffee cups. It astonishes him, the simple pleasure of doing.

He has a sudden great thirst for tasks and says to Hedquist, "I'm a man on vacation, Oliver. Point me the way to the mower and I'll have a go at your lawn."

Hedquist laughs, "You're not in Missouri anymore, Morris. Come have a look at my lawn." He motions Merkle to join him at the window. Suddenly, from the direction of the village, a piercing whistle blows.

"Is that a train?" asks Morris. "I thought we were done with trains."

"It's the local line from Williams." Hedquist looks at his watch. "Two minutes late. Come," he says again. "Stand here and behold."

There is a certain jump in Morris's pulse as he looks out at the differentness before him. It is a different differentness than the barren tableaux he saw from the train: the land loping off in all directions, frighteningly dry, easily snapped and broken or lifted and blown by the wind. He had shuddered through the plains of Colorado, gritted his teeth through New Mexico. And of Arizona he had expected the same. He had prepared himself for an awful dread. He'd seen little of the state in daylight, and that suited him fine. By the time he arrived at the Hedquists' the night was inky black, so he'd imagined a lawn or two, some hedges to buoy his hopes, a sense of civilization amid desolation. But now, as he gazes through the pine woods and small oaks that occupy and define the Hedquists' yard, and lead in some mysterious way toward an opening, becoming themselves pillars along many avenues of light, he cannot be sure whether his heart races with the unexpected vision of beauty or with relief. To be sure he feels relieved. The trees give him a feeling of home, of Missouri, though they lack the lushness he loves. He thought he might, for the next fortnight, have to do without flora altogether, but it seems Arizona can grow a thing or two. Oaks and pines. Perhaps Dotty has a garden. Hedquist seems less interested in the intervening characters of trees than in the opening they point to, and says, "Out there, my friend, that's what whupped the conquistadores."

"Whupped?" asks Morris.

"Whupped." His brother-in-law nods. "Man called Cárdenas, García López de Cárdenas, parked his horse, fell to the ground, had a kind of epileptic fit right then and there. Plans ruined. Invincibility shaken if not destroyed. Seven golden cities—a dream, only a dream. Hopes for a Spanish world dashed to smithereens. That's what did it," Hedquist says, pointing. "That right there."

"What right where?"

"See it through the trees?"

"I don't see anything," Morris admits.

"People come here expecting a mountain," grumbles Hedquist.

A Tower of Good Intentions

At 11:23 AM, in her seat on the right side of the train, Elzada Clover consults her watch and announces to her companion, "We're running a few minutes late." Miss Lois Jotter laughs and says, "Calm down, Elzie. The canyon will be there."

"It's not the canyon I worry about. It's Louis Schellbach."

"Mr. Schellbach will be there as well."

"You're an optimist."

"I'm nothing of the sort. I'm a pessimist, as you well know."

"He's a very busy man, my dear."

"Who is anxious to see you."

"I hate to keep him waiting."

"Two minutes, Elzada!"

"We're now four minutes behind."

"You're impossible, as usual!"

"I'm not," says Miss Elzada Clover, briskly dusting the knees of her trousers. "I'm nervous. Quite a different kettle of fish."

She sighs and leans back in her seat, trying to relax. But the movement of the train is so jarring. It never used to be. What has happened? she wonders. Is it a change in her or in the railroad bed? Could it be that teaching all these years has made her soft? Lois was right to leave the university behind and sail off into married life.

She sees that they're approaching Red Butte. Not long now, not long. They cross into piñon-juniper country, a distinct line on the landscape that she calls to Miss Jotter's attention. "See, it hasn't changed, Loie. Twelve years later—"

"Thirteen."

"Thirteen, then, and still no transitional zone whatsoever. The abrupt shift in species. Highly anomalous. What purpose does it serve? And does grazing affect it? The uplift of the plateau? We must put our minds to it. That's another mystery I'd like to solve before I die." She glances at her watch again, her father's gold pocket watch. "We've made up some time."

Miss Jotter regards her skeptically. "How in the dickens do you know?"

"Do I know what?"

"Whether we're two minutes late or four?"

"Red Butte is a landmark, of course, as well as the piñon-juniper, and that outcropping there—it has no name—that's precisely twenty-two minutes from the South Rim station. We're due in at 11:45, and it's 11:26 at the moment, so forty-five minus twenty-six equals nineteen, minus twenty-two puts us at negative three, or three minutes late. It's simple math."

"Yes, I see!" laughs Miss Jotter.

"Nothing to it."

"You once told me that about playing the harmonica. Do you remember? Easiest thing in the world, you said."

"What I said was, it's no more difficult than kissing. No need to blush, Loie. What ever happened to that fellow you were so taken with on the Nevills expedition? What was his name? The actor from San Francisco? Gibson? Bob Gibson?"

"Bill. And I wasn't taken with him. He was an artist, not an actor. I don't trust actors."

"Oh, he didn't know what he was. Handsome, though. A good-looking boy."

"I wouldn't know." Miss Jotter shrugs. "I paid no attention to his looks."

"Too bad. He was really quite attractive. Pleasing. So few people are."

"Why, that's not true. Good looks are a dime a dozen."

"Ah, perhaps among the young."

"I'm no longer young, Elzie."

"Yes, my dear, I know. But you don't yet rank among the ancient."

"You don't either."

"I do, in fact. Fifty-four. It makes one shudder."

Elzada can remember, and takes this moment to do so, the last time she might have called herself young. She was forty-one, a few years older than Lois is now, a rose past its bloom, to be sure, but before her lay a tremendous adventure. She was to become, or attempt to become, the first woman to successfully ride the Colorado River through Grand Canyon. Only one other female had braved it, and she'd disappeared, presumed dead. Elzada was not the sort to let someone else's poor luck deter her, and besides, the opportunity for collecting along the way was unprecedented. No botanist had traveled the river before. The flora of Grand Canyon was virtually unexplored, unrecorded. A fellow by the name of George Vasey had been memorialized by his friend John Wesley Powell, who gave the botanist's name to a marvelous gushing spring: Vasey's Paradise. But Vasey himself had never set foot in Grand Canyon, much less sampled there, which was Elzada's highest priority. And to this purpose she'd brought along her teaching assistant from the University of Michigan, a girl named Lois Jotter. Elzada had the utmost admiration for Miss Jotter. She possessed intelligence and physical fortitude; she was young and pretty and had even rowed a boat before! And indeed, it had been a memorable expedition in every way. They'd gotten an exciting paper out of it, a groundbreaking paper. There was so much to study! So little was known about desert flora. So few had ventured out into the wilderness with their collecting bags, operating instead out of old books and defending dry theories. The historical information—so much of it was untested! And in Elzada's mind, there was no test better than experience. As she said to Lois time and time again as they stayed up into the wee hours of the Nevills expedition, listening to the river and filling their plant presses with the day's collections, "Let the old pedants sit in their classrooms spouting bombast till they're blue: the fact remains, it's difficult to dispute the sample in one's hand."

But Lois had needed to sow her wild oats, hadn't she? One

could hardly blame her. Elzada—not herself an oat sower—
nevertheless understood the necessity of the phenomenon. It
saddened her. She had in one fell swoop lost both companion
and friend. But here they were again, on a different sort of
expedition, one that required no sampling bag. Their old ac-
quaintance Emery Kolb, who had joined them those thirteen
years ago on the river, was in a bit of hot water. The call came
to Elzada from Louis Schellbach, chief park naturalist at Grand
Canyon National Park, a man she'd met only once. He asked
for her help and her strictest confidence in the matter, but beyond that she had only an inkling of what might be required of
her. At the last moment she had sent word that she was bringing along Miss Jotter, and if Mr. Schellbach disapproved, she
certainly hadn't given him time to say no. Which, right now,
seventeen minutes from him, made her nervous. Not that she
regretted her decision—she never did, any decision—but she
wished it to go smoothly for all of them, and she did not want
Lois to feel like an afterthought. She was, in fact, anything but
an afterthought, though Elzada had kept that to herself for
years and intended to continue to.

The train rattles fiercely along, swaying, thinks Elzada, like
a drunken bride. Where that image came from she has no idea.
She reports it to Lois, who laughs and says, "Well, it's common
enough, I suppose. I was a drunken bride."

"You weren't."

"I was. I was drunk as a skunk. You would have been
ashamed of me."

"Ashamed?" Elzada purses her lips. "No."

"You might have been. I wobbled up the aisle to say 'Yes, yes' and 'I do, I do.' Just the kind of thing you hate."

"I don't hate it. Why would I hate it? Agreements are noble if they're sincere."

"Sincere!" Lois laughs. "Sincerity and cherry brandy hardly co-occur. None of it made sense to me. Nothing I did that day made sense at the time. I couldn't wait to get out of my costume. I was dying for a swim somewhere, a long, cool swim."

"But it did make sense. It *has* made sense."

"Is that a question?"

"An observation."

"It's true."

"And why should it not be true?"

Lois looks at her lap. "I expect it offends you, marriage."

"It does nothing of the sort," says Elzada crossly. "Silly girl."

She had, in fact, been offended on the occasion of Lois's wedding for the simple reason she had not been invited. Perhaps this is why the girl remains Miss Jotter in her mind, when in fact she has become Mrs. Cutter. But no matter. As Norm Nevills, the great river runner, used to say, it's all upstream now. It's behind them. She sighs, thinking of Norm, the way he stood with his hands on his hips, his weight on one foot—the right foot—looking out at his beloved Colorado River . . .

"Elzie." Lois has a hand on her shoulder. "Elzada. There's Mr. Schellbach. Isn't that he?"

The train is no longer moving. How can that be? The moment of arrival has come and gone, and she's missed it entirely! She looks at her watch, sees that they are two and a half minutes behind, which puts them at somewhat less than that to the station—though, of course, she has no accurate data, which is as good as having none at all. Asleep at the wheel, Elzada! Ah, the crepuscular years. Will she nap through her fifties and on into her sixties, she wonders? Will she live that long?

Mr. Schellbach is quite difficult to miss. He's a lean fellow with a dark mustache (he must dye it) and an efficient gaze that searches the platform, regards each passenger as he or she steps down onto terra firma. The misses Clover and Jotter gather their bags—they are used to traveling lightly and carry only a change of clothes and shoes and a few toiletries and reading material, all of which fills one valise apiece. They descend from the train. Miss Jotter is wearing a thin summer dress the color of peach skins. Elzada sports trousers and a long-sleeved blouse that makes her feel boxy and mannish. Lois is a solid girl herself, but somehow she flows, thinks Elzada. And just at that moment the wind catches the skirt of the peach-colored dress and sends it spiraling upward. "Goodness!" cries Miss Jotter, laughing and batting at her clothing. "The darn thing's alive!"

Alive indeed. She looks like a daylily. *Hemerocallis.* The kind Elzada's mother used to grow in great rowdy bunches, one day there, the next day gone. Mr. Schellbach is upon them. He removes his hat and shakes Miss Jotter's hand. The mustache is certainly dyed, Elzada observes. The hair on his head is thin and gray. "Dr. Clover," says he, and the hand comes out once more. "We meet again. So glad you could come. And how was your journey? Come this way, please. Let me get your bags. This can't be all you have for luggage."

Lois says, "We're river runners, Mr. Schellbach. We've learned to economize."

He laughs, finding this charming for some reason, and Elzada feels a pang of jealousy run through her, a bolt of jealousy barbed and swift. "Yes," says she. "Miss Jotter and I used to travel the world together. We developed a habit of simplicity that's hard to break."

"Well, I don't know about the world, Elzada. We did a bit of traveling, it's true, but never what I would call—"

"We planned many trips."

"Yes, we did."

"And we accomplished one or two of them."

"We did, yes. We certainly did."

"It made us good travelers."

"I suppose it did." There is a silence; then Lois asks, "Do you travel much, Mr. Schellbach?"

"I'm afraid I don't, though Ethyl and I hope to visit Hawaii someday."

"Hawaii!"

"Ethyl is my wife."

They make their way across the tracks to Park Headquarters. Elzada wishes she had her hat, which is in her valise, which the park naturalist is carrying. She's quite forgotten how hot the southwestern sun can be, the noonday sun that casts no shadow save a small gray pool at one's feet. Miss Jotter and Mr. Schellbach carry on a conversation about the weather. The rains have arrived early, to everyone's relief. Even Miss Jotter, who has never given a moment's thought to the rains, is

relieved. Elzada follows along behind, feeling dull and unat-
tractive, unable to reconcile the Elzada Clover of the present
moment with the University of Michigan's most distinguished
professor of botany. She wonders what in the world she is doing
here, why she has made the trip, whatever possessed her to try
and recreate the past. Emery, she reminds herself. There's the
matter of Emery. And at that moment, as if reading her mind,
Schellbach turns to her and says, "I would rather introduce the
business here in the open air than in my office, which has ears."
He stops, sets down the luggage. "I sincerely hope you are prepared for a bit of nastiness, Dr. Clover. And you as well, Mrs.
Cutter. For it seems our old friend Emery Kolb has . . . There
is no way to put it delicately. Mr. Kolb has very probably . . .
er . . . committed murder." The misses Clover and Jotter gasp
in unison. "Yes, yes, I know," continues Schellbach. "It's quite
a shock. But we have recently been made aware of a body, a
skeleton at this point, stashed in his garage."

"No!" breathes Lois.

"And how does he explain it?" asks Elzada.

"He doesn't," says Schellbach. "He simply laughs. The seri-
ousness of the situation seems to elude him. Which is why I've
called upon you, in the hopes that you can talk some sense into
him before we're forced to take legal measures, which might
include," Schellbach lowers his voice, "arrest. It would be very
disruptive to the community, and we're trying our darnedest to
avoid it. But we haven't much time. Already the rumors are flying, as you can imagine. It won't be long now before the whole
grisly business explodes, and then we'll have a scandal on our

hands. Bad for revenue," he adds. "The parks, I have discovered in my time here, are about revenue, alas."

"Oh, I don't know," says Elzada. "It might be good for revenue. Scandal draws the curious, the lonely, and practically everyone else. Which is beside the point, of course. It's Emery we're concerned about. Being locked away in a cell wouldn't suit Emery. But tell me," she goes on, "why have you called upon me? May we sit down somewhere, Mr. Schellbach? I'm afraid I have rather painful varicose veins."

"Yes, of course. I'm so sorry. Let's wander over to headquarters. I have my car there, and I'll take you to the house. That way you'll have a chance to settle in."

"Settle in?" asks Lois.

"Ethyl is expecting you."

"Oh, we wouldn't think of it!" Lois exclaims. "That's very kind of you, but Elzada has made arrangements for us at the hotel. I'm sure we'll be comfortable there, and we won't be underfoot. And besides," she touches his arm, "Elzie snores."

Schellbach appears embarrassed. Clearly he doesn't care for the intimate turn the conversation has taken. He clears his throat and says with effort, "Doesn't everyone snore?"

"Not like Elzie."

Elzada smiles. "It's true. I'm an immoderate snorer."

"Well, you must at least take a few meals with Mrs. Schellbach and myself. The car's right over here. Why don't I give you a lift?"

That seems agreeable to everyone. As they walk, Schellbach says to Elzada, "My sister-in-law has varicose veins."

"Does she?"

"Yes. A terrible situation."

"One lives with what the genes dictate. Although," she adds thoughtfully, "there will come a day when we turn that around, when we dictate our own genetic makeup."

"But surely you don't believe that. Human beings are not corn, Dr. Clover."

"Why, Mr. Schellbach. Selective breeding is common botanical practice, as you point out, and being human, we can't stop there, can we? We won't. Who knows what we'll try next? Cows and fireflies—"

"But what would be the point?"

"Livestock that glows in the dark!" cries Lois.

"Yes," says Elzada. "A great boon to ranchers. No more tracking, just wait until the sun goes down. And from there it's a simple step to applying these practices to humans."

"Simple?" laughs Schellbach. "How simple, Dr. Clover?"

"When we crack the gene molecule—and we're very close, scientists in several different countries are working on it now—when we finally understand the configuration of DNA and the way mutation occurs, it will be a simple step from cows and fireflies to humans. Methodologically simple but morally tremendously complex."

"I should say so. It may be a long time before those veins of yours become a choice."

"The fact is," says Lois, "we're not so different from cows and corn, and that's difficult for people."

"To me," says Elzada, "it's a great comfort."

"But we *are* different," says Schellbach.

"Yes," Elzada says, smiling, "we can reason. And we're capable of love. And murder. Is this your car, Mr. Schellbach?" He nods. "Oh, it's good to stop thinking and talking sometimes, isn't it, and just go for a drive?" Silence. "Well, I think it is."

They drive around to the El Tovar Hotel and pull up in front. They get out and a bellhop comes and collects the two valises. When the boy has gone, Schellbach turns to Elzada and says, "To answer your question, Dr. Clover, the question of why we have called upon you in this unpleasant matter involving Mr. Kolb, I can simply report that he asked for you."

"Emery did?"

"He told Dr. Bryant and myself—"

"Dr. Bryant?"

"My boss. The park superintendent. We were told, in two different interviews, that you were not only sensible, knowledgeable, and a friend, but that you . . . ," he looks out across the canyon at the North Rim, where afternoon rain clouds are gathering, "that you . . . now I don't believe this, of course, I simply pass it along . . . he seems to feel that you might . . . how shall I put it . . . ?"

"Might *what*?" asks Lois impatiently.

"That Dr. Clover, impossible as it seems, might know, or rather, well, yes, know, something about the body."

"Good Lord!" exclaims Elzada. "Why didn't you say so?"

"He did," says Lois, crossing her arms. "He certainly took his time about it, but now he's said it. And it sounds to me like Emery's up to his old tricks. Implicating you, Elzada. Come on. We don't need to stand here and listen to any more non-sense and gossip."

"I wouldn't give that particular aspect of it another thought," says Schellbach, frowning. "And I know Ethyl will be very disappointed, as will I, if you won't join us for supper tonight. She'd like to make a fuss over you."

Lois opens her mouth to speak but Elzada says, "Supper will be fine, Mr. Schellbach. What time?"

"Six o'clock. Shall I come for you in the car?"

"We'll come on our own two feet," growls Lois.

"We'll be ready to be picked up at six," says Elzada. "We'll wait right here."

He drives away, and the women watch him go. Lois says, "That fool, Emery. I knew we couldn't trust him. It's center stage or he won't play."

"Yes, but we knew that about him from the start."

"To store the evidence in his garage!"

Elzada shakes her head. "Someone else did that. He was on the river with us, as you remember."

"The perfect alibi! He left the dirty work to an accomplice."

"Really, Loie, I must insist. It's possible but improbable. What would he want with the body?"

"I don't know, Elzie, but I'm nervous."

"You mustn't be, my dear. They'll sense it. They'll smell it, like sharks do blood. And we have very little to worry about, except Emery. My reputation protects us. In their eyes I'm a tower of good intentions."

"A tower of good intentions whose interest in genetic manipulation is no longer a secret. My goodness! I thought you'd never quit!"

"It didn't stop you from adding your two cents, did it?" laughs Elzada.

"I'm not used to hiding my opinions, I'll admit."

"Never mind. Nothing to hide here and now. Come, Loie. We need to elongate our horizon."

They climb the front steps of the hotel and Elzada first, then Lois, turns to look at the great painting hung in the open air beyond the porch—the enormous canvas that changes as they watch, as the clouds darken and descend and rain visibly lashes the far rim. It is a painting beyond price, a canvas few are lucky enough to glimpse, and the effect on the two women is one of overwhelming relief. They are here at last. Scandal, dirty business, and mystery swirl about them, but they are meaningless, as are most things, in the face of what lies here before them. The great canyon opens and offers up bars of sunlight, columns of rain, as if the sky exists below, inside it. Then a sudden crisp flash of lightning, hollow thunder. The misses Clover and Jotter jump and clutch one another and laugh, and Elzada, leading Lois by the hand, walks out under the expectant sky and waits there, until finally the rain comes hard and sharp, lashing their upturned faces and pouring in endless rivers from the roof of the hotel.

Over the Edge

Oliver Hedquist has plans this morning to introduce his brother-in-law to the wilds of Grand Canyon by putting a butterfly net in his hand. He can't imagine a more exciting adventure than a stroll down the South Kaibab Trail, looking for Behr's hairstreak or the Sara orangetip. The painted ladies will be flying, of course, and a variety of skippers, and with great good luck they may see a ringlet or two on the rim. Or a Riding's satyr—now that would be a find! He waits until the groceries have been carried in and the perishables put away before he suggests such an outing.

He doesn't know Morris Merkle well, has spent little time with him over the years—geographical distance has ruled that out. They were back east for the wedding, he and Dotty, and what a gloomy affair that was! St. Louis was veiled in drizzle, and the bride's brother, who gave her away, the father having passed on some years earlier, got rip-roaring drunk and relieved himself on

the pastor's habit or cassock or whatever it was. The cake, a four-
or five-tiered thing, was raw, the champagne flat, and tequila nonexistent. Of course. No one drank tequila. No one but vaqueros
and desperadoes and the entire population of Mexico. And Oliver, when he had a chance—he tended to overdo it, he wouldn't
be the last to admit. Oh, it was ghastly! He and Dotty had a bit of
a tiff, something about the bride being too young. His response,
regretfully, was that perhaps the groom was too old. That didn't
help matters. He liked to get along with his wife, it was so much
easier than being at odds with her, though he'd become quite ac-
customed to the odds over the years and had learned to approach
her at such times like a man swaddled in bandages.

Oliver quite likes his sister-in-law, Jane. In the five years
since the wedding she's grown up and come forward a bit,
though she's still extraordinarily shy. She is, of course, young
enough to be his daughter, or Dotty's, or Morris's, a situation
that must make her feel lonely. She has a habit of biting her top
lip after she speaks. Has she been chastised for having opinions?
He finds himself suddenly relieved that soon enough Merkle
will be on his way home and Jane, by her own choice, will stay
longer. He senses an opportunity in that girl. She's a sweet girl,
nice to look at, forehead not too high, with good strong, straight
hair the color of Brazil nuts (but just below the ears? why doesn't
she grow it out?) and eyes (he's hopeless at eye color) a piercing
blue (they're green, actually), and a small mouth that could be
larger. And the rest is a bit of a mystery. The first time they met
she was draped in bridal attire, all those billowing layers upon
layers that shroud the body, advertise virginal tendencies or

some such thing. And this time he's seen her only in the dark, wearing what he recalls to be an unflattering—though understandably comfortable—dress. No, he assures himself, she's no old-man bait. She's got an old man already and seems a bit restless with him. The opportunity, he feels, lies away from the vicissitudes of sex, in a place he can only identify as her curiosity, the wideness of her eyes and her apparent entrancement with this land, this place, this canyon, which first entranced him as well, years ago. And in she comes, just at that moment, dressed in Dotty's clothes yet wearing them in a way that Dotty never has and never will because she can't. This is youth. Youth in denim. How is it that these ordinary coverings take on such a splendid, promising look when youth resides within?

Merkle says, "Why, you look like a cowboy, Jane." He laughs irritably. "Is that all Dotty could come up with?"

"Oh," says his wife. "I think this will do, Morris. I'm comfortable enough and grateful to have clothes at all. Dotty's been more than patient. See, she even basted the hem of the blue jeans." She rolls up her pant leg to show him, but he's settling into a sodden, darkish mood and she adds, meekly, "They were too long."

"A success!" says Oliver with as much gusto as he can muster. "You look western indeed, my dear, and out here in the West we like that!"

"We've made things fit," says Dotty brusquely. "That's the best we could do and we've done it."

"Done it, and done it well!" cries Oliver, then wills himself to calm down. He doesn't want to scare the girl. He coughs to gain control of himself and makes this announcement: "Plans for the day include a picnic at Yaki Point and a foray over the edge for those willing. Willing to what? Willing to foray!" (Now, don't be an idiot, he warns himself.)

"The edge?" asks Merkle.

"The edge, yes. Precisely."

"The edge of what?"

The edge of what? Oliver inwardly groans. He says, as directly and informatively as possible, with just the slightest trace of exasperation, "The canyon, Morris. Grand Canyon. For here we are, meters away from one of the seven wonders of the natural world, and to fail to begin our exploration of it willy-nilly while the sun shines and the temperature remains pleasant and the invertebrates creep and fly—to fail to run out there right now and take a look at it and bring a net or two, why . . . why, what would we be, Dotty?" His wife gives him a blank look so he answers himself: "We'd be dotty!"

The girl laughs, then asks a surprising question: "What's an invertebrate?"

"Oh," says he. It's been years since he's had to think about what an invertebrate is, not that it requires thinking. He has to express the definition of invertebrate, which is no longer automatic to him because he hasn't come across anyone for quite some time who hasn't known it. (Though he has, of course, but in his blind passion he assumes everyone knows what an invertebrate is, what an insect is, what an arachnid is and an arthropod and a true bug.) "Well," he says, removing his glasses, polishing them up a bit, and returning them to his face, "*invertebrate* means, simply, 'without a spine.'"

"Like a jellyfish?" asks Jane.

"A jellyfish is an excellent example of an invertebrate."

"But not one that creeps and flies."

"Seldom," Oliver agrees.

"And not here at Grand Canyon."

"Oh, yes," says he. "Very possibly. Five hundred million years ago they were plentiful enough, propelling themselves through the sea." He adds excitedly, "This was a sea, my dear. Imagine it! A vast sea all around us, rimmed by sand dunes and fed by rivers. And jellyfish, or their ancestors, fanning their way through it, living and dying, falling to the sea floor as boneless piles of protoplasm. *But*, kind enough to leave trace fossils. We're not sure how they did it, but it seems to be the gas. The gas within, creating a little pocket of . . . well, gas, a bubble around which the sediments formed and were subsequently cast by time and pressure. Any of this make sense?" Jane nods and he wonders aloud, "How in the world did we get on to jellyfish?"

"Spinelessness," says Dotty with a little barbed wire fence of a laugh. "Oliver's specialty."

He laughs as well, a sign of greatness, or at least great manners, thinks Jane Merkle.

They sally forth, picnic packed, sweaters draped over shoulders, feet variously shod. The Hedquists have sturdy brown hiking shoes, Morris wears loafers, and Jane sports U.S. Keds. Off they go in the Chevrolet to Yaki Point, a short drive east along the rim of Grand Canyon. Dotty drives. Her brother sits up front with her, and Oliver sits in the back with Jane. The road comes so close to the edge sometimes, Jane finds herself leaning away from that fathomless chasm toward the safety of the forest on the other side and into her brother-in-law's formidable shoulder. Known for a certain Scandinavian boniness, Oliver Hedquist gives the impression of solid angularity wrapped in skin, like a worn paper bag of baseball bats. Against this redoubt Jane Merkle plunges in her flight from vertigo, only to realize that a dizzy spell is preferable to the strange experience of arriving alone on the uninhabitable shore of her brother-in-law's humerus. He, on his part, doesn't seem the least bit fazed by her plunging and launching. He tries to steady her by leaning ever so slightly toward her. Dotty, in the front seat, is pointing out the sights. "Moose—" says she.

"Where?" cries Jane, her heart fluttering in anticipation of a creature the size of the car, gangly and cartoonish.

Her sister-in-law laughs. "I meant your husband, silly. See the temples everyone? There's Zoroaster, Brahma, Buddha, Shiva. And over there, Wotan's Throne. It's a regular roll call of infidels, isn't it?"

Jane feels carsick but interested and peeks out across the vast space, bluish with haze. It is the first real look she's allowed herself, her first sight of the canyon in daylight. It's wider than she thought it would be. Somehow she imagined a slice, a sharp cut in the earth, but this is a ragged opening, full of what her in-laws call "temples," great vertical slabs of rock, flat-topped mountains, some of them tree-covered, others bare, rising up like islands in a dry sea. And everywhere a great convolution of folded land. Everywhere the spidery dry pathways of water etching their way downward in dark lines. If she half closes her eyes, she can see a great blue cloth, a heavy linen cloth folded upon itself in the blue haze—a lover's dress, a lover's cape, flung to the floor. And the sky a blade of blue above it all, and the snow shining on the northern shore (of course it's a rim, but to her it's a shore), the far shore of a river of air and light suspended in space, suspended in *spaciousness*, for goodness' sake! Not one bit like the river she grew up with, the muddy, shrieking, crowded, busy, bustling, big-shouldered, stevedored, hot, steamy, frozen, churning, legendary Mississippi. No, nothing like that. Suddenly it's all too much for her, the grandness, the majesty, the sheer size, the arousing sense of all that rock, sinuous rock—oh, it's too much. It overwhelms her as thoughts of death do, or the universe, which has no end anywhere, no edge. She closes her eyes and hears Oliver Hedquist say, "Ten years of looking out at that miracle and still I never see it to my satisfaction. Do you, Dotty?"

"What an odd question," says Dotty. She pulls the Chevrolet into the parking area at Yaki Point. It's a large car, and her confidence brings to mind the captain of some river barge. They choose a suitable tree, a stunted piñon pine, and plop their picnic down in the shade. Dotty unwraps a meager feast of crusty bread and a bright orange spreadable cheese that looks suspiciously like war rations, while Jane admires the tablecloth with its pattern of wildflowers and bees.

"It's just an old sheet," laughs her sister-in-law. "Can you imagine sleeping with all those bees? I never did get used to it."

"Morris is afraid of bees."

"Afraid? I should say so," Dotty replies. "You would be

too if you had his condition." Jane looks at her blankly. "Why, don't you know, dear? Hasn't he told you? Shame on you not telling her, Moose. Since he was a little boy, he's been allergic to bee stings."

Lunch leaves Dotty with a rare (for her) affliction: bad gas. And Morris, light in the head, due to the seven-thousand-foot elevation and a lumpish heart, feels an overwhelming need to lie down and nap. Oliver, with a butterfly net in each hand, stands before Jane. "Madame," says he, with an almost imperceptible bow. "Your weapon awaits you. Mightier than pen and sword combined, faster than a moving ringlet, if used well. Made of broomstick and bridal veil—the cross-pollination of virgins and witches. May I introduce you, Mrs. Merkle, to your future calling. Hark!" He cups his ear, charming and ludicrous man. "What do I hear? Is that your future calling? No, it's the dry cleaners. Your husband's suit is ready to pick up. But don't go!" he cries. "Resist! What we promise you here is the adventurer's life, guaranteed no money back, no money at all! You can be penniless, for heaven's sake, and enjoy every minute of it!" He calms his voice and says sadly, "Entomology's not a useless profession, Jane, simply a misunderstood one."

"Oliver," says Dotty from where she lies beneath the piñon, knees to her chest, trying to get some relief, "you'll scare the poor girl. Stop talking and get going." No sooner said than a great rumble erupts from somewhere near her hip, and Oliver and Jane move off swiftly in the direction of the South Kaibab Trail.

At first she isn't any good at all. Oliver shows her how to hold the net with both hands, but she feels too encumbered. Her sweeps are awkward and way off the mark. She has only slightly better luck slapping the net down and catching things on the ground. The targets, he informs her, are *Vanessa cardui*, otherwise known as painted ladies. "These butterflies," she pants, after one of her more dazzling sprints and misses, "stand a very good chance."

"One in ten," he laughs.

"One in ten?"

"Only one in ten is captured."

"I'm not surprised. But there must be dozens of nincompoops like me to balance out sharpshooters like you."

He is quite marvelous with a net, and she watches as he leaps and swings and pirouettes and swings some more. An old man! He rarely misses. He's airborne most of the time, and his wrist seems made of many moving parts—his whole arm does. It's like watching a delicate machine in flight, a delicate, deadly hunting machine. "You're a bird!" she cries in admiration, and he was but moments ago a doddery old fellow. He swishes his net. Like the tail of an angry cat, it makes a slicing sound in the air. Then she sees it. She sees the very thing he's doing that she's not, the source of his unhinged acrobatic joy: he's got only one hand on the net! He's twice as long that way, his reach is doubled, and he can sweep and slash unhindered; he can miss and turn and try again on a backswing. A backhand, that's what it is!

As luck would have it, she herself has a formidable backhand and a fifty-five-mile-an-hour serve, and the moment she sees how the Ballard Park Tennis Club ladies' division championship has prepared her for a life of collecting, a life of predation in the name of science, it's a sad day for butterflies.

No Traces

Jane cannot remember if the young man's name is Earl or Ewell, and this bothers her to the point where she's kept awake by it, a terrible night, not one wink of sleep. Pulling on her blue jeans in the morning, she wonders if Ewell is even a name, and if so, is it spelled Ewell or Yul or Yule? Not Yule, she decides. Might as well call a boy Christmas.

She has grown quite attached to her blue jeans, which she purchased against Morris's will on her seventh day in the West. She and Dotty drove to Flagstaff, where they ate their sandwiches at the Hotel Weatherford. They sat on the upstairs balcony with a charming view of the train station to the south, that fearsome mountain to the north. It was a surprisingly hot day and Jane wanted something cool and slightly wicked to drink, so they crossed the street to the Black Cat, where she ordered a beer. "A beer!" whispered Dotty. "I didn't have any idea you drank beer."

"I never do," said Jane. "I thought I'd try it."

It was, in fact, the first time in her life she'd ever ordered an alcoholic beverage at lunchtime, and she wasn't prepared for the wooziness she felt for most of the afternoon. But it made the shopping interesting. And Dotty became more fun. There was an underwater feeling to the day, which Jane quite liked. Nothing seemed very important. There was a sodden dullness to the world, and it was restful. Had she not had that beer, she wondered later, would she have felt comfortable enough to equip herself with an almost entirely western wardrobe? Probably not. She chose four new pairs of blue jeans and three western shirts, one in red and two in white. She bought an untooled brown leather belt with a silver buckle, and a long, loose, red cotton skirt. A flame of a skirt! That, she would wear to the party. For Louis and Ethyl Schellbach, the park naturalist and his wife, were having a party to which she was invited, along with the Hedquists, of course. Morris would be gone by the weekend. She needed a jacket of some sort, and Dotty recommended a black wool riding jacket, cut straight just below the waist, with wide lapels and a small slit up the back—very "caballera" she called it, whatever that meant. They picked up socks and bras and underpants at Fine's Ready-to-Wear, though the underpants, in their sheer lack of material, resembled nothing Jane had ever worn before. "Why, there's nothing to them!" she puzzled. Dotty cocked her head and passed along her decision: "There's enough."

The icing on the cake was a pair of jet-black cowboy boots, pointy and shiny, yes indeed, to be worn with the red skirt,

Dotty explained, or to dress up the blue denim trousers. "Blue jeans," said Jane. "They're blue jeans, Dotty. Get with it."

"*You* get with it," Dotty chuckled. She seemed to be enjoying herself as much as Jane. "Now, one last thing, dear. We need a hat."

"What kind of hat? I loathe hats. Oh, Dotty, Dotty, don't make me wear a hat!"

"Why, out here a hat is your best friend. A hat is your Saint Bernard, your salvation—"

"I can't. I won't."

"It's a must, my dear, an absolute not-to-be-done-without. You'll perish, it's as simple as that, if you step outside without your hat! Oh, I'm not talking about a pillbox, Jane. Or a beret, for goodness sake. Or one of those terrible tams my mother made me wear to school. I wore a pillbox to church, poor me. Can you imagine, me, little Dorothy, in her dark blue pillbox hat and her little white gloves? Oh, I never was much of a believer, I'm afraid. Maybe I would have been if Mother hadn't believed so strongly in starch. I think she believed in starch the way I was meant to believe in God. I sat, every Presbyterian Sunday, in a good bit of pain as a result. I don't think one is susceptible to abstractions when one is in pain, do you, Jane?"

But Jane had formed a question of her own. "Was Morris a Presbyterian?"

"Well, of course he was."

"He's always said he was an Episcopalian."

"An Episcopalian! How very odd. What does he know about Episcopalians?"

"Nothing, I imagine."

"Does he go to church?" asked Dotty. "Well, of course, you were married in a church."

"We aren't much for church," said Jane. "I don't know why we got married in a church. A park would have suited me more, a meadow by a stream. But I suppose a church is expected."

"Yes, when it comes to marriage, many things are expected." Dotty forced a little laugh. "Children, for example."

"Yes," sighed Jane.

"Now, you would tell me, wouldn't you, if there was a bun in the oven?"

"I would," said Jane.

"I could never, frankly, imagine Morris with a child."

"No."

"But you, dear?"

"Well, I'm married to Morris."

Dotty cocked her head. "Where there's a will there's a way, that's what I say. To every problem there's a solution."

"Oh, I don't know that it's a problem—"

"Not at this moment, perhaps."

They wandered down Beaver Street after that, saying very little, looking in shop windows. An inexpensive yet well-made straw hat was what they were after, and what they soon found. Dotty used the word *handsome* to describe it, and it was, in fact, a handsome hat for a man as well as a stylish hat for a woman. It had a slight crease in the crown and a widish brim, and the hatband was a simple leather cord that came down to tie under the chin. It was made of pale straw, a blond straw that complemented Jane's dark hair. They bought it at a small shop on Route 66 that sold hats to tourists, and at the time of their transaction it was crowded with a whimpering, red-faced group for whom it was already too late. "You see," Dotty poked Jane in the arm. "Cooked lobsters! That's how you know who's from here and who's not."

Jane was startled by a sudden feeling of wanting to be "from here"—perhaps brought on by the sight of these human crustaceans. The feeling passed, but the shock of it lingered. Hadn't she but a week before been unequivocally, if not happily, from St. Louis?

She thinks of this again as she dresses. It must be very early still; the sky is just beginning to lighten. She knows how quickly the light comes when it comes, here in Arizona, an avalanche of gray becoming white, a sudden opening of the day, which doesn't happen in the same way back east. And here there is a sky. Such a blue one—a turquoise one! Oh, for heaven's sake, she thinks, my ring! Where on earth is my turquoise ring? She hasn't had it on or thought of it since she took it off on the train. She bought it at the station in Albuquerque, from an old Indian woman selling jewelry on the platform. The woman had a blanket draped across her shoulders, and she leaned across the table and put the ring on Jane's finger herself. Suddenly, quite irrationally, she's afraid it's somehow gone back home with Morris. But of course it couldn't have. It's here somewhere, she has it, she must. Take a deep breath, she commands herself. Now, think. A likely place for it would be . . . ?

She's tempted to throw herself into action, to search the

small room from top to bottom, but she makes herself try to remember. The few things she brought from the train ... Sometimes she wonders where her clothes have ended up, in what drear lost and never to be found, or given to the poor of Kansas City or Albuquerque. Oh, she's glad to be rid of them! What did she bring from the train, then, besides her purse? Her purse! That must be where it is. It's in her purse. She remembers now tucking it away in the inner pocket of her purse. But where is her purse? It's not on the bureau, where she has been in the habit of leaving it. It's not on the chair by the door. She had it last night at the party, yet she has no memory of leaving the Schellbachs' house with it, no memory at all.

She had, in fact, felt a strange lightness, which she attributed to the wine, a lightness of limb and mind as she returned by car with the Hedquists. She sat in the backseat, looking directly at the back of Dotty's head (her hair was in its usual social bun), and felt tingly and light all over, a feeling that stayed with her all night, she now realizes, which was the reason for her wakefulness. To think that leaving one's purse behind gave one one's freedom! She will absolutely not indulge in the thought that sending one's husband home might do the same. She tries to imagine the contents of the purse, and all she can come up with, besides the hidden ring, is a rather too red lipstick, some nail scissors, a pack of Chiclets, and a small hanky from her maiden days, monogrammed with her pre-Merkle initials. Of course there must have been money, her coin purse at least and a few odd dollars. Oh, and of all things—*quelle horreur!*—the pocket-size notebook in which she jots the names and identifying features of those she meets and wishes to remember: Unsightly Wen, for example, or Spits When Speaking. It isn't malice but simple necessity that drives these laconic asides. She has a terrible time with names, and creating visual prompts has greatly helped her in social situations in the past. But now, she fears, she's done herself in. What if her purse and its contents have fallen into the hands of Rust Spot on Collar, or Ears That Protrude, or Jewelry Not Fit to Pawn? Her hope, this morning, is that Mating Habits of Tarantulas, who spent most of the evening in earnest conversation with Insect Rape!, is now in possession of her purse, or Insect Rape! himself is, as they are the two least likely to examine its contents for fear they will come across something feminine and unseemly. They are both young men at the age of embarrassment, she believes, a period of life in a man's early twenties. Insect Rape! is a scrawny redhead whose name she can't recall, and Mating Habits is a more mature-looking, dark-haired fellow with very white teeth and a squint that gives the impression of intelligence—or suspicion or sleep. His name is Earl or Ewell, the name she puzzled over in the night, and she has several reasons to remember him.

First and foremost, he's a dead ringer for the Duke of Windsor, despite the obvious age difference. Jane Merkle is much taken with the Duke of Windsor, though she frankly mistrusts that carpetbagger Mrs. Simpson and imagines her capable of inexhaustible bossiness. A second reason is that all the while Mating Habits huddled with his good friend Insect Rape!, he held a plate of Swedish meatballs in one hand, each meatball speared by a toothpick, each toothpick decorated with a lively pink ruffle. It seemed to Jane, herself no more than a few years older than this young man, that she was watching someone right smack in the middle of wildest youth, to whom small pink-tailed birds flocked. At one point the hand holding the plate imperceptibly drooped—a small shift of angle to be sure, but enough to encourage a greasy drip of meatball juice to leap out onto the toe of Earl or Ewell's boot. The hand shifted again, causing the drip to become a trickle, and suddenly, with the noise of liquid spattering the hard black linoleum of Ethyl Schellbach's floor, the young man seemed to awaken and adjust, as bewildered as he could be to have fallen into a world of plates and consequences.

Something childlike about him, then. That's the reason he impressed her. A boy who did not want to be king, who wanted instead to chase down tarantulas. And beetles, as this scrap of conversation revealed. She had eavesdropped shamelessly, and was able to recall it almost in its entirety.

Mating Habits I was out at Rowe Well last Thursday, just about dusk, and all around in the rabbitbrush these little darkling beetles were having a group grope.

Insect Rape! A what?

MH An orgy, ferrethead. They were doing it. In multiplicate.

IR! It's called lekking, you know.

MH No, I didn't know. Lekking? Sounds like what you lek in brains, you make up for in imagination.

IR! Mock me if you want, Charles, but it's right there in Jaques.

MH Don't call me Charles.

IR! If you studied a bit, you know, put your nose in a book instead of wandering around watching beetles buggering each other—

MH Buggering's interesting. To everyone but you.

IR! It's interesting to me. But I'm old-fashioned and sentimental and silly, I guess. I prefer *Homo sapiens*. I'm a little less keen on the bumping and grinding of insects. Theirs is a world of rape, Charlie. Now get on with your sordid tale.

MH The darkling males were completely indiscriminate, trying to breed with anything and everything they bumped into—

IR! *Invertidos!*

MH Worse. I dropped my cigarette butt and one of those boys climbed on and tried to hump it.

IR! Ah! They don't call them Lucky Strikes for nothing.

Silly boys, thinks Jane Merkle. She slips into the left Ked, then the right, takes one last look at herself in the long mirror behind the door, and tiptoes through the house to the kitchen. It's too early for Dotty and Oliver to be up, and for this reason she likes this hour. The house, which doesn't belong to her, nonetheless seems to be hers, and she goes about toast and coffee with the confidence of a resident.

She is staring into her empty coffee cup when Oliver enters the kitchen. "Oh, hello," says he. "Looking for minnows?"

"Minnows?" asks Jane.

"In your cup."

"No," she laughs. "My fortune."

"I had a lady read my tea leaves once. Said I was going to live a long and happy life. Then she poked around, just like some old forty-niner sifting for gold. Sifting for gold and turning up bear turds. I should have known the bad news was coming. They save it for the end, after the long and happy."

"Goodness! What was it?"

"Blindness."

"Oh, how awful! Blindness? What a terrible thing to say! They shouldn't be allowed to say things like that. Not if you pay them."

"I asked her how blind and happy went together."

"I don't like this story at all."

"She said if I looked around while I still had my sight, I would see not one happy man who wasn't blind."

"Good heavens! What sort of person *was* this?"

"Happiness demands blindness, said she, but if I wished to explore a different sort of satisfaction, I might see clearly for the rest of my life and on into the future."

"Gosh."

"Those were her very words."

"She sounds like a gypsy, Oliver."

"Dotty's Aunt Gretchen? She was a Communist."

Jane has never heard of Aunt Gretchen. Probably dead, she thinks. She knows so little about Morris's family. He's never spoken of a fortune-teller. Or a Communist, for heaven's sake. Good Lord! Is he a Communist too? It's certainly possible. He's not been entirely forthcoming about certain things. He's allergic to bees. And he's a Presbyterian, while all this time he's presented himself as an Episcopalian. It's very possible—likely, in fact—that her husband of five years is a Presbyterian Communist, and she is nothing but his unknowing dupe of a wife. It's unbearable, suddenly. She feels alone on an island in a sea of barracudas. She watches her brother-in-law pour himself a glass of orange juice, and then, to her astonishment, he kneels down and reaches into the cupboard under the sink and pulls out a bottle of something. He adds a generous dollop to the juice. At first she believes it's Lestoil and gives a little cry of protest, which she regrets.

"There's nothing to fear, my dear," says he. "Hair of the dog, bit of tequila. Ah, forgive me. I didn't even offer." He waves the bottle at her and cocks his head.

"No, thank you," says Jane nervously.

"*Chacun à son goût* and all that," he shrugs. "Call it my different sort of satisfaction. Possibly not the one Aunt Gretchen had in mind—though she was a dragon wrestler, she was. Born the day Robert Lee signed away the South at Appomattox. Five days later Lincoln took the bullet. Some of us, my dear, have unrest in our veins. That one did."

He caps the bottle and tucks it back under the sink, behind a frail wall of sponges and soap powders. He sits down across from her at the little table and says, "I know almost nothing about your habits. That seems a shame."

Habits? Jane can't think of any habits—except, according to Morris, she clicks her teeth in her sleep. There's one. And she's caught herself picking at a rough place on her elbow, fearing it will become a wart. But that's not the kind of thing he needs to know. She offers something unincriminating: "I read," she says.

"Ah! Whom?"

"The French at the moment."

"*Vive* the French! They write the way they cook. Rich, heavy stuff. Though in my opinion it makes better eating than reading."

She nods, though she's not sure she agrees or whether agreement is expected or necessary.

"I'll tell you who I like," he says. "I like that Mr. Tolstoy. Anna Karenina—now there's a gal with spunk."

"Oh, I wouldn't call it spunk, would you? I'd call it a tragic fate."

"Women have their own words for things."

"But not *spunk*."

"She's a rebel, dear girl. She's led by her passions, doomed passions, to be sure, but passions nonetheless, leading her—"

"Leading her around," says Jane, "like a harnessed mare, the promise of a good trot ahead of her, a long fine trot through exquisite country, pulling a well-made wagon."

"That's not far off," says he.

"But without choice, Oliver."

"What would she choose, then? How much choice does she require?"

"She would choose what you and I would."

"And what's that, young lady?"

"Why, no harness. No traces. No wagon."

"I wouldn't choose that," he says bluntly, "and neither would you. Anyway, in her case, it's either out there in the wind or back in the barn. Two important choices. It's the wind she chooses."

Dotty, at that moment, appears in the kitchen wearing a housecoat so old and worn it might better serve as compost in her garden. "Good morning one and all," she says cheerily. She favors cheer at this hour.

"Jane and I have been engaging in the most fascinating conversation," says Oliver. "Fascinating," he repeats, shaking his head. He stands up and excuses himself, taking his orange juice with him.

"He's in a rare mood," says Dotty. "He hasn't been fascinated for years." She looks around the kitchen. "Now what do I want for breakfast? Meat loaf! That's what I want. Have you ever heard of such a thing? Cold meat loaf on a nice white bun, with mustard and a slice of apple? Oh, this will impress you, Jane."

"Dotty, I need some help," says Jane.

"Help, dear? What is it?"

"I've misplaced my purse. I had it last night and don't seem to have it this morning."

"You don't think it was a prowler, do you?"

"A prowler? In the house?"

"It's terrible to think of," says Dotty, "but perfectly possible. Why, every year or two Babbitt Brothers is broken into. They take canned goods and such, because of course there's never any money left in the till overnight. Now, you'd think whoever does this would learn there's no cash to be had and they should just quit and get an honest job."

"Maybe the food is what they want."

"Oh, it can't be worth it to them. The risk is so great. Besides, Jane, it's not food they want, it's . . . I hate to say it . . . drink. The Indians have a terrible time with it."

"These are Indians, then, these prowlers?"

"I'm afraid so. They've never been apprehended, but it's the work of Indians. They're very stealthy, very crafty. They leave no trace and move like noonday shadows. Oh, if they weren't engaged in unlawful acts, we might admire their skill. They enter and leave the store through locked doors. They really are the closest thing to ghosts."

Dotty starts constructing her breakfast, and Jane experiences a sudden yearning for her turquoise ring, wondering if she will ever see it again. "I don't think it was a prowler," she says. "I'm quite sure I left it at the Schellbachs'."

"Well, that's a relief," says Dotty. "Why don't you take the car and go on over."

"I might just walk. I feel like a little exercise."

"Take my bicycle! There's an idea. We'll pump up the tires and send you off! What fun!"

A Man's Plate

Morris Merkle is a man of ritual. His red leather slippers live beneath his red leather armchair; he reads the newspaper before dinner and history after; he pulls on his left sock first, then his right; he has smoked the same cherry tobacco all his life, though pipes come and go, and has, as long as he can remember, parted his hair down the middle and visited the barber every other Tuesday, unless the barber is ill or on vacation. In twenty-five years he's owned only six suits, due to parsimony on his part and the fact that he loathes new clothes of any kind. On Friday he eats fish (though he doesn't pretend to be Catholic), on Monday and Wednesday red meat of some kind, on Tuesday and Thursday chicken, and on the weekend he allows himself to be somewhat spontaneous, catch-as-catch-can. In Jane's absence he has had to hire a cook, a temporary woman named Catherine, who won't come on the weekend but will leave him casseroles to reheat. She's not a bad cook but terribly sloppy in the kitchen, and because, as she reminds him, she's an artiste not a potwasher, he spends a good deal of his time cleaning up after her. Which he is content to do. As he discovered in Arizona, dishwashing calms him. It collects him. Its logic is plain and simple, quite the opposite of marriage.

After Catherine serves him dinner and says good-bye— *cheerio* is her word—the house feels too quiet. Morris eats and listens for the sound of her husband's car driving away with her in it, then he calls the dog, a chocolate brown and white springer spaniel. "Up," he says, and Martin jumps up onto the dining room chair that Jane usually sits in. It's now covered with a sheet. "Good boy," says Morris. He gets Martin's plate, an unbreakable one made of a new material called plastic, and sets it on the table and takes not just the scraps but often the juiciest bits from his own plate and places them in front of the dog. When they are finished eating, the dog goes into the library to wait beside Morris's chair, and Morris goes into the kitchen to clean up. He is learning Spanish, and he keeps the book propped above the sink, as his sister does. He is proud of his progress through the verbs, but the reflexive stumps him somewhat. Those Spaniards certainly must admire themselves with all of that *me me me* business.

As for Jane, she comes to mind often, especially at night. He doesn't miss her, exactly. He doesn't really know what his feelings are. He doesn't think about feelings, or feel them much. He knows she's always been good to him, and at the same time he's aware of a certain relief in her absence. Without her there, he doesn't have to keep up his end of things, or so it seems.

Yet the house is well cared for. The kitchen is actually cleaner than it ever was, and meals proceed in an orderly fashion. She, of course, would never allow Martin at the table. She tolerates the dog without being overly fond of him. When it comes to living things, she has a certain reserve that mystifies Morris, for he does not share it. During their brief courtship, though he saw no sign of her wanting children, his expectation of it was so complete—a woman her age would naturally set sail toward motherhood—he never thought to bring it up. He remembers the exquisite sensual delight of the first fortnight of their marriage and how responsive Jane was, how grateful to be his wife. He had thought then that surely they would make a baby, in gratitude to one another they would make a baby, that somehow in the warm light of their lovemaking a baby would arise. But it did not. And then to his surprise, one night Jane brought to their bed a *thing*, a rubbery thing the size of the palm of her hand, which she, with the boldness of new sex—a daring they had given each other—asked him to insert inside her. He was horrified. That was the end of their innocence together.

Morris is not in favor of spoiling children, but dogs are a different matter. One evening, while lingering at the dinner table with Martin, whose interest in staying seated wanes dramatically after his food has been devoured, he decides it's time for a chat. "Martin," he says. Their names are so similar in sound and form, he sometimes wishes he'd just named the dog Morris instead. "I don't know whether you've given this any thought. I suspect you haven't." Martin is licking his plate and seems not to be listening. "Martin!" Morris commands. "Pay attention here! Now, it may not have entered your brain that our Jane will at some point return home. We certainly look forward to it, but at that time, my dear boy, your life will cease to be the rich and fanciful thing it is today and will become more or less the same drab monster it once was." Martin delivers a quizzical look in the direction of his master's unlicked plate. "Which isn't to say we fault her. No, it's nobody's fault. We're not perfectly suited to one another, there's the rub, but we do love each other. On our best behavior is what we are. And I'm afraid my best behavior is at odds with your best interests. I cannot see a way to satisfy Jane and continue our— Martin! Feet off the table! Right now! What in the world has come over you? This is exactly what I'm speaking of. Jane has no patience for this kind of performance, and if presented with it, what am I to do? Who am I to protect? You leave me little choice, dear fellow. It's in the future, I know, yet soon I must turn my mind to it in a serious fashion." He scratches Martin behind the ears. "You're a scoundrel, and I'm tempted to let you clean my plate tonight for a special treat, but we'll not make it a habit, will we? We'll not expect it every night. And when Jane comes home we'll button up a bit, won't we? We'll make everything shipshape. We'll straighten up and fly right. Oh, don't look at me that way, sir, if you please. We'll still have our evening walks together, our romps in the wet leaves. Now, I won't have those sad eyes, Martin, I mean it."

Morris carries his plate into the kitchen and the dog follows. He sets the plate on the floor, and Martin, with one long swipe of his fat pink tongue, cleans the plate, which is quite an attractive plate, Morris realizes, though he doesn't remember where it came from. He picks it up and examines it. Jane would know. She would know everything about that plate. She would know both the long and short histories of it. It was probably a wedding present. Though one was seldom presented with a single plate. Unless it was some sort of award. Could Jane have earned an award? Has he forgotten a shining moment in her life? His heart sinks. Then he notices with relief that the plate is not a woman's plate, it's a man's. It has red-coated fellows riding in a circle around its outer edge, and within that circle a circle of hounds, and in the center a running fox. Over hill and dale it runs, its pointy face to the wind, its bushy tail streaming out behind. He realizes, to his surprise, he feels just like that fox, and in his imagination it runs and runs, never to be caught until it reaches the sea, where it stops and turns to meet its pursuers. Then, by the power of its magnanimous and reasonable personality, it turns back the hounds; it turns back the red coats. This sequence of events puzzles Morris. It's true he often feels dogged by obligations to wife and home, but never has he thought of himself as a man driven to the *brink* of something. And more surprising still, when riders and hounds have trotted away and he is alone, he can scarcely imagine a life without them. So back over hill and dale he runs, pursuing his pursuers in order that they might once again give his life purpose and meaning.

The Myth at Home

As Jane Merkle pedals through the village, past Babbitt Brothers where Supai Mary is sitting on the porch on a milk crate, past the post office, past the train yard where the train is disgorging dozens of French tourists chattering like phlegmy squirrels, Louis Schellbach is having a difficult morning. He has already anticipated, with the invitation of a certain female personage to lunch, a difficult afternoon. It's Sunday, and to his great dissatisfaction he does not go to work on Sundays. Nor Saturdays. And he is simply not the myth at home that he is in uniform. He would like to be a family man but finds domestic life full of annoying little knots he cannot untie. He feels at times disrespected by his son Donny and overlooked by his well-meaning wife, Ethyl. As a result, he has fashioned a little laboratory for himself, consisting of one long table at the back of his study. At one end of the table is a microscope, a large bottle of formaldehyde, an enamel pan containing surgical tools, and half a dozen boxes of Lepidoptera (butterflies, moths, skippers) or Hemiptera (true bugs) or Odonata (dragonflies and damselflies). It is nothing more elaborate than this, but the presence of the table allows him to feel mythical, which in turn allows him to do his work. This morning he tried, unsuccessfully, to interest Donny, age fourteen, in the variations in wing venation in dragonflies, and he showed him a green darner, *Anax junius*, one of the largest and most terrifying-looking dragonflies, under the microscope. Donny, his eye to the scope, only commented that "This whole business of bugs is sort of sick, Papa, and you're obsessed." At least he didn't run away in tears as he used to.

It is in this mood of glum rebellion against fatherhood that Louis Schellbach hears a faint knock at the door. Ethyl has gone shopping, and Donny has either locked himself in his room or run away from home to throw off the burden of an obsessed father. Outside, Jane leans the fat-tired blue Schwinn up against the low rock wall enclosing Ethyl Schellbach's garden. Apparently Oliver has never ridden a bicycle, or has limited knowledge of them, because the bicycle he bought for Dotty is not equipped with two of the more practical elements involved in transport: basket and kickstand. With an unexpected case of nerves, she walks to the door and, finding no doorbell, knocks on it. There seems to be nobody home. She readjusts her hat, which she has grown quite fond of, and knocks again. Inside, a dog starts yapping. She doesn't remember a dog from the night before. She guesses it's long haired and under five pounds and its eyes leak and it has a flattened nose that looks like a culinary mistake. A man cries, "Reginald! Reginald! Reggie!" Footsteps approach. The yapping approaches as well. The footsteps stop, followed by a bout of coughing. The yapping continues and little nails scratch at the inside of the door. The coughing grows louder, accompanied by horrible gasps. "Goodness," she thinks, "he may be dying! While I stand here as useless as Reginald!"

She turns the doorknob: nothing. She leans her shoulder against the door, preparing to knock it down if necessary. It is at this moment that Louis Schellbach recovers himself and opens the door from within, and little Reggie bursts forth to administer sharp nips to the ankles of the unexpected visitor. Jane Merkle suddenly finds the top half of herself in the arms of the park naturalist, while the bottom half is severely buffeted by the park naturalist's pug. There is a brief, confused readjusting among the humans: a straightening of the tie by Schellbach, who is seldom seen without a tie, and a rearrangement of the hat by Mrs. Merkle. The dog is told to "Stop that, Reginald!" and made to sit, which he's poor at. Finally he's banished to the back of the house.

"My deepest apologies," says Schellbach, wheezing ominously. Jane hopes to heaven he won't start in again with that racking cough. "It's the dog," he manages to say. "Allergic," he gasps.

"Is there anything I can do?" asks Jane.

He shakes his head. Finally he's able to speak again and says, "Annoying little fellow, isn't he? Ethyl's dog, really. Ethyl's watchdog. Takes his job rather seriously, I'm afraid. Now,

I think we better have a look at your ankles. Little devil's been known to break the skin."

"Oh." Jane smiles, with effort. She's determined to keep her ankles to herself. "Oh, no no no. They're sharp little teeth all right, but no harm done. I have a dog myself," she adds. "It's Morris's dog. They're useless, aren't they?"

"Useless?" Schellbach raises an eyebrow. He has a long, comical face, a neatly trimmed mustache, and gray pouches under his eyes.

"Did I say useless?" asks Jane.

"You did."

"Useful is what I meant."

"Useless may be more accurate," says Schellbach, winking at her. "Shall we go inside?"

"Oh, well. I don't know about that. You're probably busy and I—"

"Nonsense. It's true, I'm up to no good, but you might find it interesting." He sweeps her down the hall into a room that smells of tobacco. There are several large windows covered with shades, two tall shelves of books, and a desk with a cow skull hanging over it. This must be his study, though the skull seems as poor an invitation to sit and think as Jane can imagine.

"The truth is," says Schellbach, leading her to a long table at the back of the room, "I've forgotten your name."

"Jane. Jane Merkle. I'm Oliver Hedquist's sister-in-law."

"Of course you are." He motions to the table. "Here lies a dilemma."

What Jane sees is puzzling, to be sure. A stole. In the middle of the table. It's a dull fur, obviously an inexpensive one or poorly cared for. It must have been left behind by one of last night's partygoers.

"I have no more understanding of what killed this fox than I do of my son's preoccupation with anomaly," says Schellbach. "Do you have children, Mrs. Merkle? Oh dear," he adds suddenly, "I always assume marriage. Forgive me. Ethyl tells me it's an insult to a lady. It makes her feel old."

Jane laughs and says, "But surely *Miss* may be taken as an insult as well, a sign of undesirability. It's a fickle world, Mr. Schellbach."

"Louie," he says quickly.

"Jane," says she. "I don't have a child, but from what I've heard, your son's preoccupation with anomaly may well be inherited from his father. I hear you're quite taken with the variations in wing patterns in dragonflies. To see the odd and unusual can be a kind of perception passed on in the blood. I certainly don't have it. If anything, I have the opposite."

"Which is what, may I ask?"

"I take great comfort in the familiar, I'm afraid. At least I always have. The familiar and universal. The ways in which we are the same."

"Well, what could be better than that?" pronounces Schellbach. "Room for both, I say. This fox, for example. Come around here and have a look-see. I've opened her up, gullet to gizzard, and what you see in there ought to look pretty darn familiar. Stomach, liver, kidneys, the old ticker. Her . . . thingamajig. She's carrying kits, isn't she? No sign of trauma to her body. She wasn't shot or hit by a car or mortally wounded by a coyote. I suspect poison. But have a look at this, Jane. The much-maligned intestines. Three meters of small intestine alone. Can you imagine all that intestine? Packed in there like a nest of nematodes. It's a marvel, isn't it? An absolute marvel."

This fox, thinks Jane, is beginning to smell. Under the fruity fragrance of pipe tobacco she detects the sweetish smell of death. She is suddenly dizzy and sick to her stomach. "I . . ." she begins. "I'm afraid I must go."

"Of course," says Schellbach. "I've bored you, and I apologize."

"No no," she says. "It's been very interesting."

"A bit of forensic science to start your day."

She nods agreeably, wondering what on earth that word means. *Forensic.* She's got to sharpen her mind. It's been idle too long, sitting with its feet up in St. Louis. Schellbach leads her back through the house. She's aware of a radio playing in the distance and wonders if Ethyl has come home, or the son. Or perhaps it's to soothe the dog.

She can't bring herself to call him Louie, so she calls him nothing at all. She thanks him for his hospitality, and it isn't until she's mounted the bicycle that she suddenly remembers the reason for her visit. Good Lord, she thinks. What is the matter with me? My mind is a muddle. Schellbach answers the door once more, and once more Reggie applies himself to her ankles. This time she discourages him with a few discreet kicks, overlooked by the park naturalist.

"I'm so sorry to bother you again," she says, "but I believe I left my purse here last night."

"Purse," says Schellbach carefully, as if exposed to the word for the first time. "I don't know of a purse. What kind of purse would this be?"

"Oh, nothing the least bit unusual. A brown purse. A brown leather purse. It has a long strap that can be shortened."

"A long strap."

"An adjustable strap."

"Yes, I see. So it might in fact be a short strap at the present moment. In our search for your purse we should not overlook straps long or short, is that right?"

Jane nods.

"Well, Ethyl's the one in charge of purses. I would have to speak to Ethyl."

"Of course."

"We'll find it," he assures her, and closes the door.

The Perfect Confidante

Ethyl Schellbach is seldom satisfied with the quality of beef at Babbitt Brothers. She often buys pork or chicken instead. She has, on odd years, bought a whole spring lamb from Neez Charlie, but as soon as she makes space in the freezer, Louie fills it up with his dead rattlesnakes and birds. Today there was a nice smoked ham that beckoned to her, and as she drives home she's trying to decide how to do the potatoes. Whether or not Miss Clover will eat potatoes is anyone's guess. Perhaps, as a botanist, she's against the consumption of plants. What Ethyl does know is that Donny likes potato salad with pickles, olives, and onions, but Louie likes good old-fashioned mashed. He's not a fussy eater, whereas Donny is as picky as the day is long, declining this and that, demanding something else. Who, thinks Ethyl, would it be wiser to coddle? Her irascible son or her extremely even-tempered husband? "Potato salad it is," she says to herself, and just then she spots Dotty Hedquist's sister-in-law bicycling up the road.

She toots her horn and waves. The sister-in-law, whose name she can't remember, waves back. But what a coincidence, thinks Ethyl, the very person I need to see. She drives onto the shoulder of the road and stops, expecting the sister-in-law to stop too. But the sister-in-law is traveling in the opposite direction at quite a clip. She has the proverbial devil on her back, thinks Ethyl. She turns the car around and comes abreast of the bicycle and gives another little wave to demonstrate harmlessness and good intentions. "Hello," she says, but the window on the passenger side is rolled up. She stops the car, leans over, and rolls it down and says, "Hello again. Ethyl here. Ethyl Schellbach."

"Ethyl," says the girl sadly. She really is quite young. "I've lost my purse."

"I know you have, dear, but you can stop your worrying, it's been found."

"Found?"

"By a very nice young fellow by the name of Hugh. Don't know his last name."

"Hugh? Hugh! Insect Rape!" cries the girl.

"I beg your pardon?"

"Oh, I'm relieved."

"He promised to bring it by today," says Ethyl. "I said today was far too busy, I'm expecting someone for lunch, an important someone, and I thought he might as well talk to you since it was your purse."

"That's right."

"So run on home. He may have left it there already. I told him you were staying with the Hedquists. Hope it's no secret."

"Of course not."

"Well, you never know, dear."

In fact, when it comes to secrets, Ethyl knows more than most. If she hasn't seen it all, she's certainly seen the lion's share, including Dorothy Hedquist's various transgressions over the years, though Ethyl, whose mind is sharp and tongue is not—the perfect confidante—has never judged them to be more than misadventures. One thing she's learned is that those who harbor secrets are often the last to know the secret's true nature. There's an innate innocence, a blindness, that shields a person from woe, and as this drops away like childhood, and the terrible weight of a wrongdoing makes itself felt, the bearer of a secret is as close as she will ever come to self-inflicted death. Indeed, Ethyl has talked more than one individual away from the brink. Sometimes she wishes she did not live in such an easy place for death, that Louie was stationed in a peaceful valley. But he is not, and she, who is at heart a nurse in the trenches, has found a way to be useful.

Her prescription for the guilt-ridden, remorseful, and brokenhearted is to take themselves into the trench itself, to walk into the canyon and lie down among the shattered bones of deer and bighorn sheep, grateful for their own human kneecaps, shinbones, and thighbones that carried them there. To hike their own lucky bag of appetites and excretions over the trail from Hermit Creek to Indian Garden and on to Grapevine,

Cottonwood, and Hance, while gossip and ill intentions run their course on the high ground like a bunch of skinny coyotes howling. If only the words were as harmless, thinks Ethyl, whose private opinion is that employment in the government regularly sends people upside down over the precipice. She walks among the fallen like a swami, like a saint. Saint Ethyl of Disappointment has a good nose for where trouble lies—an uncanny nose. In fact, her presence is ever-so-slightly suspect, for wherever she goes, trouble and disappointment are not far behind. The truth is, they're already there. They're everywhere to begin with.

So Jane Merkle pedals home in her temporary state of grace, thinking only of her imminent reunion with her turquoise ring. Nothing of the chance encounter with Louis Schellbach's wife troubles her. It strikes her only as felicitous, and she arrives at the Hedquists' in a very good humor. The young man, Hugh, has not come by, but he has left a telephone number where he can be reached in the evenings and on Saturday and Sunday afternoons. Well, thinks Jane, it's a Sunday, isn't it? Oliver has gone back to bed, and Dotty is rooting around in the garden. She stands in the den, which since his retirement has become Oliver's study, and dials the number of the young man on whom she feels her happiness depends. But the telephone rings in an empty house, or perhaps it fails to awaken the sleepy fellow. It isn't yet afternoon, she reasons, though it's pretty darn close. And then there's the question of what is afternoon? To some it means a lengthening of shadows, a certain quality of light; to others it's what follows the stroke of noon or the drowsy period brought on by lunch. To Jane it's a feeling, usually an unpleasant one. It's the time of day when she feels dulled to the world around her, wrapped in gauze, like Siam (which Morris's friend George Runge once described as a kingdom of cocoons where every bed in every hotel is draped in mosquito netting). She decides to take her mind off the extraordinarily pokey passage of time and read her book.

One thing that may be said about Jane Merkle is that she is a diligent reader. She is working diligently through *Madame Bovary* at the moment, but she is not in love with the woman. And this is the problem. The book and the woman are, to her, the same. She cannot help but compare it to *Anna Karenina*, in which Anna's personality and circumstances are only one tragic strand of what Jane feels to be an uplifting story. Hadn't Kitty had her baby at the end? She turns the pages of *Madame Bovary* with apprehension, feeling quite dreary, as if she too must take to her bed—or take to Emma Bovary's bed. The bed looms so large in the novel that Jane begins to consider it a sort of protagonist. She reads distractedly until lunchtime, when she joins the Hedquists for tuna fish sandwiches outside on folding chairs.

Oliver is wearing a wet towel on his head, turban fashion, and is terribly out of sorts. Dotty tries to ask the right questions about Jane's morning, but when it comes to a dead fox in Louis Schellbach's study, she can hear no more. "A smelly old thing like that in the house, with a party going on! Oh, it's too much—it really is."

"It wasn't that smelly," Jane lies.

"Of course it was," snorts Oliver, who up until that moment seemed to be napping in his chair. "By the time things get to Louie they stink. That's the nature of the job."

"The butterflies don't," says Jane quietly.

"I'm speaking of the flesh, dear girl, the *flesh*."

"Please!" cries Dotty. "Not another word about it!"

Jane glances at her sister-in-law with some alarm. Dotty has gone pale and sits staring in front of her, her mouth twitching in an awful way, as if the words are hammering at her lips from the inside, unable to force their way out. In the silence that follows, Jane is aware of many things, which she later recalls in detail: the butterscotch smell of the pines; the narrow plank of shade where the Hedquists have placed their chairs; the warmth of the sun in her lap, as if a cat has been sleeping there; the taste of mustard on the inside of her teeth; the sound of a jay calling, which reminds her of Missouri. She watches as Dotty gets up and gathers the plates, asking if anyone would like dessert. Oliver would. Jane would not. The telephone rings far away in the house, too far away to bother with—until she remembers her purse, the young man, her happiness. She runs off to answer it.

No Place for Corpses

Lunch went smoothly enough until Elzada Clover, amateur gumshoe, questioned her hostess about her relationship with one Lowell Dunhill, former ranger naturalist at Grand Canyon National Park. She later regrets her egregious timing but cannot figure out how the business of mystery solving is to be accomplished without making innocent people squirm. If she'd accepted seconds of potato salad, would Ethyl Schellbach have taken less offense?

"Innocent or not so innocent," Lois reminds her. "We really have no idea."

They are walking vigorously westward along the rim of Grand Canyon, on a narrow trail that leads to Hermit's Rest. Elzada writes in the morning, or pursues interviews such as the one she attempted with Ethyl, but in the afternoon her intention is to keep fit. "Oh, come," she says, breathing raggedly but determined not to pant, "Mr. Schellbach didn't invite us here to investigate a murder in which his wife is a suspect."

"Not as far as he knows. But they don't, you see, always know."

"They?" asks Elzada.

"The husbands. And anyway, Elzie, everyone in the village is a suspect."

"Why, what an extraordinary idea! That makes our job impossible!"

"Yes it does," says Lois, "and I, for one, am ready to go home."

This is discouraging news but not altogether surprising. Elzada has always known that Lois thrives on doing, while she herself is all too content to reflect. But even she has grown impatient. They've been here more than a week and have had no luck with Emery Kolb. He refuses even to see them, much less talk. Whatever his game is, it seems Lois is right: the entire village is suspect and willing to let the matter drop. More than willing—determined. Summoning "the professors," as they've been dubbed, is only a way to satisfy some higher-ups who feel the national parks are no place for corpses. If anyone really wanted to get to the bottom of the matter, they would have hired a detective, not a botanist.

But Elzada Clover has a stubborn streak, a combination of raw ambition and a dislike of authority. Add to that the fact that the accused, Emery Kolb, once saved her life—she feels more inclined than ever to clear his name. At the same time, it's entered her head that the skeleton in his garage *isn't* Dunhill, which opens the fertile question, who the deuce is it?

"I have an idea," she says suddenly. "But you'll have to slow down if you want to hear it. You're impossibly long-legged, did you know that?"

"I suppose I have my genes to thank," says Lois crossly.

"You do indeed. Now listen. Mrs. Schellbach did mention something that might be important. It was a bit of information she offered me out of earshot of her husband. She had a strange look on her face as she said it, a look of disgust. She asked if I'd ever heard of . . ." Elzada struggles to recall that brief exchange, and specifically the name that entered her consciousness between bites of unpleasantly sweetened potato salad. Suddenly its foreign syllables form on her tongue and fly from her mouth, startling her and stopping Lois in her tracks. "Skłodowska, Loie. The Skłodowska Institute, that's what she said."

"What on earth does that mean?"

"I have no idea."

"It's not enough!" cries Lois in exasperation. "There's nothing to go on. Two words that make no sense and a body in a garage."

"A skeleton," Elzada corrects her.

"Yes, bones. Nothing but bones." Lois sighs and starts walking again. "I know what you're thinking. Two words is two words more than we had yesterday. If there really is a Skłodowska Institute, I'll find it. Libraries, telephone books— I'll talk to Mrs. Schellbach myself, if she'll allow it. I don't guarantee anything," she says over her shoulder. "It's madness, as usual, tagging along with you."

Madness? Was it madness to ask Lois to come? Madness to ask her to join the Nevills expedition of 1938, the chance of a lifetime? Was she, Elzada, mad to feel strongly about the girl, who is now no longer a girl but a tough and sensible woman? As a teacher she had strict rules about conduct with students. She was drawn to many of her students. So many of the young women were intelligent and attractive. But Lois had never been a student of hers. She arrived as a teaching assistant, a brilliant one, and this immediately posed a possibility and a problem. Elzada was thirty-seven years old, Lois twenty-two. Fifteen years separated them, as well as a good many other things, including Lois's sincere attraction to the opposite sex. Elzada was not, and never had been, one to wear her heart on her sleeve. She did not believe that was what the sleeve was for. The sleeve was created to cover up, not to display. She expressed her feelings for Lois to no one, for she felt it was no one's business but her own. Occasionally, however, after a glass of wine in the evening, she wrote in her diary, in prose unlike any she had ever used elsewhere in her life, entries that later embarrassed her, but because they embarrassed her she didn't destroy them. They were mortifiers, humiliators, deterrents to any future peccadilloes. The entries acted as the pillory had in Puritan America—though in Elzada's case she added effort to insult by having constructed the diabolic contraption herself.

Since that time she has written almost nothing of a personal nature—not in letters and never again in a diary. She keeps her field book, of course, and publishes the odd paper, but other than that, her involvement with words is as a reader, not a writer. "Like taking the bus" is the way she thinks of it. Letting a professional driver drive. There are several such buses in her life, operating in different neighborhoods at different times of day. On the bus of mystery novels, Ngaio Marsh is inevitably at the wheel. Elzada rides with her in the evenings when she's too tired to think. She likes that bus at that time of day because it flies along, stopping infrequently, and the gentle hum of its motor often puts her to sleep. In the mornings, when she's alert, she's apt to ride the bus of scientific tomes, a slower, heavier vehicle. At the moment her preferred driver is Madame Marie Curie, whose understanding of radioactivity is of great interest to Elzada, who has taken it upon herself to explore the little-known relationship between nuclear fallout and deoxyribonucleic acid, or DNA.

The business of DNA has for some time attracted Dr. Clover. The chemical properties of this fascinating molecule were known at last, though the great race to define its structure continued to occupy some of the most fertile minds of the century, including hers. Recently, without the necessary time and equipment, she has fallen toward the rear of the pack, and accepting her position, has allowed herself to explore other aspects of the critical substance, namely the role it plays in mutation. The interrupted or abnormal growth of plants and animals in the state of New Mexico, downwind of the atomic test site, caught her attention five years earlier, when it first became known. White cattle, hairless sheep, plants that would not flower and birds that could not sing—these were the rumors, discredited as quickly as they arose. But in scientific circles the anomalies were duly tallied and the evidence examined. What seemed obvious to Dr. Clover and her many colleagues was that however great the destruction wrought by A-bombs, however insidious the danger posed by fallout from these explosions, the government of the great nation in whose defense these weapons were produced was not the slightest bit interested in letting the truth be known. Those who knew it were encouraged not to know it, and those who refused to pretend ignorance lived in fear of the consequences. Dr. Clover, who was not a cellular biologist, nor a physicist, used her position as a mere botanist, a mere woman, to advance in the study of radiation without drawing suspicion to herself. As a result, in a few short years she became a pioneer in the field of genetic mutation caused by nuclear fallout. And no one knew. Not even Lois Jotter Cutter, whose life and family she did not care to jeopardize. Her interest in mutation and manipulation of DNA was considered a perfectly acceptable, if not heroic, pursuit in a country of farmers. But the other side of it, the unknown side, the dark side, where science traveled well beyond God, and some would argue, beyond Darwin, caused in her a loneliness, a bitterness, that were it not for her daily obligations as a teacher—or a gumshoe—she would find impossible to live with. Without work, or the possibility of love, she would not necessarily find life in an atomic age worth living.

She considers running after Lois who has hiked far ahead, but decides against it. Let the girl lope away and be free. Instead Elzada Clover walks to the rim and looks down on the

Orphan Mine, all but abandoned since the end of the copper boom. But surely something else of value lies below the surface, something worth clawing from the ground. Uranium, of course. And if she's right, someday soon the bright thread of Horn Creek, just below, will run a horrid yellow, spilling its radioactive poison into the muddy Colorado. And the river will dump it into the sea, and the sea will bring it to the shores of friend and enemy alike. Our human lives, thinks Elzada, are ever more connected by a grand ignorance and folly.

A Patriot

Euell Wigglesworth may look like the Duke of Windsor, but looks aren't everything. He has never acquired the dukely habit of social ease, with which to hide the chip on his shoulder. The chip, weighing 117 pounds unclothed, goes by the name of Sally Domani and lives in Dorsey Corners, Pennsylvania, Mr. Wigglesworth's hometown. After going steady for three years in high school, Miss Domani suddenly left Mr. Wigglesworth one day after Latin class and took up with Douggie Warren, class clown.

At Cornell University Euell had a full scholarship in classics, which he dumped sophomore year for a major in ecology. "A major in *what*?" said his father, holding a tuition bill. "Classics wasn't useless enough? Classics is what they're paying you to study, boy. This . . . this other thing is not."

He left Cornell for points west shortly after that.

On his own he studied the bugs, birds, fish, mammals, and

plants of North America. He had, to his great relief, missed
the war by a few months, seventeen years old at its close, but
through his studies and wanderings around the West, he became a patriot. He hadn't felt such things before, things like
love of country. It astonished him. He hiked the mountains
of Idaho, Montana, California, looking under every rock. He
hiked the San Juans, thumbed a ride down the Rio Grande. He
was happy but for the chip on his shoulder, which followed him
everywhere, his shoulder heavy with that silly girl's rejection.

Work, a steady job, finally became imperative. To his surprise he was hired as a summer ranger on the North Rim of
Grand Canyon, a place he'd never laid eyes on. His duties
included the maintenance of outhouses and mule corrals, the
emptying of trash cans in the vicinity of Grand Canyon Lodge,
and the inspection of campgrounds, including the ability to
issue warnings if necessary, though the only violations noted by
young Wigglesworth were those that involved personal mor-
als (the woods were dark and deep), and every so often a city
dweller would play a radio after nine o'clock in the evening to
quell longings for home. There was little of what he considered
"rangering," but the land left him in awe, the great size of it,
like a sea, and he was happy, if occasionally bored out of
his wits.

Every eleventh day he had four days off, and he took himself down the North Kaibab Trail into the canyon, swinging
a homemade butterfly net. It was on one of these adventures
that he first encountered Hugh Huddleston. They met in the
middle of the bridge spanning the Colorado River, one

young man approaching from the south, the other from the north, each brandishing a net. As Euell remembers it, Hugh suggested a beer at Phantom Ranch, to wait out the heat of the day; and as Hugh remembers it, Euell suggested a walk uphill in the blazing sun, in pursuit of anything that flew. On this occasion, victory went to the beer, though up the creek, in the hot white light between patches of cottonwood shade, Euell had his satisfaction as well. He gave chase to a cloudless sulphur, a magnificent yellow butterfly, which he brought down not with a sweep of his net, it being tangled in a mesquite, but with his hat. It boded well for the friendship.

Now it's summer again. Hugh, in his third year as a temporary hire on the South Rim, has pleaded homelessness, and the two friends are cohabiting for a brief time before Euell moves across the canyon to take a permanent job as assistant park naturalist, working under Louis Schellbach. Which is why, when invited to a party at the Schellbachs', he considered it his duty to go and allowed himself to be dragged along by Hugh, whose enthusiasm for free liquor was akin to a pole vaulter's attraction to the sky. He ate meatballs, dripped meatball juice on Mrs. Schellbach's floor, and remembered little else until it was time to go home. He searched for his jacket and found it on a chair in Donny Schellbach's room. Oddly enough there was a purse half concealed in the sleeve. It was a brown leather purse with a long strap, and alas, the last of the ladies had left the party. Hugh suggested with drunken good humor that they rifle through it to discover its rightful owner and carry it in their fairy-tale coach to that particular Cinderella. But they had no coach, only their bicycles. And, as Euell pointed out, because of the sensitive nature of the location in which the purse was found—Donny's lair, which may or may not have served as a coat room—they would do better to say nothing of the incident to their host and hostess, just teeter on home to deal with it in the daylight. Now, over a nauseating (to Hugh, sipping a warm beer) breakfast of scrambled eggs and homemade pecan pie, made by Euell himself, they discuss the situation and come up with a plan.

Because Euell's chip inhibits him from attempting social intercourse with any member of the opposite sex who is not old enough to be his mother, he decides, given the unknown age of the purse's owner, that Hugh must be the one to track her down. It will make his friend feel manly. Hugh, for his part, decides that Euell will be the one to pursue this Mrs. Morris Merkle (a charming little notebook bears her name on its cover). She's a married woman, after all, and therefore risk free, and Euell could use a little gratitude coming his way from a female, a little adoration. Each argues his case, Hugh loses, and off he goes to call Mrs. Schellbach, who informs him that the lady in question is staying with the Hedquists. He calls and speaks with Mrs. Hedquist, who promises to pass along the message to Jane. Knowing he's done all he can do for the time being, he allows himself a little glass of whiskey to soften the edges of what has turned out to be a surprisingly hard day.

When Euell Wigglesworth comes home from Rowe Well that afternoon with a killing jar of blister beetles, he finds Hugh snoring on his bed with the perfume of whiskey wafting up from his inert body. "You drunken Goldilocks!" he cries, shaking the mattress. "The queens are flying. *Queens*, batbreath! Get up!" But Hugh is beyond rousing. He grunts like an armadillo and rolls onto his side and within seconds is fast asleep again.

The queens are indeed flying, though it is already July. Euell has never seen them on the rim and guesses the wind has blown them up from a lower elevation. He likes the queens, has always preferred them to their better-known relatives, the monarchs. They're a smaller and less dramatic butterfly, with white wing spots and a soft, uniform rusty color. They lack the dark venation that makes the monarchs seem a brooding bunch, backstabbers and conspirators—the Brutus factor, Euell calls it, though in general he tries to keep his prejudices in check. He appeals to science and logic, eschews the irrational tides of emotion and anthropomorphism that plague . . . Hugh, for example. For while Hugh is a fine marksman, a fine collector in most respects, it remains only a passionate hobby for him. Euell has observed him in hot pursuit of what certainly appeared to be a dark buckeye, *Junonia nigrosuffusa*, a rare sighting indeed and a first for Grand Canyon, only to give up the chase at the critical moment when the creature flew across a creek and he, the New York City boy, didn't want to get his blessed feet wet. Maddening.

Euell has captured three queens, though two are really all he needs, and sets about pinning them. He pins the first and finds himself at odds with the day, restless and bored and particularly annoyed with his friend, whose nasal music fills the small and only room of Euell's house. He pins the second butterfly and is about to apply himself to the third, when his eyes come to rest on an object he thought he was done with: the wayward purse of Mrs. What's-her-name Merkle. He sighs. Hugh's mission failed, apparently. It's getting on in the afternoon, and his lush of a friend lies as if dead, with his mouth slung open and his limbs askew—hit by lightning, that's the look of it. Not a pretty sight. Euell pushes back his chair, knowing what he must do. He has a queer sense of elation as he dials Mrs. Schellbach's number. He's felt this way before scrambling up cliff faces with no rope. She informs him, as she did his friend Hugh not two hours earlier, that Mrs. Merkle may be reached at her in-laws', the Hedquists. "Has there been some mix-up?" she asks, to which Euell Wigglesworth would like to respond that the mix-up lies inebriated on his bed. Instead he says, "No no. We're right on track here. We'll get the thing settled shortly, Mrs. Schellbach. We will." He would also like to add, but refrains from it, that if money is missing from the purse, he will see to it that little Donny is strung up by his thumbs until he confesses. "Thank you, Mrs. Schellbach," he says in exactly the tone of voice his mother taught him to use with older women of a certain status, on whose good will he might someday depend.

Assured that Mrs. Merkle is of a reasonably advanced age, being sister-in-law to the Hedquists, Euell feels a lightness in his limbs and shoulders, a sense of being airborne—the same feeling he gets when chasing a butterfly. He is therefore not prepared for the youthful voice that answers the Hedquists' telephone. He guesses it must be a daughter. Then he remembers there are no children, for he knows Oliver Hedquist, enjoys picking his brain about bugs and enjoys a beer with him every so often. Perhaps it's a niece. To her breathy hello (does she know the distraction she causes with the simple passage of air through her lips?) he says, "Hello. Yes," then immediately becomes tongue-tied. Oh, idiot! He momentarily regains composure, his sense of purpose, and battles on with, "May I speak to Mrs. Merkle, please?" At which point he's done in and needs a rest. But Whoever she is says, calm as could be, as if the world were not forever changed because of it, "This is Mrs. Merkle. Would this be Hugh?" And he, being so taken aback, responds in the affirmative, not knowing how to undo it once it's done.

An Impersonator

Oliver Hedquist has seen many things in his day, and expects to see a few more before it's over, but never has he seen a young man in such a high state of excitement over a purse. The poor lad comes pedaling up the road, and instead of leaning his bicycle against a tree, he kicks that useless kickstand thing, which does nothing but delay the inevitable topple. The bicycle falls before he reaches the door. The boy returns to the bicycle. (Oliver watches all this from his window.) He's got a lady's handbag slung over his shoulder. Oliver knows Euell Wigglesworth and finds this odd, then remembers his sister-in-law and her missing purse. The bicycle goes up again, young Wigglesworth again moves in the direction of the door, and once more the bicycle responds to gravity. Wigglesworth must have the mind of a sow bug today.

By the time he finally decides to leave the bicycle on the ground (doesn't he recognize a ponderosa pine for what it's worth?), the poor fellow's got a look in his eye that says to Oliver: SOS! Nonetheless, being the rugged ranger he is, he puts the immediate past behind him and moves on into his future. He rolls his shoulders a couple of times and knocks on the Hedquists' door. Oliver hears Jane's light running step—wearing her Keds, no doubt—and her call of "Coming, coming, coming!" There is the slow slide of the door opening, then a silence followed by a single, echoing "Oh."

The lad, on his part, is a sudden rush of words. Oliver can't hear exactly what's said, but Euell Wigglesworth, always tight-lipped around the ladies, seems to have come unbuttoned. He stumbles on excitedly, like a mynah bird on truth serum. Curiosity drives Oliver out of his study. He is surprised to find that his sister-in-law hasn't asked the young man in. Inexplicably her rudeness goes beyond that, and she calls poor Euell an impersonator. "Goodness," says Oliver, approaching the scene. Jane looks unabashed and Wigglesworth says, "Afternoon, Mr. Hedquist," and hangs his head.

Jane says, "There's simply no explanation for it."

"There is," says Euell. "I mean, I think there is."

They ignore Oliver.

Jane puts one hand on her hip and says, "I'd like to hear it."

"I'm trying to tell you!" cries Euell.

Never has Oliver seen either of these usually placid individuals so ill at ease, so ruffled. What can be the reason for it?

"Well," says Jane, "tell me one more time. Tell Oliver too. Maybe he's quicker than I am. And what do I care anyway? I've got my purse. That's all that matters."

Euell looks like he is about to sink through the ground. Oliver says, "Come in, Mr. Wigglesworth. Come in. I would introduce you to my sister-in-law, Jane Merkle, but it seems you've already met."

To his relief, Euell Wigglesworth attempts a smile. "We have," he says, "and the pleasure is entirely mine. Solely mine, I would say."

"He introduced himself as Hugh!" cries Jane. "I knew he wasn't Hugh. I knew it right from the start. And yet he had the audacity to go on with—"

"Not audacity," says Euell, shaking his head.

"To go on with the deception."

"Just dumb."

"This constitutes a crime, then?" says Oliver.

Jane nods, and says almost contritely, "You see, I . . . I watch people. At the party last night . . . I mean you mustn't think I was *spying*. I don't *spy* on people, I . . . Oh, how to say it? I . . ."

"You pay attention," Euell offers.

"Yes. Yes, thank you. I pay attention. I notice those around me, take mental notes, if you will. It's quite harmless, isn't it? It's harmless. And that's how I knew you weren't Hugh. I knew you were Earl."

"Euell," says Euell.

"Of course," says Jane. "Ewell. With a *w*?"

"A single *u*. E-u-e-l-l."

"My goodness. What a lot of vowels."

Oliver Hedquist excuses himself at that moment. He

isn't particularly interested in why one man masquerades as another—or rather he has felt the temptation himself and has from time to time succumbed to it. It seems the most human thing in the world, to wish oneself into someone else's life. Or at least out of one's own. During several dark periods in his marriage he pretended to be a man never at home, a man so busy, so caught up in his work, he had no time to darken the door of his own house. And all this in order to widen the gulf between him and his wife, whose actions, he knew, came of a desperation he could not soothe, an absence she felt in his presence. "More absence!" his body cried, so acute at times was his desire to remove himself from her. He understands, yes he certainly does, the need to be who one is not. Though why Euell Wigglesworth would choose to be that dissolute sissy fruitcake Hugh Huddleston, that's a bit of a mystery.

Her Rubicon

Jane stands in the doorway and watches him bicycle away. The relief she thought she would feel with his departure does not arrive. Instead a terrible restlessness overtakes her, and she goes to her room and empties the contents of her purse onto the bed. No ring. She shakes the accursed purse, holding it upside down and sweeping her hand around inside it. No ring. Ah! she remembers. Of course! The inner pocket. She tugs on the zipper and there it is, right where she placed it a fortnight ago. A simple silver ring, set all around with light blue stones. The turquoise thrills and astonishes her anew. She looks at her wedding band, remembering for a brief moment the incident that came to represent that day for her. It eclipsed the nuptial vows, the scratchy kiss Morris dutifully planted on her cheek at the altar (she had anticipated a kiss on the lips and stood there like a beached fish, smacking the air), the oversize tent under which a motley band played "Boogie Woogie Bugle

Boy," "Chattanooga Choo Choo," and what sounded to Jane
like "Giovinezza," a Fascist marching song—all too difficult
to dance to, Morris not being much of a dancer to begin with.
But the jewel in the crown of that less-than-fairy-tale day was
the stream of urine unleashed by Jane's brother, Willis, onto
the lily white surplice of the minister. Poor man, ghastly as he
was with his buck teeth and malfunctioning salivary glands
that caused him to swallow and drool all through the service,
he certainly didn't deserve what Willis bequeathed him. Such
is Jane's thought as she removes her wedding band and tucks
it into her underwear drawer and slips on the turquoise ring in
its place. She feels a guilty thrill, and at the same time a sense
of standing at the bow of a boat, looking toward the far shore,
the gray waters of the Rubicon passing beneath. Or is it the
Delaware? Anyway, launched is what she feels, and it is at this
moment in her trajectory that her attention falls on the folded
piece of paper thrust at her by Euell Wigglesworth as he fled
the house. It lies on the bed amid the contents of her purse. She
picks it up gingerly, her hand trembling for reasons she cannot
imagine, and slowly, carefully, unfolds it. She expects a note,
some word of apology perhaps, but clearly this is not young
Mr. Wigglesworth's way. For when the paper lies open in her
hands, there is not one ink mark upon it. Instead, a freshly collected butterfly.

A Gentleman's Correspondence

Louis Schellbach sits in his study at home and meditates on the Texas longhorn skull above his desk. It seems to resemble him in ways he never considered before, in ways he was blind to. What brings a man to fruition is neither ordinary nor extraordinary—bones, flesh, blood, and a riot of chemicals. He must admit, the same can be said for this cow.

Before him lies a pile of old correspondence, a stack of carbon copies that his job this morning is to read and discard with a ruthlessness to which he is not suited. His wife, Ethyl, is taken with the notion of running a tight ship. He's tried to argue that her ship and his are two different vessels, that she commands the navy while he's just a fisherman hauling in his nets. But as she points out, his nets tend to drift beyond the bounds of his study, so an innocent guest searching for jam might come upon a dead snake stored in the icebox. What that has to do with a clean desk, he's not entirely certain, but in order to maintain peace in the region, he has chosen this day to sit and review his past. The fact that the past can be so easily removed—a toss into the wastebasket—intrigues him. Is it really so?

At the top of the pile is a letter from the great naturalist John Garth, who named a butterfly for him, *Speyeria atlantis schellbachi*. Some day it will be said, Schellbach muses, that he left a trace of himself in the world of butterflies, though the truth is quite the opposite—those evanescent creatures have filled his days for as long as he can remember, and all but carried him on their wings. They know what sort of man he is. He loves his wife and a mule named Dark Eyes. He's curious about every living thing, as well as rocks, weather, water, and briarwood pipes. There is only one area that holds no interest for him whatsoever, which he assiduously avoids: the realm of human psychology. And tragedy in particular. Unlike Ethyl, who attracts the downtrodden, the trials and tribulations of his fellow human beings largely pass him by. He does not sightsee nor rubberneck should he happen to encounter another man's misfortune. He has two children, two boys, and knows in a little-used part of his brain that planted in his sons are innumerable adolescent misfortunes, from which all the butterflies in the world cannot save him.

The next letter causes him to pause as he revisits the state of agitation in which it was composed, as well as the balky *U* key on his old Royal typewriter:

Dear Mr. Dunhill,

It is with great sadness and regret that I write to you today to inform you of the death of your brother, Lowell. He died in an accident while serving the park he loved so well. All of us here at Grand Canyon mourn him as our own, and take comfort only in the fact that he died in the place where he was happiest, surrounded by the natural beauty he gave his life to protect. He was an accomplished photographer and a great outdoorsman, admired by all. We shall miss him. As we have no knowledge of Lowell's wishes for burial, please advise about these matters with due haste. My deepest sympathies go out to you and your family at this time.

Stapled to the first is a second letter:

Dear Mr. Owen Dunhill,

Allow me to extend my sympathy to you at this unfortunate time. I am certain you are reeling from the shock of your brother's death, as are we here at Grand Canyon. Regretfully, we still have no instructions as to the disposal of his body and feel it outside the bounds of our jurisdiction to make such decisions, which are rightfully the family's. It is with some urgency, therefore, that I write to request once again that you make your wishes known to us, so we may do everything within our power to lay your brother's body to rest in the way you deem suitable.

That was a disagreeable business if there ever was one. It was the summer of 1938, his first season as chief park naturalist. He was new and green, yet from the evidence in his hand, tactful as a man could be. Had he abandoned diplomacy and said it straight, it might have sounded like this: "Dunhill, you fool! Death isn't pretty. Come and get the poor soul, come and bury your brother. Have you no human decency? A man like Lowell deserves a better lot!" But the family never came, never uttered a peep, and the very next day the unclaimed body walked out of the house, Schellbach's own house, and disappeared! Not a sign, not a trace, no twenty-one guns, no flag-draped coffin—Lowell had his way even in death. If the sheriff knew of a corpse gone missing, he decided against the paperwork, and the county coroner was a sad Norwegian on a bender. Schellbach diligently hopes (though he fears otherwise) that the whole unsavory mess hasn't come back to haunt them. He has his own theories about the skeleton in Emery Kolb's garage, theories founded on things he doesn't believe in, like intuition.

What he remembers most about that summer of 1938, before the incident, is the appearance of a comic-book character, a recent immigrant from the planet Krypton, a young fellow by the name of Superman. Plagued by insomnia, Schellbach would make his way to the kitchen in the wee hours of the morning, drink a glass of milk, and eat a plate of cookies while he pored over his son's *Action Comics*. There was something fresh and raw in those pages that he found nowhere else in his life, not even out in the field. It was a guilty pleasure he sought, as he had once sought romance, though soon enough the guilt disappeared, leaving in its place a simple enjoyment, a rest and reassurance found only in the company of fallible superheroes. And then one day, as if to test his powers, the pack mules hauled up something other than garbage and dirty linens from Phantom Ranch. It lay in the mule barn, a recognizable human shape wrapped in a sheet. By the time he got there the stench was unmistakable.

As he backed the car to the door of the barn to retrieve the body, Schellbach reviewed his rationale for this course of action and found it to be sound. There was no good reason to leave the poor man here. In Schellbach's home, packed in ice, the bundle (easier to call it that) might happily await the vultures of law enforcement whose probing and prodding, slicing and eviscerating would confirm what he already knew: identity and cause of death. He knew both without having laid eyes on the man. Accelerating cautiously backward, he wondered at the circumstances that made him, Louis Schellbach, what he was—*Homo sapiens*, living and breathing—while the other fellow was suddenly a bundle. The answer was love, the circumstances of love. But might he not have done the same, followed his heart—unto death if necessary? Certainly had he been a bachelor, in the days when he was Don Juan Schellbach . . . But wasn't every man, married or unmarried, prone to the same appetites? And apparently some women as well? (He still found it troubling, the identity of the woman involved.) What was it that made one man resist the onslaught of love and another succumb to it? And who was the better man in the end, the resister or the succumber? Which one would evolution smile upon, the living celibate or the dead lover? Or perhaps there was a narrow path in between, where walked the gentleman.

His breakfast suddenly pirouetted in his stomach—two eggs over easy and a buttered English muffin with marmalade—as Oliver Hedquist, of all people, loomed in the rearview mirror. "Another two meters, Louie!" he called hoarsely, motioning the car back. "That's it. That's it. Stop 'er right there!"

Schellbach got out and slowly closed the car door. "Oliver." He nodded. Hedquist nodded back. "What brings you here to the mule barn?"

Hedquist held out a bunch of carrot tops. "Just saying hello to a friend of mine."

"Not Dark Eyes."

"Howdy is the poor creature's ignominious name."

"I see. Well, I'm afraid there's been some trouble."

"I should say so," said Hedquist.

"The wrangler came and got me at the house."

"I was here when he brought the . . . when he brought him up."

"Did he tell you the circumstances?" asked Schellbach.

"Just that he found the fellow washed up on the beach under the bridge. Hard to say what happened."

Schellbach nodded, then loosened his tie and stepped inside the barn. A terrible syrupy odor came to him, mixed with the sweet smell of hay. The bundle lay on the floor, where a large tomcat was sniffing the length of it. He shooed it away and stepped outside again. "Anyone else in on this?" he asked.

"In on it?"

"Has anyone else been by? Seen the . . . er . . . evidence?"

Hedquist shook his head. "No one's been here. Just me and the mules. But I don't know where the wrangler's gone to. He's an unstable sort of character, that Amadeo."

"He's waiting at the house."

"Your house?"

"To help me lift the fellow in."

"In? You're taking him to your home?" asked Hedquist, startled.

"Ethyl's away."

"Glad to hear it."

"The children are with her."

"I would expect it."

"Listen," said Schellbach. "I don't have much choice, do I? I can't leave him here to rot, and I can't very well drag him into the office, can I? He's in a delicate state. He might lose an arm or a leg. At any moment his head might fall off. Why, the smell's enough to— Do you see?"

"Well, of course, but I—"

"And what makes it worse is that we all know the individual."

"How can that be? You haven't even looked under his wraps!"

Schellbach sighed. "I don't pay much attention to cries for help, I'm afraid. I leave that to Ethyl. This time I wish I had. Lowell Dunhill would be alive now."

"Dunhill!" Hedquist exclaimed. "How could it be Dunhill?

He's the most experienced ranger we have—in the outdoors and all. Not a likely one to end up in the river. Not Dunhill."

"I'm afraid, yes. Dunhill."

"But that's impossible. I don't believe you." Hedquist took a deep breath. "I'll look for myself."

Schellbach did not try and stop him but instead walked away and readied the backseat of the car. When he returned to the barn, the look on Hedquist's face was one of horror and disbelief. The bundle lay with the head exposed, covered with flies. It was, of course, Dunhill.

"A terrible thing," said Hedquist, "the way a man's face changes in death."

"It's no longer his," said Schellbach. "Help me with this, will you?"

Together they lifted the body into Schellbach's car. It did not fit across the seat, and to have the feet hang out the window was out of the question. In the end they wired the door shut.

"But how did you know it was he?" asked Hedquist.

"He told me," said Schellbach.

"Look here, I don't believe in ghosts, the talking dead— none of that nonsense."

"Oh, he was quite alive when he said it."

"I don't follow."

Schellbach took his pipe from the glove case of the car and slowly filled it with tobacco. "Lowell was alone so much of his life. His great companion was his camera. He didn't understand life—and love—as a game, the way most of us do. If it was a game, it was a very serious one, and he felt, I believe, that he was beginning to lose the game and he had no solution but to remove himself from it."

"So he—"

"Yes. There's a sheep trail down to the river just above Grapevine Rapid. That's where he often went to think things over, and that's where I believe he did it. He always said that's what he'd do, throw himself in above a big rapid and let the river do the rest."

"Am I to understand there were . . . *women* involved?"

"A woman, yes."

"How extraordinary. I guess I . . . well, I suppose I didn't know the man worth a hill of beans."

"He was hard to know. I don't know that any of us really knew him. I had the impression that, being a trim fellow, his heart was too big for his body. It certainly outweighed his sense."

"Well, it wouldn't be the first time a man's lost his head to a woman."

"But his life," sighed Schellbach. "I must ask you not to tell anyone, Oliver. Not just yet."

"Of course not."

"I'll want to notify the family. I know there's a brother."

"Of course. Mum's the word."

But by the end of the afternoon the news had spread all over the village: Lowell Dunhill was dead. The source of this information wasn't Oliver but Amadeo, whose cowboy tongue loosened considerably when indulging in alcohol. The minute Dunhill's remains clunked onto the table in Louis Schellbach's laboratory, the wiry little wrangler turned and fled the house. Soon enough everyone in the cowboy dorm was saturated with cheap whiskey and hearing the grisly tale for the nth time. By evening rumor had created several bodies on the beach below the bridge, many of them disfigured, their faces clawed and mutilated, their bodies hacked at—clear evidence of cannibalism. And Schellbach, knowing better than to fight the swift onslaught of a tall tale, instead let it exhaust itself and limp on to its own demise—a strategy for which he was rewarded. Within a day, equilibrium had been accomplished and grieving had begun. Shortly after that, Lowell Dunhill had roused himself from death, it seemed, and disappeared, taking his body with him.

Suddenly weary, feeling wrapped in a kind of mothball stupor, the park naturalist drops the Dunhill correspondence in the wastebasket and rises from his desk. The past feels like a heavy, choking thing, not easily disposed of, and he allows himself to wonder once again: where are the bones, the flesh, the blood that made up that man?

A Packet of Liverwurst

Every July the Hedquists pack the car with sleeping bags, cots, mattresses, an old Army tent, the camp stove, pots and pans, plates, cups, utensils, kerosene lanterns, canned food and staples, jugs of water, and extra gasoline, and off they go to the North Rim to live in the woods for a week. Jane is curious about the North Rim. It sounds so arctic, so far away, and besides, she has looked out across the canyon and seen it shrouded with mist or hovering behind a thick pall of smoke, and it is all such a mystery. She has informed the Hedquists she would like to walk around inside that mystery, if they are willing to include her. Oliver and Dotty at once say yes. Oliver, on his part, likes Jane very well but his excitement further rises when he thinks of having another net along—and not just any net, for Jane, in a remarkably short time, has become an enthusiastic butterfly collector of admirable skill. Dotty has her own reasons for welcoming her sister-in-law on this year's journey. She often feels lonely out in the woods, for she doesn't have the interests Oliver has, and she could use the company. Her interests are at home, in the garden, which she hates to leave for any length of time. Who will mulch and fertilize and do the watering? It all must be arranged in advance, and there is no one she can count on, except perhaps Amadeo.

The household is in a flurry of preparation. Jane is sent to the store for lunch meat, coffee, and cheese. Dotty adds sugar, flour, and frankfurters to the list. Oliver would like marshmallows and a good supply of candy bars. Off goes Jane, every day more wedded to her hat, the ample shade of its brim a reassuring presence. She's on her bicycle (she's come to think of it as hers), an empty rucksack on her back for bringing home the groceries. Halfway along the road to Babbitt Brothers she stops, as she always does, to gaze at the canyon, to judge its mood, perhaps, or discover her own mood reflected by it—Narcissus and his pool. Today it's a dramatic sight, the clouds gathering thickly to the north in long dark columns. As she watches, a thin silver line of lightning jumps from cloud to cloud—a hairline crack moving outward. She feels the wind pick up, a pressure in the air. Yet above her the sky is clear and untouched. A marvel.

Her first stop is the post office, where she collects the Hedquists' mail and sends off her weekly letter to Morris. She can't help but notice that her epistles have lost their verve, their vigor, and perhaps their vim as well. At first she wrote to her husband daily, recounting in great detail how the hours were spent, what was eaten at each meal, what was said, where her bicycle had carried her, and whom she'd met. She had a vague

sense she might be boring Morris to tears. He, on his part, tele-
phoned twice a week from the office, a two-minute call that assured little time for anything but news of the dog—Martin, it
seemed, was now running the household. And though he continues to call, she feels a slight unraveling of their connection.
Perhaps he's put her aside in order to tolerate her absence. This
makes him gruff and unapproachable on the telephone, which
does nothing to bring them closer. "A sad state of affairs," sighs
Jane Merkle. Though common enough in a marriage.

Today Dotty has a letter from a Mrs. T. E. Gastrofoil of
West Branch, Iowa, which Jane recalls, from an article in
National Geographic Magazine, is the birthplace of Herbert
Hoover. What an odd and useless thing to remember! Mrs.
Gastrofoil may well be a descendent of the unlucky president,
whose name inspires thoughts of hobos and the electric carpet
sweeper. Does a person in this position take pride in the ances-
tor or hide behind the name Gastrofoil? Jane herself was a Yarborough of no fame at all, nor infamy, Jane Meese Yarborough
in her larval stage, as Oliver would put it, pupating as Jane Yarborough Merkle. Though pupation, she has learned, is a sort
of live mummification, an immobile, nonfeeding state before
emergence. Is this the truth, then? She has not yet emerged?
She laughs out loud at the thought. Almost twenty-six years old
and married to Morris? She feels positively long in the tooth!

A second letter for Dotty has neither stamp nor postmark.
It's addressed to "Mrss Dorathy Hedqist" and the addresser is
"AV, Grn Canon, Arzona." Jane looks around to be sure she's
alone in the post office—except, of course, for the ubiquitous

prune of a postmistress who rules the roost. To her astonishment, never having thought of herself as quite this kind of person, she rips open the envelope and retrieves the piece of paper inside, which is folded twice and contains this message:

> meat 12 noon bhind mule barn
> I em yors Deo

Well, now she's done it. She tucks paper and envelope into her rucksack along with the rest of the mail and runs out and leaps on her bicycle, neglecting to wish the postal prune a good morning. She pedals next door to the store, the peace of her day swallowed up by the single act of opening a letter. She can't imagine what came over her. She can't account for it. Mere curiosity? A desire to catch Dotty in the act of something—which she now has, though the act of what, exactly? What might her sister-in-law be up to, meeting I Em Yors Deo behind the mule barn? Or not meeting him, if it's a him. Because, as Jane realizes, the note is in her possession and will never get to Dotty. And yet if it doesn't, there will be no meeting and the mystery will end there— the trail will lose itself in the underbrush. Or at least the communicants will grow leery of their present system and never use the mail again. They'll resort to a hollow tree or a crack in a rock, squirreling away their love letters where the prying eyes of snoops will never find them. Snoops? Is she a snoop, then? Didn't she recently claim she wasn't one to spy? "I don't spy on people." Hadn't those exact words escaped her lying lips just a short time ago? They had. She had spoken them to Euell, Euell-With-a-*U*, as she has taken to calling him. Not that she ever speaks of him to anyone except herself. She wants to—too much, that's the problem. The one time Oliver mentioned his name in conversation, a conversation that happened to be about the labial palpi of the snout butterfly, she was horrified to feel a flush along her arms and up her neck and across her forehead and cheeks. When her brother-in-law asked if she had a fever, she lied and said yes. It was easier than saying, "Oliver, dear Oliver, I don't know what's become of me!"

The clerk at the store is a pale, bulbous, middle-aged woman whom Dotty refers to privately as Mrs. Jicama. "Hello there!" she cries. "Hot out, isn't it!" If one were to write her into a play, thinks Jane, entering the store and standing for a moment in the blinding darkness, one would punctuate her entirely with exclamation points.

"It is," says Jane. "Very hot."

"June's hotter!" cries Jicama. "Before the rains!"

"Thank goodness the rain is here," says Jane, shifting her mind from weather to lunch meats. "I wonder if you have any bologna today."

"No bologna!" Jicama shakes her head. "But the nicest liverwurst you ever saw!"

"Thank you," says Jane, and she starts down an aisle, picking up flour and sugar and coffee as she goes.

She has nothing against liverwurst. Liverwurst with apple makes a very nice sandwich. She can't remember if the Hedquists harbor some ill feeling toward liverwurst. Many people do. She's never been offered it in their home, in almost a month of

lunches. But Morris likes liverwurst quite a bit, and therefore Dotty might be prone to liking it as well. Perhaps it's Oliver who shies away from it. Yet he's admitted a fondness for
caviar, and liverwurst and caviar have a certain strong fishy
taste in common. Now how, thinks Jane, could something that
comes from a cow taste like a fish? Oliver's love of caviar may
go hand in hand with his admiration for Tolstoy. Don't the
Russians eat fish eggs? The old Russians, not this new breed
of hotheaded Communists. Suddenly she remembers that her
own husband may be a Communist—she hasn't had the nerve
to ask him. Wouldn't it be awkward on the telephone? "Morris," she imagines herself saying, "what's this about you being
a Communist? No no, dear, of course I don't disapprove. Why,
your own Aunt Gretchen was a Communist. *And* a fortune-
teller. *And* a Presbyterian. It's hardly your fault." In any case
she'll take a close look at this liverwurst and see if it's fresh and
then decide.

Ahead of her looms the delicatessen counter with its glass
case of assorted raw meats, sliced meats, and roasted chickens
arranged to look peaceful in death. Jane approaches, her eye
on a perfectly decent-looking roll of liverwurst. She asks the
butcher whether the liverwurst is fresh. "¡Ah, sí!" he says, "is
fresh, is fresh!" He too is prone to exclamation points. "I'll take
three inches off the roll then," she says, wondering if *roll* is the
right word or whether *log* or *loaf* might be more correct. She
can't remember if she was instructed to buy cheese. There are
several different cheeses in front of her, as well as potato salad
and egg salad and coleslaw and a scarlet Jell-O salad bedeviled

with tiny marshmallows, which reminds her that she must get marshmallows for Oliver, and candy bars, and, oh, what else? She'll do that while she's waiting for the handsome man to cut her liverwurst, which seems to be taking forever. But wasn't she a bit stingy with the liverwurst? Maybe she should tell him four inches, not three. Those who like liverwurst like liverwurst, after all, and those who don't wouldn't go near it for all the tea in China. Oh! All this wretched decision making! She turns to pursue an easier task—Mars Bars or Hershey bars, which will it be?—and in a clumsy rush runs smack into the person behind her, whom, in her agitated state of mind, she hasn't noticed. He cries out as a man would when he's been walloped in the chest, then to her great surprise says, "Mrs. Merkle?"

"Mr. Wigglesworth!" she gasps. She's aware of a sort of fishlike gape overtaking her lower face, but she manages to say, "Or is it Hugh?"

Euell Wigglesworth smiles. He has a very pleasant smile, Jane notices, not elfin, which she finds difficult to trust, but large and open, showing good teeth. "I'm pleased to report that Hugh and I are no longer the same person."

"Well," she laughs, "that's a relief."

"It is," says he, and he looks at the wooden floor for what seems like a very long time. Finally Jane looks there as well, seeing nothing but sawdust. Sawdust and the bottom of his uniform trousers and his shiny brown boots.

"What a pleasant surprise," he says at last.

"Yes," she agrees, but her tongue feels maddeningly reluctant, like an old dog ordered off the bed.

"Well," says he.

"It's hot out, isn't it?" says she.

"Hot? Yes, yes. Hot!"

"And humid."

"The rain is about to—"

"Perhaps you saw the thunderheads just now—"

"Yes! The North Rim is—"

"Isn't it a sight!"

Then there is nothing more to say. Jane Merkle cannot imagine what two people talk about, though she herself is usually a capable conversationalist. She's flummoxed. Everything feels new and strange. Which it is. She's not prepared to understand it, but this is the first communication between herself and Mr. Wigglesworth that has nothing to do with the topic at hand (and how quickly they exhaust it!) but is instead an intended expression of goodness, of suitability, of interest in the other, after which each feels a certain sadness and guilt, a failing of energy, like the coming of winter. Neither party knows what to do with such a feeling, or what name to call it, and neither imagines its existence in the other but feels alone with it, dumb and inconsolable. Jane Merkle is the more desperate to escape her discomfort. Her skin feels on fire and her heart feels waxy and dead. She's a little sick to her stomach, as if she's swallowed a lump of toothpaste. Finally she can tolerate it no longer and says the first thing that presents itself to her disturbed and distracted mind: "Do you by any chance know whether the Hedquists like liverwurst?"

Euell Wigglesworth considers the question. He feels somehow he owes her this consideration. He furrows his brow, quite a charming furrow, and his lower lip protrudes slightly in a boyish wondering way. His effort seems to produce a flush in his cheeks, and he loosens his tie ever so slightly without even knowing he's doing so. His tongue, however, is as locked up as hers is.

She sighs and says, "So many people don't. Like it, I mean. I suppose it's too strong a taste. Too . . . alive. And the silly thing is, I went ahead and ordered three inches but I don't know if that's enough. Do you think four might be better?"

"Four?" he says dully.

"The cut. The cut off the loaf, or the length, or the roll, whatever it's called."

"Oh," he laughs, feeling suddenly untangled, free. "Oh, I see. Well, four is four inches too many for those who don't like liverwurst, and three isn't enough for those who do, so I'd go with four and hope they're in the 'like it' category. Though you could telephone them and hear it from the horse's mouth."

"Oh, there's an idea!" cries Jane, clapping her hands. She ought to feel silly and childish in her glee, but she doesn't. She feels she can breathe again. She looks at Euell fully, for the first time, and realizes she's never seen him in uniform before. She doesn't generally like olive green but it lends something to him. He looks manly and in charge of things, well prepared for any adventure or emergency. The hat is unfortunate, but he has the good sense to take it off indoors and hold it by his side. He inspires confidence, and but a moment ago, he was young looking, shy as a girl. Oh, he's boy and man all mixed up in one, thinks Jane. It's a thought that pleases and frightens her in equal parts.

At that moment the butcher flops her liverwurst on the counter, and she thanks him, saying she might be back for more.

"Or less," teases Euell Wigglesworth as he steps up to order eight roasted chickens and a pound of sliced cheese.

"Goodness!" cries Jane. "What an awful lot of chickens!"

"It's for the boys," says Euell.

"The boys?" Jane is suddenly dizzy, panicky. She manages to say, "I didn't know you had children, Mr. Wigglesworth."

"They act like children." He smiles. "The boys I work with. I'm over on the North Rim now, heading back there this afternoon. I like to bring them something so they're happy to see me again, so they don't forget about me when I'm gone."

"Oh, I can't believe anyone would be unhappy to see you. Or forget about you when you're away. I . . . I myself am going to the North Rim tomorrow."

"No kidding!"

"Maybe our paths will cross on the far side of the river."

"That would be swell!"

Jane laughs and says, "*Swell* is a word I haven't heard in years. Do you know the time, Mr. Wigglesworth?"

He consults his watch. "It's quarter past eleven."

"Oh!" she cries. "I must make that telephone call." For she has a plan now, thanks to Euell Wigglesworth, and there's no time to waste. In forty-five minutes it will be noon. She holds out her hand and says, boldly, "May we meet again."

He takes her hand solemnly but does not shake it. He holds

it in much the same way she holds her packet of liverwurst. "I hope so," he says.

Suddenly she remembers something. "Oh, I almost forgot to thank you. For my butterfly, Mr. Wigglesworth. It's the most beautiful thing."

"You like it?" he says, his eyes on the floor again, his cheeks suddenly aflame. "It's royalty in the butterfly world. Its common name is—"

"Queen. I know. And I took the liberty of pinning it, and I meant to ask you where you captured it so I can write that on the tag."

"You know butterflies, Mrs. Merkle?" He is genuinely astonished. "You know how to pin butterflies? Do you collect them?"

"I do, Mr. Wigglesworth. I'm a fast-moving amateur, as my brother-in-law would say. I believe it refers to swift of foot rather than any prodigious qualities of mind, but I'm happy for the compliment."

"I'm . . . I'm speechless."

"Well, you needn't be," laughs Jane. "Oliver is far too generous with his compliments."

"No. No, I doubt it," says Euell thoughtfully, and just then the butcher arrives with a tray of eight wrapped chickens and slides them onto the counter.

"What you want for cheese?" he says. "Swiss, Monster, American?"

"Cheddar," says Euell.

"We no have cheddar."

"Then I'll take American."

"How much? Five pound?"

"One pound."

"You pay for it?"

"Charge it to Hugh."

"What you gonna do when he's not your friend no more? The chickens too?"

"I'll pay for them," says Euell.

"If I was you," says the butcher, "I pay the cheese and let my friend pay the chickens!"

Jane says good-bye once more and leaves Euell Wigglesworth to his packages. She has her own little packet of liverwurst, wrapped in brown paper, tied with white butcher string, and the way it fits in her hand, and the small but solid weight of it, and the color of the string against the color of the paper— all of it soothes her as she walks to the front of the store. She gathers the rest of the things on her list and pays for them at the register. She counts out the money into the hamlike hand of Mrs. Jicama and finds herself on the verge of tears. Tears that seem to spring from her throat and chest, tears of release—from what or to what, she cannot tell. From her calm self the tears come, tears in response to some promise, some hope, some new opening onto a world she had no idea she was closed to, or hopeless about, or seeking a promise from, a conversation with. A new territory from which tears arise like rivers in flood passing through drought-stricken fields where life has not moved for years, and where the reapers have not reaped because the sowers have not sown, and where birds, bees, and butterflies are unknown, as foreign as a picture language to those who alphabetize. Mrs. Jicama looks at her with some concern and cries, "Find everything you were looking for?!"

"Just a telephone," says Jane.

"You want a telephone?!"

"To call my sister-in-law."

"Mrs. Hedquist!"

"That's right."

"You come with me and we'll find you a telephone! I see you got yourself some of that liverwurst! Don't you worry about nothing!"

The Hour of No Shadow

At 11:25 in the morning, Dotty Hedquist receives a telephone call from her sister-in-law who seems to be in an uncharacteristic flap about what kind of lunch meat to buy. Liverwurst? Anyone can tolerate liverwurst. As far as liking it? Well she, Dotty, won't go as far as to say they like it, she and Oliver, but certainly, if Jane has in her slender midwestern hand a hunk of already-purchased liverwurst, that will do. Dotty prepares to hang up the receiver. She doesn't like telephones, she feels she can hear the nickels and dimes being sucked into the wires. But there's more. Jane says, "Oh, and I got the mail, and Dotty, you have two letters, one from Iowa, a Mrs. Gastrofoil. I think it's Gastrofoil—"

"That's fine, Jane, just bring it home."

But the impervious Jane is not to be stopped. "And a second one from an AV right here in the village. I wonder who that would be? Anyway, I have both letters and I'll be home soon, as quickly as I can, though it won't be . . . no, certainly not before noon. Would you like me to do anything with the letters, Dotty? One or the other of them might be important."

"Yes," Dotty manages to say, her head spinning, her heart thumping. She's gone pale, but of course her sister-in-law can't see that. "Yes. Very good, Jane. Read them to me. Well, no. Just the one from . . . what did you say the initials were?" She's proud of this little performance.

"AV, Dotty."

"AV, then. Why don't we look at that one."

She hears the rustling of a paper, and Jane reads: "Dear Mrs. Hedquist, I have adjusted your stirrups and would like to make sure they fit. Meet me behind the mule barn today at noon and we'll take care of that business. Repectfully yours, AV."

"Stirrups?" Dotty wonders aloud.

"Perhaps you had a plan to go riding," Jane offers.

"I'm not much of a rider. You're sure it says 'stirrups'?"

"It seems to," says Jane. "Though the details are sometimes misleading. I think the message is clear enough: mule barn at noon. That's the way I see it, at least. Well, I'd better be on my way. Anything else I can do for you?"

"No no. Well, yes, actually, Jane. You might just throw that letter away, not even bring it home. Now that you've read it to me, I mean."

"Certainly. One less thing to carry."

Dorothy Hedquist stands in her own kitchen, as confused as she has ever been. Why on earth would he throw in the business about the stirrups? Unless he was afraid the letter might be intercepted. But by whom? Not Oliver. Certainly not Oliver.

The clock says almost twenty-five minutes before twelve. She hasn't much time. However, she likes to look her best on these occasions and takes a few minutes to fuss with her hair (the bun comes out) and change into a clean pair of blue denim trousers and one of her (one of his, Lowell's) old but practically new Oxford shirts. The pink one. It makes her feel strong and capable and not too feminine, in the weak sense of the word. She dons her hiking boots on the good chance she'll be walking through mule poo, and with a little good-bye to Oliver, who's dug in in his den identifying water beetles, she leaves the house on foot, cutting through the woods until she catches the heady odor of digested grass and turns toward the mule barn. It is now, by her dainty gold watch, five minutes to noon.

Back at the house Oliver Hedquist has answered the telephone, which rang and rang and rang until he could stand the noisy intrusion no longer. On a small notepad kept beside the beast for just these purposes, he jots a message for Jane: "Rowe Well, nr. Supai Camp, GCNP."

"She'll know what this is in regard to?" asks Oliver.

"Yes, sir," says Euell Wigglesworth.

"And how are you keeping yourself these days?"

"Just fine, sir."

"It's a good life, isn't it?"

"What life would that be, Mr. Hedquist?"

"All of it, damn it!"

"Yes, sir. It's a good life."

"Well, it ought to be," says Oliver.

Dotty stands at the edge of the ponderosas, considering her options. Noon is the hour of no shadow and therefore the wrong time to go unnoticed. Between her and the mule barn is the corral—an acre of open ground dotted with unpredictable, ill-tempered animals. But if she stays outside the fence, she will surely be seen by someone, which wouldn't be the end of the world as long as she doesn't act furtive. Perhaps he won't come at all. Or he'll be as late as he was the last time, and their half hour together will come down to a matter of minutes. No. She won't risk her reputation for a few minutes alone with him. No matter how pressing the matter is or how much new information he has for her: heard with his own ears, seen with his own eyes. How dearly she would love to catch Emery Kolb in the act, to illuminate his foul deed for all the world to see! But she must be patient. She's nobody's fool. Her watch reads five minutes after twelve and she'll give him till quarter past. She steps back into the concealing pines and waits for Amadeo.

A Road Trip

Euell Wigglesworth and Hugh Huddleston are not getting along as well as they used to, which is why Ranger Naturalist Wigglesworth has invited Ranger Naturalist Huddleston up to the North Rim for a few days to catch bugs by day and light-trap moths by night and generally clear the air between them, an air resembling the dirty brown gunk hanging over New Jersey. But Hugh, it seems, has forgotten. In Euell's absence he has taken over his house and fallen in love with his bed, and it is there Euell finds him, sound asleep in the middle of the day, wearing only his shoes. Mysteriously, he has a pillow over his head.

"Huddleston? Are you ill?"

"Hullo!" cries Hugh from under the foul-smelling pillow. "I might be. Can't tell."

"Why don't you come up for air and find out?"

"Can't."

"Can't?"

"It's too much for me, Charles."

"What a sop you are! What's this with the pillow?"

"I need the pillow. Don't take the pillow."

"Well, I'm not talking to you with that thing over your head."

"It's not a thing. It's a pillow."

"Hugh," says Euell evenly, "I will count to three."

"You can count to three hundred. I need the pillow. I don't like today and I don't feel very well and I like being in bed and I won't come out just because you want me to. We can talk like this. Don't be so bloody stubborn."

"I'm not talking to a pillow."

"But you are."

"All right. Never mind. I've left you some cheese. I'm sorry you won't come with me. I think it would do you some good."

"Where are you going?" asks Hugh, sliding the pillow away from his face. "Are you going somewhere? Have I driven you away?"

Euell comes and sits on the bed. "To the North Rim, Hughie. In search of butterflies—the elusive Riding's satyr and all the bonnie sulphurs, clouded and cloudless, and red-spotted purples and swallowtails the size of cow's feet and hairstreaks and silvery blues and red and Weidemeyer's admirals. And at night, my friend, the moths—sphinxes, tigers, Pandoras, and underwings, and all other manner of noctuids, some never seen before by hominids. You don't remember, do you? We planned a trip."

"It sounds like a good trip," says Hugh, sitting up. "And we have enough cheese for the two of us?"

"We do."

"Well, I'll pack my things, shall I? My net and my canteen?"

Euell nods. "Very good. I'll wait in the truck."

At the trading post in Cameron they stop to buy Coca-Colas, and Hugh would like to buy a blanket from an old Navajo woman, but he's forgotten his money. "Trade?" he says hopefully. She points to the back of the truck. "I can't give you the truck, m'dear. I wish I could. It's a government vehicle. My friend, he's the one I want to buy the blanket for, he'd be in a lot of hot water. He'd be given the boot. He's inside getting sodas." She points again and Hugh shrugs. "No deal, I guess. It's not even a good truck. You don't want this truck. I bet you've got a better one at home. Husband?" he asks her. She laughs and stands up, brushing the dust off the back of her purple skirt. She comes over to the truck and points and says, "Chickens."

"Chickens? Well, I'll be damned," says Hugh, peering into the truck bed. "Look at that. Look at all those chickens. How'd you know there were chickens in there? Bet you smelled them, didn't you?" He sniffs and points to the chickens. The woman laughs and holds up eight fingers and nods at the blanket. "Eight?" says Hugh. "You want all eight of them? What's your name? Name?" he asks again. "I'm Hugh." The woman watches him. "Hell," he says, "take them. They're yours," and he lifts the box of chickens out of the truck and sets them on the ground in the shade of the trading post. The woman folds the blanket and wraps it in brown paper and ties it with a piece of wool.

Euell comes back with two bottles of Coca-Cola, straws sticking out the top. They cross the Little Colorado, stopping on the bridge to look down at the dry riverbed. "She'll be running tomorrow," says Euell.

"Rivers aren't she's," says Hugh.

"Some of them are."

"Not the Hudson. Not the Mississippi. Not Ol' Man River. He just keeps rolling along."

"You're feeling better," Euell laughs.

"It's a road trip. I love a road trip."

By the time they arrive at the North Rim ranger station the truck is spitting dark fumes, as are the driver and passenger, each one having counted on the other for certain amenities, like cigarettes. And Hugh, to his profound dismay, has neglected to bring a bottle of something with him, something nice to drink. He realized it halfway across Indian land, somewhere in the Chinle formation, the blue humped hillocks so clownish, so bone dry it caused a thirst in him, which excited the memory of liquid refreshment. Which was not for sale on the reservation, nor beyond in the little town of Jacob Lake where they stopped for gas. The boy filling the tank was solemn when Hugh conveyed to him his hopes for a beverage stronger than Coca-Cola. "You won't find that here," said the lad. "I mean the Coca-Cola. But we got 7 Up and we got Nehi."

"Nehi?" laughed Hugh bitterly. "What the bloody hell is Nehi?"

The boy, a pale boy, clean and scrubbed, turned red as a ripe tomato and backed up a step or two. "Orange drink. You can get it in different flavors, but all's we got is orange."

"You've got nothing with, let's say, alcohol in it?"

"Alcohol?" The boy gaped at him.

"No beer or fine wines or perhaps an aged Scotch. Or a nice malt whiskey. Or a—"

"No sir," the boy interrupted. "We don't have none of that."

"Cigarettes, then. I'll have a pack of Luckies. Two packs. One for my friend."

"We don't have no cigarettes. But we got gum."

"Gum?"

The boy nodded.

"Gum, then," said Hugh. "Gum it is. A round of gum."

Across the front seat he passed Euell a stick of Doublemint. "Let's hear it for gum," he said. "And enlighten me, Charles. Who the hell were those very strange people? I felt like I was ordering moussaka in Sweden."

"Mormons," said Euell.

"They were Mormons? That ghostly little kid was a Mormon?"

"This is Mormon country."

"Well, bless my soul."

"Utah's thataway."

"I know where Utah is," said Hugh huffily. "Do they really have all those wives?"

"Some of them do."

"All those women and nothing but gum? How the Sam Hill do they do it?"

"It sounds like paradise to me."

"Oh, it doesn't, Charles. You sound like every silly red-blooded American boy. I'll tell you what, though. Right now I'd give anything for a good bottle of Scotch."

"Or a smoke," said Euell.

"Hell, I'd settle for a modest rye."

"A beer would taste good. A beer and a smoke."

"I'd give up the smoke to upgrade the beer."

"You won't have to," said Euell. "We've got the chickens."

"Chickens?"

"I'm bringing the boys some roast chickens. It loosens them up and they become generous."

"With smokes, you mean?"

"And a stash of the best Glenlivet I personally have ever tasted."

"Ah," said Hugh. "Damn."

More Than One Secret

Pretending to doze in the backseat of the Hedquists' car, Jane Merkle considers the events of the day before. In retrospect she shouldn't have done it. It was far too risky. She was lucky, yes, but it could easily have been otherwise. It was a day that divided itself right down the middle, the two halves as different as pepper and salt. That extremely pleasant encounter with Mr. Wigglesworth on the one hand, and on the other a furtive, perhaps even sordid, business that made no sense to her, though it involved someone known to her, to whom she was practically related. She opens one eye and sneaks a look at Dotty, or rather at the back of her head, as if her sister-in-law's bun might start to speak. Ordinarily a neat pincushion of hair, this morning it resembles a dog turd, and Jane is overcome with the giggles, which she expresses as a coughing fit, which in turn captures the Hedquists' attention. "Are you quite all right?" asks Oliver, who is driving. "Yes, yes," she murmurs, as if drifting back to sleep. She snores lightly to authenticate the ruse and goes on with her accounting.

She had been careful to arrive in the vicinity of the mule barn a few minutes before noon and no earlier. She went around into the woods to find the best place to wait, and as the time approached, she made her way to the edge of the woods and practically ran smack-dab into Dotty. But fortunately Dotty had her back to her, her attention focused on the barn. Minutes passed. Jane watched her anxiously scan the road and guessed that whoever he was, this Deo, he would arrive by car or truck, and it would not seem out of the ordinary for him, so he was therefore almost surely connected to the mule operation. If he was a he, she reminded herself. Just then Dotty spotted something. Jane heard her catch her breath (she was that close) and watched her walk out of the woods and along the corral fence. She walked quickly at first, nervously. She seemed to be talking to herself, trying to calm and slow herself down. Jane noticed a green truck coming along the road from the other direction, the back of it piled high with hay bales. It stopped at the barn and she saw a figure get out. It seemed like a man, though she was too far away to tell. It was small for a man, but it walked stiffly, the way a man walks, as if wearing a heavy iron belt. She would have to get closer, she realized, or she would miss everything.

Jane waited until the figure went behind the barn, followed a minute later by Dotty, then she slipped into the corral and, weaving her way around the back ends of mules (she'd heard they were steadier than horses), she made her way toward the scene of the intrigue. The voices came from inside the barn, and she crouched down behind a water barrel near the door. Dotty spoke in an angry whisper, and the man, for it was a man, replied in a pleading, subdued voice. He had an accent like the butcher's in the general store—a Spaniard then? A Mexican? "It's no good," he declared. "I cannot do it."

"What are you saying?" asked Dotty, her voice rising. "All these months and you want to walk away from it? It means nothing to you, does it? I should have known."

"It mean something. It mean I lose my job."

"Oh, your job," she scoffed. "Don't be ridiculous. You've been here almost as long as Mr. Kolb has, and you're too colorful. You're almost as colorful as he is."

"What means this, *colorful?*"

"It means you'll never lose your job. They need you. The visitors love you. Except when you're drunk."

"Please, Mrs. Dorothy."

"And I need you too," she went on. "Come here, Deo."

Jane wanted desperately to peek out from behind her barrel, but she didn't dare. From the corral came the sound of a mule sucking water from a trough, then a bird of some kind flew over going *cheeeeeeee cheeeeeeee*. She couldn't tell what was transpiring in the barn. Whatever it was, it went on for several minutes. Finally Dotty spoke in what seemed to be a breathier-than-usual voice, saying, "That's better, isn't it? We can go on, can't we?" The man, Deo, said nothing, but he must have indicated yes, because there was another brief period without conversation, and then Dotty gave a little yelp and said, "Oh, I must go! You've promised me, remember?

We'll be away for a while now, and when I get back I want you to give me everything."

"I give you something, Mrs. Dorothy."

"Everything," she repeated.

"I do good for you. But I don't want I lose my job."

"We've talked about your job, Deo."

"I need my job. I have wife and kids. They need my job."

"I know all that," said Dotty. "I know. I don't have time now. What will it take?"

"Money."

"Money!" she laughed. "You're joking."

"No. This is not joke, Mrs. Dorothy. This is America. Money is America."

"Your ideas are childish, Deo. And corrupt," she added. She was no longer whispering, and Jane could feel her own face growing hot. Suddenly she realized she was hardly invisible. She was squatting behind a barrel and any moment now Dotty could come storming out of the barn, hot as a hornet, chasing or escaping from her lover or blackmailer or whoever he was, and to be in her path would amount to suicide. It would be, in plain English, as ugly a scene as one could imagine. Rather than imagine it, Jane stood up and tiptoed away. Tiptoed, then ran, and when she reached the road she slowed to a brisk walk. She walked back to Babbitt's where, what seemed like a lifetime ago, she'd leaned her bicycle against the building. She got on it and was halfway home before she remembered the groceries. She turned around. She was in no hurry. She wanted Dotty to get home before she did. If she were Dotty, she thought, if she had a secret to keep, she would live for those moments when she could be alone with her secret, not only for the deliciousness of it—though Dotty's seemed a bit unsavory—but for the simple relief of not having to lie. Not having to lie with one's words or one's face or a trembling hand. And Jane did not want to be lied to. For she in turn would then have to lie, because she had a secret now too, didn't she? More than one. In a matter of hours she'd opened a letter not addressed to her, fabricated its contents, tracked her hapless victim, and eavesdropped on a conversation clearly not intended for her ears. And there was something else. She had tried to ignore the signs, hoping they were of no importance, like an allergic reaction to béchamel sauce that occurs once and never again. She herself had experienced such a thing and abstained for years afterward, then quite by accident had eaten it with no ill effect, which left her annoyed at all the time she'd wasted on abstinence. But. *But.* The signs she was thinking of had not abated. She continued to grow flustered in his presence, her heart beat faster, her words felt clumsy and inadequate. She noticed things about him that she had never noticed in any man before, such as his teeth and shoes. And worst of all, she could hardly wait to see him again! She had not been away from him for more than an hour and she . . . what was it exactly . . . ? She *missed* him. What an extraordinary sensation. She wasn't sure she had ever felt it before, not even for her parents, though she had loved her father very much and missed talking to him, missed their games of badminton and helping him set the table. But this was different. It didn't rely on a past together, a history of daily life. It was immediate and physical. It had to do with the presence and proximity of skin, and then its absence. His skin, his form, his—good Lord, might she use the word *spirit*? It was all a jumble in her mind. Yet clear as could be.

At the store Mrs. Jicama yielded up her packages and she started out once again, pedaling as fast as she could with the enormous rucksack of groceries on her back. She pedaled faster and faster, faster than she ever had before, even as a child. She remembered something her father used to say—he said it often, and she never understood it: "Thoughts are impediments. They're flies in the paint, pebbles in the soup. They break your teeth in the name of food." It was still obscure to her, but as she sped along, she knew that whatever kept her upright on her bicycle, it was not thought. Thought might have cautioned her to slow down, and slowing down on a bicycle meant falling over. No, it was something else; it was something she had learned to trust without knowing it, the way she trusted her feet and calves, hips and thighs to carry her through her day. It was more than instinct, more than nerve endings. It was a place, a country, a whole continent, and she had tried to live beyond its borders and had succeeded quite well, navigating by her mind, until . . . She could not put her finger on the transformative moment. And who cared anyway? It was all too philosophical. This thing, this gap, this gape of canyon over her right shoulder, it didn't care in the slightest that she, Jane Merkle, felt herself to be—oh say it, Jane!—taken, somewhat, by a young man, younger than she, certainly, who seemed himself to be somewhat smitten by her. But then, who could tell? She resolved right then and there to invite Mr. Wigglesworth to dinner. Dinner around the campfire. Followed by a walk in the moonlight. Oliver would wonder, perhaps, but perhaps not. And Dotty, caught up in her own intrigue, would hardly have time for someone else's. There was a certain assumption that went along with being a wife (it didn't hold for husbands) that Mrs. Jane Merkle now wished to use to her advantage. Wives were trustworthy and loyal, and the whole world knew it, and even when the proof lay elsewhere, they knew it all the more. They wanted it to be so, and it was so. This was a revelation to Jane. It meant freedom where she had believed there was none. Oh, freedom! she thought, bicycling into the Hedquists' yard. Terrifying freedom! And for one fleeting moment she wished to be back in St. Louis, the old Jane, Morris's dutiful helpmeet, making supper, shoveling the walk, smiling and nodding at those long pointless stories of his, which were not the sum of his life, though perhaps he thought they were. The feeling passed. She leaned her bicycle against a tree, a pine that smelled of butterscotch, and marched inside, calling out, "Yoo-hoo! Oliver! Dotty! We have food enough for weeks!"

Guessing Game

It is on the third evening, after begging a couple of Rheingolds off Ranger Naturalist Warren Haas in exchange for future favors, that Euell Wigglesworth finds an opportunity to express certain feelings to his friend Hugh Huddleston, feelings not connected to Hugh himself nor of a kind with which Hugh is directly familiar, but nonetheless floating blobs of emotion that have been bumping around inside Euell Wigglesworth's rib cage until he can stand the jarring and jostling no longer. He feels as if a crowd has gathered in his chest, an excited banner-waving crowd, not an unpleasant sensation at first but by the end of forty-eight hours unmanageable. The two young men sit on the porch of the Grand Canyon Lodge, dressed in dungarees and wool shirts. It's a cold night, following a cold and wet day. Even the hardiest guests have retreated inside, and they have the porch to themselves. Which means they can drink their borrowed beers without attracting the disapproving look of the Harvey Girl named Betty sent to serve them. Betty (written on her name tag as if she were a prize cow at the fair) is a girl of a ripe old age, at least thirty years old and plump, no longer a paragon of propriety in her too-tight-at-the-bust Fred Harvey frock. Hugh takes an immediate liking to her, which Euell suspects has something to do with the parts of her that remind them both of the buxom pillows on Euell's bed.

He has spent all his money on the chickens—or rather on the blanket that was Hugh's gift to him by way of the chickens for which he paid. And Hugh never has any money, so between the two young men there is a distinct lack of capital, which has resulted in a booze-deprived, low-nicotine, hungry few days. And the weather is raw, no good for butterflies. Euell is restless as a cat in a cage, and Warren Haas's beer has gone right to his head—literally, for he feels himself expand, sprout mandibles. Suddenly he's a hellgrammite—ugly, voracious creature, though one he finds beautiful in that hideous larval way—becoming a . . . prince! But who wants to be a prince? Who really and truly wants the job? No. He'll go along with what nature designed for him to begin with. He'll follow the career track, metamorphose as he ought to, become a dobsonfly. He has a vision of a winged insect the size of his hand, a small airplane called *Dobsonfly* with the head of a hellgrammite visible in the cockpit. God in heaven, it's a strange world—not the world of bugs with which he is familiar, but the world in which he is afloat at the moment, afloat or awash, he can't tell, sitting on a damp porch at sunset, a chilly sunset at that, feeling three sheets to the wind on half a lousy Rheingold beer.

"Shall I bum you a smoke, Charlotte?" Hugh offers congenially. "You seem a bit twittery."

"I'm not twittery."

"You are. You keep scratching your behind. And look. Look at your leg."

"What's the matter with my leg?"

"You're jiggling it."

"I'm not jiggling it. And I'm scratching my bum because it itches. It's this dratted wool shirt."

"The offer stands," says Hugh. "I'd be happy to bum you a smoke."

"And who would you bum it from?"

"From whom would I bum it? I would bum it from Betty, who else?"

"Betty isn't interested in you," Euell says crossly. "Not the slightest bit."

"What an extraordinarily rotten thing to point out. But it's not her interest I'm interested in, it's her cigarettes. And not for me but for you, m'love. Me m'self could personally give a baboon's ass for a smoke. I'm happy as a duck in pig shit with this Warren f——ing Haas's f——ing beer. Cheers." He raises his glass. "To friendship, love, and lepidoptera. And for the ones that elude the net."

"Cheers," says Euell glumly.

"You've got to do better than that, Charlie."

"I can't."

"What's eating you? You have that Edgar Allan Poe look. Something dark and dreary about you. High school yearbook: 'Best friend: Raven.'"

Euell snorts and says, "But you're my best friend, Hughie."

"I know. That's just what little Virginia Stokes-Hyde said to me in kindergarten, right before she broke my heart. Last girl I ever had." He eyes his friend. "This wouldn't be lady-love business, would it? If it's something about a girl, you would tell me? It couldn't be about a girl anyway, could it? There isn't a girl from here to kingdom come."

"It's not about a girl, exactly."

"Euell," Hugh says, leaning forward in his chair, "what the hell does that mean?"

"It's about someone, I think."

"You think?"

"But she's not a girl."

"She's a gorilla?"

"She's . . . older."

"How much older? A lot older? A little older? Help me out here."

"A little older. Older than a girl."

"Is she married?" asks Hugh.

"I . . . " Euell shrugs.

"You . . . what? She's married or she's not. Let's try this: does she have a husband?"

"Yes."

"Then she's married, nitwit. You don't want a married woman, right?"

"Right."

"End of conversation."

"I know. But I can't stop thinking about her."

"Nobody suggested not thinking about her."

"I've been thinking about her so much I feel sick to my stomach."

"That's the way I felt all through kindergarten. It turned out I was allergic to chalk."

"Do you think I should write to her?" asks Euell.

"I think you should consider the very strong possibility that all your impulses in her direction are part of a temporary insanity that will, if you let it, lead you into hot water the likes of which you've never imagined. I forbid you to write to her. *Unless.* Unless you are willing to be maimed, preferably killed, in a duel, by her furious husband. In which case, be my guest. Write to her. Does she have a name, this fair maid?"

"You know her."

"That narrows it down to several dozen married women, not counting all my parents' friends."

"You know *of* her, and you've been in her presence once without realizing it."

"Charlotte," says Hugh in exasperation, "I had no idea you had such a natural feel for suspense. But it's not a guessing game I'm interested in, it's the unveiling of the object of your desire. The dove in your heart. Who the hell is she?"

"It's Jane."

"Jane?"

Euell nods.

"But, idiot, Jane who?"

"Jane Merkle. Mrs. Merkle. Of the purse."

"Mrs. Merkle of the purse!" cries Hugh. "Our dear Mrs.

Morris Merkle of the purse! *Whoo-aah!* You sly devil!" He shakes his head and laughs.

But Euell feels neither sly nor devilish, only somewhat embarrassed by his confession. He wishes he had never mentioned any of this business and wonders why he did. Why was it so much easier to talk about a girl in a bar, or a friend's sister who once made your knees shake, than it was to talk about Jane? It would be easier to talk about Sally Domani. He never had, but he could, couldn't he? He could remember the fleshy parts of that girl and yet he couldn't remember her eyes. It was strange, a strange business.

He turns to his friend and says, "Hemple's going back tomorrow. You can catch a ride with him if you want."

"Hemple wouldn't be my first choice."

"He's not so bad. And he's your only."

"I'm sorry we didn't have a few more bugs to catch, bonnie boy," says Hugh. "It's been shit for weather. You don't know this, but I've enjoyed it. I've enjoyed your company. I'll come up again if I'm invited. As long as I don't have to ride with Hemple."

"He's all right."

"Until you have to ride with him. His idea of fun is to verbally masticate everyone known to both of you, and on top of that he farts nonstop."

"Just ignore him."

Hugh shifts in his chair. "You haven't told me anything, you know. I know there's more to tell. I'm a patient friend, Charlotte. Just don't get in over your head."

"I won't."

"You probably will."

Euell agrees but says nothing. He may possibly be in over his head already. He may have been in over his head ever since he knocked on the Hedquists' door. He thinks of her here on the North Rim (something he's forgotten to mention to Hugh), possibly close by, eating supper with Mr. and Mrs. Hedquist in the last of the gloomy light. The long, lingering summer light, and she's sitting on a log or at a picnic table somewhere just beyond his reach. What is she thinking? The bats are flying, and she's never seen bats before. She's never heard the high chirping sounds they make. She's not afraid of bats. She's not afraid of anything. She's happy to eat off a tin plate and drink out of a tin cup. The night doesn't scare her. She stands up and stretches and says good night to the Hedquists and brushes her teeth and her hair and goes into her tent. It's not yet dark and she sits on her cot in her nightgown, watching the dark outline of the trees, the pines. She's surprised at how cold it is, how exposed she feels sleeping outdoors. In her bedroll she allows herself at last to think of him, and her thoughts are delicious, like the first bite of a long-awaited meal. Lying there she places her hands on her body and imagines what his hands might feel like. There is no husband, no home somewhere else, nothing but his hands on her and the long summer light and later a saw-whet owl, though she doesn't know what to call it. She's never heard a saw-whet owl, Euell is quite certain. She can't imagine what animal might make that faraway whistling sound. It doesn't frighten her. It's a new world to her, one that keeps her awake at night, daydreaming, wondering what things in the dark look like.

The Cause of Suffering

A cloudburst such as this rivals the magnificent summer storms of Illinois and excites old memories in the gray matter otherwise known as Oliver Hedquist's brain. He sits on his camp stool in the doorway of the large canvas tent. Behind him, in the shadowy interior, Dotty lies napping. Jane is off on a hike somewhere with young Wigglesworth, without her raincoat, the silly girl. Rain pummels the tent and shakes it from top to bottom, front to back. Hedquist, age fifty-six years, three months, decides to strip off his clothes and run out into it.

He is in a state of naked abandon, wearing only his socks and sensible hiking shoes, waving arms and legs and whooping croakily, when he spies his sister-in-law and Mr. Wigglesworth heading in his direction. The young man is gallantly trying to shield the lady from the elements with his jacket, which he holds above her as they run through the forest. It's fruitless, of course. Anyone can see that. She's soaked to the skin, as is he, and the wise thing would be to lay aside gallantry and gallop for the barn. Both of them. For he has slowed down to lay his cloak across her sky, and she, sensing knightly action, has slowed down to accommodate it. Odd to Oliver how crisply, cleanly, he can read this interaction. Which amounts to courtship, doesn't it? *Well, I'll be damned.*

Reluctantly he ducks into the tent and returns his body to his clothes. Dressed, he feels duller. His clothing hangs about him like a pupal casing, a shield through which he must grope with effort in order to sense the pulse of other lives. As Jane enters, panting and laughing, followed by Wigglesworth, he is just enjoying the memory of his aunt Millicent Graves of New Hampshire, whose nudist tendencies shocked the family but excited him no end. She taught school and took her summer vacations in France and other exotic places, where she could lie on the beach *sans vêtements*, as she put it, and not be bothered by small-minded gentry and Peeping Toms. She told him, and he understood it, that the naked body could feel things, things in the air, the ether. The skin was sympathetic. It was an organ of sympathy, and clothing kept humans from knowing the truth about one another and was therefore the cause of much of the world's suffering, including war.

After a conversation with Aunt Millicent, Oliver always sat up late thinking about things, trying to make up his own mind about misery and joy. It was only when he finally undressed and lay on his bed and let the summer night air of New Hampshire slip over his body, and the smell of Aunt Millicent's two cows, Borage and Brownie, penetrate his skin—for he had learned that smells touch the skin and enter it—it was only when he was naked and quiet in his upstairs room in her old farmhouse, twenty miles south of Canada, which felt like the rest of the world to him, only then could he think in a way that thinking was meant to happen, think with his whole body and not just his mind, and in this state of openness and aloneness he knew that people needed walls because without them the earth became a glorious garden. They needed socks and shoes and shirts and trousers because they couldn't bear to feel what he was feeling now, the tingling on his arms and on the inside of his legs and even on the tough soles of his feet. The next morning he woke up as he always did, to the smell of frying bacon, and sadly put on his clothes. He was only halfway there and he knew it. Why couldn't he live and play in that garden? That was the rest of the question, and it bothered him that day and the next and the next, and he imagined soon he would find the answer and yet years went by and he didn't, and now as a man closing in on sixty, he still hasn't. It is the question his life was made for. Sometimes, swinging his net and finding a butterfly in it, a particular joy comes over him after the initial surprise of the catch, and just like that he's in the garden. *Brief, oh brief dream.* And sometimes, under the influence of a particular liquid vice of his, he senses the garden is near, yet ever moving, lumbering away like a three-wheeled caravan. And just now, clothes off in the rain, his body stung and bruised and beaten by the sheer force of a bailing sky, the garden approached him and he could see inside the minds and bodies of those near to him and could, if he wished, even decipher the epic poem scribbled on his wife's heart. But he did not wish to. And now the power is gone. Jane and her young man come inside, still laughing. They shake like dogs, the heavy droplets flying off them, and only then turn to say hello. Oliver feels like an overstuffed chair, a piece of ludicrously padded furniture hauled out into the African bush to satisfy effete bottoms. He says, with uncharacteristic grumpiness, "You're too wet, both of you."

"And what are they supposed to do?" asks Dotty, sitting up from her nap and arranging her hair. "It's raining buckets, Oliver. They can't dry off outside."

"We've been very bad," says Jane merrily.

"There's no avoiding it!" cries Dotty, rising from her cot. "Has anyone invited Euell to eat with us?"

"He ate with us last night," says Oliver.

"Last night was last night and tonight is tonight. He was Jane's guest last night; tonight he'll be mine."

"Thanks," says Euell Wigglesworth, "but I—"

"Stop!" Dotty holds up her hand dramatically. "No excuses, please. Remember, Oliver and I were young once too, young and poor as church mice. We'd say no to any invitation that seemed an act of charity, then we'd go home to our grilled cheese sandwiches. That's all I knew how to cook. Oliver knew how to boil water and open cans."

"I'd love to stay—"

"Good. That's settled."

"But I have to be back at the station this evening, and with these roads and this rain, it'll be muddy as heck."

"What do you figure it will take you?" asks Oliver.

"I won't make it by dark."

"You better stay the night then," Dotty insists. "We can't offer you a cot, but we have a mattress."

Jane, throughout this interaction, says nothing. She has pulled herself together and is once again the wife of Morris Merkle. Or so it seems to Oliver. Her sparkle is gone, her merriness. She seems suddenly older and more staid, more like Morris himself. Oliver, who is not by nature a jealous man, feels his jealousy waning. He opens and closes his hands a few times to enliven his organ of sympathy—his skin. He looks at Euell Wigglesworth with a new appreciation, for it no longer matters to him who brings this girl to life, whether it be he or Euell or anyone else, as long as she is brought to life. Brought there and kept there by whatever means necessary. Is this true? he wonders. Having wasted a fair amount of his own happiness and self-respect on lip service to gods and idols he never believed in, he knows, yes, it's true. By whatever means. "Stay the night," he hears himself say to the young man so eager to linger. "When this rain lets up we'll go out and hunt for *Speyeria atlantis schellbachi*, shall we? I can't imagine your boss would stand in the way of a man with a net and his prey, especially if the creature bears his name. Come with us, Jane?"

She looks uncertain.

Dotty says, "Of course she'll go with you."

"Oh, I don't know!" cries Jane.

But Oliver senses that somewhere, in the preternatural dimness of the tent, a glove, a gauntlet, has been thrown down. "She'll go with you," Dotty repeats, and this time it is impossible not to hear it as a challenge and a command.

An Inconsiderate Omission

Morris Merkle feels the telephone has turned against him. Lately Jane's voice has carried a tone of accusation, and he can't think why. There was a time early in their marriage when she had every right to accuse him and chose against it— or so it seemed. In the evening, slumped in his red armchair, de Tocqueville's *Democracy in America* unopened in his lap, the dog at his feet, he considers the mystery that is his wife. She is young, of course, and he is not. He has always suspected his role in her life is that of a father, yet her father would not have approved of him, he is quite sure. Mr. Yarborough. He has seen only one photograph of the man, sitting on a sloped lawn with a furry terrier in his arms. It's a pose Morris understands, relaxing with one's faithful companion on a hot summer day.

He has begun to drink again, a little sherry before dinner. This time he feels confident in his ability to stay alert to the temptations of hedonism. He finds himself lonely, yet not drawn to womanizing, as are so many of his colleagues. It is Jane he desires, but he must remind himself it was Eleanor before that. Things change. The heart changes course. It's the way a man copes. And a woman? His mind wanders to his sister, Dotty, whose affections seem to swell this way and that, like a sail on a blustery day. He realizes, suddenly, that he admires her for it, for her peregrinations. If he were wed to a man like Oliver—a woman in his case—steadfast and content as Oliver seems to be, he too would need the occasional voyage to Mount Olympus simply to feel the blood in his veins.

His Mount Olympus came to him in Eleanor, and he, foolish idiot that he was, believed in that craggy, permanent heaven. This sad thought propels Morris from his chair in search of something to drink. Jane is quite strict about drink, but Jane is gone. He pours himself a glass of sherry—sadly, that's all there is. He'll have to get in some decent whiskey. "Hello, Martin," he sighs, patting his friend on the head and sinking into his chair. The red leather holds him like a buffoonish pair of arms.

They were engaged to marry, he and his Eleanor. He was a young man then, climbing in business, gaining momentum in ways that blinded him. He felt he was proving himself worthy of her, but each success sent her into a jealous rage. He had never before seen anger of a physical nature in a woman, and after these outbursts he was flushed with thoughts of sex. And then one day he opened a letter from her, a paragraph in which she sent him away. He fell to his knees—he was alone in the room—and uttered a sound he had never heard before from his own throat, and never since. Many years later, when he met Jane, he was still a man with an arrow lodged above his collarbone. His first response to her unexpected affection was: never again.

Jane, Jane. She chided him, quite rightly, for not loving her enough, though he did what suitors do, carried chocolate to her door, inundated her with roses (only to discover that roses reminded her of funerals and her parents' deaths). His heart wasn't in it, yet he hadn't the courage to desist. Somehow, shortly after that, they married.

It is the central mystery of his life, how he came to be Jane's husband. He addresses the question to the dog, who raises his muzzle at the sound of his name. A neat appearance, Morris believes, won her confidence. He was courteous and kind and reminded her of her father. Naive youth was on her side as well. But *his* capitulation is something else altogether. He wonders if it's happened yet and knows it has not—or not, at least, in the way he expected, which was the quick, fleshy, treacherous way he had fallen in love with Eleanor. To Jane he never spoke of his engagement so many years in the past. He doesn't even remember the circumstances by which the matter was raised, but it came not long after the wedding. Jane was entirely undone by what she called his "inconsiderate omission." Generous of her to speak of it that way when it caused her such visible distress. It grew her up a notch. It turned her inward in a way that, he would never admit to anyone (except the dog at his feet), made her more attractive. It was then he began to fall in love with her, just as she was falling away. The whole episode made her more spicy, more complicated. As time went by, he decided she had forgiven him.

A Dinner Party

Ethyl Schellbach serves up a delicate pork roast garnished with apples, cheese, and pine nuts. Dotty Hedquist has never understood pine nuts. If she wanted the flavor of turpentine in her food, she would take up oil painting in the kitchen. And the cheese seems a bit out of the ordinary. A little too experimental for her taste. She sits between Louie Schellbach and the older of the two visitors. The younger one—she's quite attractive really, for a professor—is seated next to Oliver.

The Hedquists have just that afternoon returned from the North Rim. Ordinarily they would spend a few days settling in before accepting a dinner invitation, but on the telephone Ethyl practically begged, and in the end they lifted their weary backsides into the car and drove over. From her brief conversation with her hostess, Dotty is led to believe the two professors have overstayed their welcome. They have crossed the line and become freeloaders. But from Louie she understands they are staying at the hotel, they have shared a meal or two and declined several others, the visit is longer than anyone expected, and its nature is not to be discussed. She sighs inwardly, wondering if jealousy is at play here. The younger professor certainly is interested in every aspect of Louie's work. But this must be old hat to Ethyl. Perhaps what piques the lady of the house is the fact that Louie is interested, or pretending to be, in the work of the young professor. And the young professor is not, as anyone can see with their own eyes, a bearded, slightly simian, bespectacled, socially inept male, but an intelligent, pretty, and enthusiastic female. Not a temptress, but one of those of her sex who, precisely because they pay no attention to it, cannot help but be noticed.

The older one, Miss Clover, is a bit drab in her presentation. She wears trousers and a man's shirt and sturdy shoes that give her the appearance of someone on the eve of a great adventure. Something alpine, involving ropes and picks and axes and those things for the feet with the French name—oh, what are they called? Having to do with female problems. Anyway, Dotty, who is just her age, has not felt the proximity of that kind of adventure for a long time, not since she and Lowell Dunhill used to walk all day and by nightfall would find themselves in places far from anyone—once on a ledge only wide enough for two—and they'd throw down their bedrolls and share an orange between them and lie out under the stars without a care. But it's been some time since then. Thirteen years, in fact. How extraordinary.

Crampons! That's the word. It comes to her as she is listening to Miss Clover lecture on the merits of dry farming. Dotty, never much of a student, feels she ought to be taking notes. "Dry farming," Miss Clover informs, wagging her butter knife in the air, "is practiced in very few places, and we aren't sure whether the reasons for that are cultural or—"

Dotty suddenly feels sure she is about to be called on, and to prevent this from happening she interrupts with a question of her own. In a glorious non sequitur, and to the surprise of everyone at the table, she blurts out, "But if crampons are for the feet, what are the things for the rock?"

There is a leaden silence. "For the rock, my darling?" asks Oliver.

Dotty cannot remember a time when he has ever addressed her as "my darling." It has an ominous, sickening feel to it. "Yes," she insists. "You know. The little things they pound into the rock. They sort of pull themselves up with them."

"Up?" asks Oliver.

"Who are *they*?" asks Ethyl.

"Oh, all of you!" cries Dotty. "The alpineers, of course!"

Miss Clover starts to laugh, then suddenly to cough violently. She grabs her napkin and covers her mouth and shudders noiselessly for some time, until Dotty realizes she's choking and they'll never hear the rest of the lecture on dry farming because she, Dotty Hedquist, has with her ill-timed interruption caused the poor lady to inhale Ethyl Schellbach's glorious pork roast. She turns and taps Miss Clover on the back and Miss Clover, her eyes round as teacups, nods vigorously, which Dotty interprets as an invitation to tap her again, harder this time—more of a whack—which she does, half rising to her feet with the effort. With a gust of air, the offending bit of gristle and flesh is launched from the distinguished botanist's windpipe, and a gasping Miss Clover collapses against Dotty, practically knocking her out of her chair.

"Elzada!" cries her young companion, whose name, Dotty seems to remember, is Lois. Lois Cutter. Or Jotter. Or Jotter Cutter, or some such thing. She seems about to leap across the table, her pretty face pale and elongated with concern. The two men jump to their feet, Oliver shouting, "Stay calm everyone!" and Louie silent but nimble as a cat. Then the crisis is over. Refusing assistance, an embarrassed Miss Clover groggily pulls herself up, straightens her shirt, and pats her hair. "I must look a sight," she says, frowning.

"No no, not a hair out of place," laughs Dotty nervously.

"Good gracious!" says Oliver. "That's enough excitement for one evening, I should say."

"Interesting," says Louie thoughtfully. "I've never before witnessed a choking incident that wasn't accompanied by the classic hands-to-the-throat motion."

"And you've watched many people choke?" wheezes Miss Clover, rubbing her collarbone.

"Not fatally. It's always worked out much the same way this one did. The only hurt involved is a bit of wounded pride."

"But choking is no stranger to you, Mr. Schellbach?"

"I myself have never had the misfortune."

"Yet those around you tend to—"

"Heavens!" cries Ethyl, seated on Miss Clover's left. "What

a gruesome conversation!" She stands abruptly and begins to whisk away the plates.

"Let me help you," offers Miss Jotter Cutter.

Ethyl turns to her with a chilly smile and shakes her head. "How kind of you, but you're a guest in my home, you and Elzada, and we don't ask guests to trouble themselves, do we Louie?"

"We don't ask," he agrees, "but if they volunteer . . . ?"

"Guests don't volunteer," Dotty chimes in.

"The young lady just has," Oliver points out.

"It's highly anomalous," says Louie, nodding. "I think we need to consider this case on its own merits."

"*Not* while I stand here with a load of plates." Ethyl frowns.

"Come to think of it," says Dotty, "Jane, who could be considered a guest, does more than her fair share of work. She often does the laundry and is always willing to cook, though Oliver and I don't happen to like our meat well done or raw, which seems to be all she knows. Maybe that's how they do it in St. Louis these days."

"Jane?" asks Louie. "Is this the Jane I met? Your sister-in-law?"

"Yes," says Dotty.

"She's still with you?"

"Very much with us."

"Well, why isn't she here?"

"She's at home with a headache," says Oliver. "She gets headaches, apparently. Either you do or you don't is what I think. For example, I'm an indigestion man myself."

"*Oliver*," says Dotty sharply. "This can't be very interesting for the guests."

"Oh, quite the contrary," says Miss Cutter Jotter quickly. "We're fascinated by every little thing. We've had quite enough of ourselves, isn't that right, Elzie? I get headaches myself, actually."

"Now, headaches," says Dotty, "in my opinion, are mostly in the mind."

"In the head, you mean," laughs Louie.

"What about indigestion?" asks Oliver.

"In the mind as well," says Dotty.

"Your point," says Miss Clover, "seems to be that illness is psychological."

"Perhaps."

"Including that which results in death?"

"Yes. Oh, yes."

"But not all deaths are due to matters 'in the mind,' as you put it?"

Dotty is silent, considering.

"Drowning, for example," Miss Clover continues. "Is that too a psychological matter, Mrs. Hedquist?"

Dotty stiffens, lets her gaze fall on the table. Her tongue feels like a great big shoe in her mouth. She reaches out to lift her water glass and finds her hand trembling. She returns it to her lap and says, "No. Of course not."

Ethyl, who has finished removing the plates, now sweeps in from the kitchen with an enormous brown cake. She lays it on the sideboard, along with the dessert plates and utensils, and invites everyone to come and help themselves. Dotty rises with the rest, though she is suddenly feeling strange and dizzy and could use a little lie-down. What she was going to say before the old professor cornered her was that, in her opinion, Jane wasn't suffering from a headache at all but a heartache. Wasn't that interesting? She thought it was. She'd watched it coming on as they drove farther and farther away from the North Rim. Jane had become increasingly more silent, more lost in her thoughts. By the time they got home she looked peaked indeed. She had gone to bed immediately and stayed there, bestirring herself only to call out a faint good-bye.

"May I serve you some cake?" asks Oliver, bending over her. Dotty discovers she is no longer on her feet but sitting in her chair at the table. She nods absently and he leans forward, a look of curious excitement on his face. He reaches for her water glass and picks it up. "What the devil?"

"Oh my word!" she whispers, for something sways at the bottom of the glass. Pale and ragged looking, curled up like an embryo, it is, of course, the piece of pork roast launched from Miss Elzada Clover's windpipe.

"Drowned in your drink," he murmurs close to her ear. His eyes sparkle and he goes to cut her a rather large piece of cake.

Humming

She lies on her bed and listens to the noises of the empty house. A clanging pipe seems to call her name: *Jane Jane Jane.* Something in the wall behind her starts to buzz. It sounds like bees. She imagines honey seeping through the plaster and wallpaper of her little room, touching a finger to the dark spreading wetness, tasting it. Sweet.

Her head pounds strangely but does not hurt. What she is feeling is the beating of her heart. A car goes by outside, and she sits up and hopes beyond hope it's him. But it isn't, of course. She knows it isn't. He's 210 miles away and doesn't have a day off until next week.

She's acting childish. No, childish may not be quite right. Children don't have such feelings, do they? What on earth does she know about children? As far as she can tell she never was one. Perhaps she's becoming one now. She certainly isn't ruled by reason. In a matter of weeks she seems to have lost her reason and perhaps the rest of herself as well. Though something has been gained, surely. Oh, it's all such a muddle to her!

The noise in the wall is more of a hum than a buzz, though the difference between the two seems purely geometric. A hum is round. Even the letters *h-u-m* are softly rounded. A buzz is a different matter entirely and has those two angular *z*'s to prove it. But what could it be, back there behind her head? Suddenly the cause of the humming interests her. Just weeks ago her thought would have been, "Call the exterminator!" and now, because she's lost her reason but gained something else, she would like to know the name of the creature responsible for this mellifluous intrusion.

She and Morris had quite an adventure with cockroaches. The St. Louis house was a magnet for them, and her duty in the early days of their marriage was to discern when an infestation had taken place and call the cockroach man. He arrived in an unmarked truck, which unfailingly aroused the neighbors' suspicions, and Jane came to enjoy the feeling of espionage that shrouded these visits. The poison itself had a soporific effect on her, but even the grogginess seemed high adventure. Once, early on, she forced herself to ask the cockroach man whether the "problem," as she had learned to call it, was due to some failure in her housekeeping. When he assured her that a single crumb could keep hundreds of cockroaches alive for weeks, and that without that crumb they could live indefinitely on invisible bits of lint, a weight lifted and without thinking she flung her arms around him, to which he responded by trying to kiss her. She was dumbfounded and unprepared and yet intrigued that a gesture of gratitude might be construed as a passionate invitation. Perhaps the nuances of intention were lost on most people. Or perhaps love was its own kind of high adventure. She had never thought about such things, for her life with Morris was new and unformed, and she was young, and though her love for him and with him was not what she would call adventure, high or low, she lived inside it in a daily way and was comforted by it, content.

Now, thinking back on this, she feels at least a century older. A new possibility occurs to her: the cockroach man kissed every young wife he could, simply because he could. And some of them, Jane is now certain, kissed him back (she had not). It astonishes her, the world she has been blind to. A world of washing machine repairmen, and Fuller Brush men, and men selling magazine subscriptions, and men hired to paint or poison or mow the lawn. Men dressed in neat suits, Jehovah's Witnesses, selling religion. Men making their way inside the house, to fix this or that or bring something or get a glass of water. That's how it happened, didn't it? The milkman, the exterminator, the florist carrying armfuls of roses into her kitchen—a gift from her husband, who left at eight and returned at six and never ever surprised her at the door. Strangers with jobs to do and to whom she said, "Yes, come in." Well, that was how it happened, and whether it was good or bad she couldn't say, only that it was easy as one, two, three and she had never known it.

But Dotty knew it, had known it for quite some time by the look of things. Jane feels too warm all of a sudden. She wonders if the humming in the wall generates heat. She gets up and goes into the Hedquists' bedroom, promising herself this will be the last of her snooping. She tries to imagine being her sister-in-law and having something to hide. Where would she hide it? In her bureau drawer? In a shoe? Somewhere Oliver would never come across it. And what might be hidden anyway? A love letter? A scrap of clothing? She cracks open the closet but it's too dark to see, and she doesn't want to turn on another light. She's trying to think like a detective. Dotty's bottom drawer calls to her, and she kneels and opens it and carefully lifts out the slacks and blue jeans, even feeling the pockets. But nothing. The drawer above is full of men's shirts, some still in the package. They're the kind Morris wears to work, good-quality Oxford cloth, white, yellow, and blue. There's even a pink one, and suddenly Jane remembers Dotty wearing a similar shirt to her rendezvous with Deo. But what could a shirt mean? If she were really a detective maybe she'd know. She replaces the clothing and tiptoes out of the room, though there is no need for stealth.

She's tired of her bedroom and goes outside to look at the sky and think about Euell. He may at this moment be looking at the same sky. Well, of course it's the same sky, but he may be looking at it and thinking about her. The idea makes her happy and sad at the same time. She wonders how she would feel if he weren't Euell but the milkman. If he weren't a park ranger but the Hotpoint repairman. If he were the same man in a different uniform, or a different man in the same uniform. She doesn't know, she doesn't know, she doesn't know. The only thing she knows is that next week she will see him again, and until then she must do *something* to make the hours and days move along. She must make herself useful. Oliver has mentioned pinning butterflies. And there's always more collecting to do, more racing across the earth with net in hand in hopeless pursuit of what she has learned to call lepidoptera. The tasks of her old life suddenly come to her like shackles: cooking, cleaning, sewing, feeding the dog. She's almost forgotten the dog's name. How extraordinary. She looks up at the stars and wonders why she never looked there for wisdom before. A mirror kingdom made of change and movement: old fires burning out, new fires flaring up. An entire world beyond the pull of Earth's gravity. She hears a ringing and shakes her head to clear the sudden dizziness that thoughts of space evoke in her. The ringing continues. The telephone! she realizes. Could it possibly be Euell? Has he read her mind? She hurries inside, catches her breath, and lifts the receiver. "Hello?" Her voice sounds like a squeak. She feels like a mouse. "Hello?" she says again, sounding more like herself. On the other end Morris's voice, ragged and blubbering: "Oh, Jane, is that you?"

"What on earth is the matter?"

"Oh, Jane, terrible news. Terrible, terrible."

"What is it, Morris. Tell me."

"Oh, Jane."

"Morris."

"I'm so glad it's you."

"Yes," she says.

"Jane? It's Martin."

"Martin's the dog, Morris."

"He's no longer, Jane."

"I don't follow you."

There is a great gust of air and Morris covers the receiver. She can hear only faint snuffling sounds. He comes on again and says, "He's dead, Jane. He died."

"The dog died?"

"Martin."

"Why, that's terrible, Morris. Awful."

"I know."

"I'm so sorry."

"I know." There is a silence and her husband says, "I'll be there in a few days, Jane. I'm afraid I miss you."

"A few days? Where?"

"There. With you."

"Oh," she says, and sits down heavily on a little stool beside the telephone table, kept there for events such as these.

The Same Shirt

"**P**itons," says Lois, emerging from the bathroom with a fresh batch of rollers in her hair. "That's the word poor Mrs. Hedquist was searching for."

"Pitons?" asks Elzada, looking up from her book.

"The things they pound into the rock."

"Ah, yes. Though I'm not sure we need to think of her as poor Mrs. Hedquist."

"No?" asks Lois, flopping onto her bed.

"No."

Elzada turns back to her book and Lois laughs. "Is that all I get for an answer?" She props herself up on one elbow. "Really, Elzada. Have you nothing more to say?"

"On the contrary, Loie, I have an almost infinite number of things to say. I choose not to say them because not one of them is backed up by enough data to make it more than a random observation—a suspicion, if you will—and as we find ourselves in a situation fraught with rumor, gossip, and unsubstantiated suspicions, it seems pointless and perhaps unconscionable to add to the mess." She removes her glasses, rubs her eyes ferociously. "I will say one thing. The sight of you with those prickly gadgets springing from your head is enough to turn me insomniac."

"Oh, for heaven's sake," pouts Lois, patting the rollers. "Have a little sympathy for those of us who weren't born curly."

"I just don't know how you can sleep."

"I sleep like a baby and you know it."

Elzada does, of course, know it, but she has always found the rituals of beautification somewhat beyond her—or she beyond them. Why in the process of becoming a goddess did a woman have to look like a clown? Yet there were parallels in the plant world. The cacti's unrivaled efficiency and delicacy always caused in her a tingle of reverent awe, but to most of the world they were cartoon characters, alien and ugly—until they flowered, when there was no mistaking their beauty.

It's well past midnight by the time she closes her book, a Ngaio Marsh mystery that she has solved, she believes, though Marsh is almost always one step ahead of her. Elzada cannot trust her own sleuthing until she reads the last word on the last page, and even then she holds her breath, as if the book might come alive and stand up smartly and say: "Not yet! No! This is not the ending I choose for myself, not the fate I have in mind! Out of my way, reader—and writer too!" It's a strange fantasy for a woman as practical as Elzada perceives herself to be, but there it is.

She prepares for bed, slipping on her pajamas in the dark. In the bathroom she brushes her teeth, pulls her lips this way and that in the mirror, checking for gum disease. Her hair catches her attention. She has never before considered the curliness of it, nor thought of it much at all. It is something that grows on her head, something she seldom has to fuss with. Up until this evening she was content to forget about it, but now, suddenly, she feels remiss, a clod, insensitive to the world of hair or the world of curliness, she's not sure which. Lois has once again opened her eyes to what lies right before her—or more accurately, right on top of her. This is what friends do for one another: they forestall blindness.

A touching business, friendship, Elzada knows, as she climbs between the covers. And quite her stock-in-trade, though the so-called loftier pursuit of marriage eludes her. Loftier? Rubbish! It is, in fact, an economic arrangement as corrupt as any other, prone to falsification, mudslinging, bribery, and debt. It's its own detective novel, with enough insoluble problems to keep Inspector Roderick Alleyn busy for a lifetime. If only he were here, she thinks. He could untangle the mess our old friend Emery has made. Or rather, he could sift through the mud and murk created by Lowell Dunhill's body when it wed itself to the Colorado River thirteen years ago—a wedding *not* envisioned by Ranger Dunhill himself, if the evidence speaks true. For what would be the odds—and frankly the point—of a man shooting himself in the head before jumping to a second death in the river below? All Elzada knows is what she does not know: Why on earth would Emery

Kolb decide to keep the body? And if not, how did it come to rest in his garage?

Her thoughts turn back to dinner and the admittedly plain but strangely provocative Mrs. Hedquist, with whom Elzada shared an odd and perhaps enlightening conversation. After the meal—the murderous pork roast followed by a delicious ginger cake—the party retreated to the living room where Mrs. Hedquist, looking tired and agitated, approached her. "May I share a word with you, Professor?"

"Of course," replied Elzada, "but only on the condition you call me Elzada."

"Well," said Mrs. Hedquist, "I'll certainly try."

There followed a long silence. Mrs. Hedquist fussed with the top button of her shirt, which closely resembled Elzada's own Oxford-cloth shirt, a style she'd come to appreciate in the field for its roominess and durability. She waited uncomfortably for the other woman to find her tongue and finally gave up and started the conversation herself. "We seem to be wearing the same shirt, Mrs. Hedquist."

"Oh, I wouldn't say so. Yours is white and mine is yellow."

"I was referring to the style. And the material." She reached out and pinched the sleeve of the other woman's shirt. "Yes, just the same. Oxford cloth. Some call it broadcloth. It's a man's shirt, of a very fine quality I might add. The only way to tell the quality is to feel it."

Mrs. Hedquist drew her arm away with a frown. Elzada sensed they had arrived at a conversational cul-de-sac and perhaps so much the better. She was weary. It was time for bed. She looked around the room for Lois, hoping to catch her eye, but she was deeply engaged with Mr. Schellbach, a charmed man if there ever was one.

"Professor!" said Mrs. Hedquist, her voice an urgent whisper. "There is one thing. It's odd but I can't seem to shake it from my mind, and now that you've brought up the shirts, well, it's even odder, because now that I think about it, it's your shirt that reminds me of him—"

"Of whom?"

"Of . . . of someone I once knew. He drowned, actually."

"I'm sorry."

"Yes. It was years ago."

Thirteen, thought Elzada. Lowell Dunhill. How in the world . . . ?

"I don't know why I felt compelled to tell you," continued Mrs. Hedquist. "I suppose the resemblance—oh, not physical, you look nothing like him, but in spirit, the spirit of adventure—it startled me. It got me thinking and I wanted to . . . well . . . mention it to you. I wondered, in fact, if you knew him." She lowered her voice. "If that might be the reason you were here."

"Mrs. Hedquist, I—"

"Now I don't expect you to be able to answer that!" she cried, then smiled angelically. "But I did want you to know I was wondering."

What Elzada cannot recall, as she lies in her bed at El Tovar, is whether or not the woman ever told her the name of the particular "someone she once knew." She is quite sure she did not, which meant that she, Mrs. Hedquist, knew that she, Elzada, knew his name already. So the rumors Mr. Schellbach feared would fly, have flown, and somehow the not-so-innocent Mrs. Hedquist has made the connection between the skeleton in Emery Kolb's garage and her unfortunate . . . lover. For how could he not have been her lover? Women like Mrs. Hedquist didn't just start up conversations about someone they once knew, unless that someone was lodged in their heart as one longed for. As one missed. Elzada had felt the woman's longing as she spoke. And yet, no stranger to longing herself, she knows it hardly exempts one from culpability. It isn't only stage characters who feel the tug of passion and are driven by it to commit crimes unthinkable, even against the object of their desire.

"Ah well," she sighs, squashing her pillow into a more manageable flatness. (The trouble with fancy hotels is they equate luxury with a lofty pillow, and she has always preferred to lay her head on flat ground.) There is no point in casting about for villains, not at this time of night. There are villains enough already, including herself and Emery. It's Emery who holds the key. She must get him to talk. They have spoken on the telephone on two occasions, but he reveals nothing, remains stolid and stubbornly silent about the whole business. Frustrating man! Is there anyone to whom he will freely speak?

The answer is suddenly plain as day: his brother, of course! Ellsworth Kolb. Why hasn't she thought of him? She will call him in the morning. He lives over in Los Angeles and could be here in a matter of hours. If the situation were explained to him, the grave consequences of Emery's silence, he would surely come as quickly as possible.

The dratted pillow has regained its original shape, rising like a mound of bread dough. Elzada gives up and casts it aside. Some problems are simply beyond solving. But she feels she has solved a more important one tonight: the problem of how to coax language from Emery Kolb. The sooner he talks, the sooner she and Lois can go home, and the sooner they go home, the sooner she can get on with her studies and her books. She never thought she would wish to be away from Grand Canyon. Of course it isn't the canyon she wishes to flee, but the terrible, sticky feeling of involvement in human drama, which is like slogging through deep wet underbrush when her heart lies with the cacti. Oh, the cacti! *Opuntia basilaris*, *Opuntia chlorotica*, *Carnegiea gigantea*, she recites, as if she were counting sheep. And soon enough the words lull her—*Echinocactus polycephalus . . .*, *Mammillaria tetrancistra . . .*, and her own *Sclerocactus cloveriae*—into a fine, dreamless sleep.

Clark Kent Calling

It is the first time Ranger Naturalist Euell Wigglesworth has considered taking a nap on the job, and he feels nervous. He wishes his friend Hugh were there to advise him. But if Hugh were there other things wouldn't be, such as peace and quiet. The air would be filled with Hugh's high-flown tales of der-ring-do, for he has gotten himself into quite a bit of hot water recently, due to girls. Too many girls. Girls not exactly stolen or rescued but certainly borrowed and shared. It is something Euell was once in favor of and now wishes he hadn't been. The excitement of it—Hugh's excitement—fills the airwaves. It is surprising anyone on the planet can sleep.

For the first time in his life Euell has been doing poorly in the sleep department. All day his mind jumps around, and at night he lies down and closes his eyes and nothing happens—nothing faintly resembling sleep. He tells himself it's Hugh's fault, Hugh the Casanova, but in fact he knows it has nothing to do with the tempestuous love adventures of his friend—not really. It's his own heart that needs arranging, like a roomful of chairs.

He drives out to Kanabownits Spring where the large and velvety *Speyeria atlantis schellbachi* are flying in the meadow. Schellbach's fritillary, the color of a Bengalese tiger. The hind wing sports a silver-spotted cocoa color on its underside. It's one of the prettiest butterflies he can imagine. He parks his truck in the shade of the pines and goes to the spot where a week ago he sat with Jane. Now, as then, the air is full of nymphalids— brush-footed butterflies—tortoiseshells, painted ladies, and Schellbach's fritillary among them. The same fallen log lies across the stream, the same grasses and sedges grow along its verdant, diminutive banks. The breeze is cool, the sun is hot, just as it was that day. But it's far from the same. He feels a gap in his chest, like a missing lung. He thought he would lie down here in the comfort of his memories and go to sleep. That day, that long ago day last week, as he watched her run and dodge in the wake of *Speyeria*'s fluttering, feinting genius, he had come to feel this place was hers and his together. But it's not. It's a place of the past.

The stream too is a different stream, the water different water. He sits by it and does something he hasn't done since he was a boy—he fashions a boat from an aspen leaf and sends it down the river. It runs through the first narrows and over a waterfall made of twigs and through a series of rapids with boulders the size of pebbles. He runs after it. It's upright still. He promises himself if it stays upright he will call Jane. He will call her that evening from the telephone at the station.

No, he thinks, that would be folly. May the boat capsize.

But how wonderful to hear her voice. He'd like to tell her the goshawks are flying. May the boat stay upright.

What is he thinking? A married woman. The Hedquists' sister-in-law! May the boat capsize!

But Mr. and Mrs. Hedquist themselves insisted he eat with them, insisted he spend the night. They were *quite* insistent. May the boat stay upright.

Jane had been the only one to hesitate, come to think of it. May the boat capsize.

But her hesitation had vanished like the rain, out here chasing butterflies. He and Mr. Hedquist both seemed under her spell. May the boat stay upright.

And then, as the sun left the meadow and Mr. Hedquist announced he would go and see if his wife needed help boiling water and opening cans, they had had a little time together, and they sat by the stream, where Euell felt an almost irrepressible urge to press his lips against her skin. He would have settled for the skin of her elbow had it been offered. But it was not. May the boat capsize.

Instead he showed her how to tie a bowline, and the sight of her rather small hands going out of the hole, around the tree, and back into the hole nourished him all week. May the boat stay upright. He trots along the stream. May it stay upright and never capsize, never sink, never fail. The odds are against it. If it survives this stretch there'll be another and another and another, and even as he thinks this he sees it drop into a whirlpool the size of a soup bowl, and while it's down and out of sight he knows what he wants, and without waiting to discover the fate of the leaf—it's just a leaf!—he hurries back to his truck, and with the energy of a well-rested man, drives back to the station.

It proves a very busy afternoon. A group of Swedish tourists can't find their vehicle, and Ranger Wigglesworth discovers it unharmed and, inexplicably, where they left it, at the North Kaibab trailhead. A man named Sayer and his wife, two British malacologists, come looking for Ranger Naturalist Warren Haas, who is AWOL. Admitting a rather sketchy knowledge of snails, Ranger Wigglesworth offers his services, but it seems the couple's greatest need is in putting up their tent. There's paperwork to do, then a short lull. Ranger Wigglesworth, becoming Euell again, gets himself a Coca-Cola and sits in the kitchen and thinks about Superman. All day long he feels like Superman. Every ranger does. But does he like that feeling? At night, and at times like this, relaxing with a caffeinated beverage intended to restore his humanity, he feels like Clark Kent. He's always trusted Clark Kent, always felt Superman was lucky to have him. Without him, Superman would be a dull fellow indeed.

He stops thinking about Superman and thinks about Jane. He'd like to drink his Coca-Cola and think about her for the rest of the afternoon. No he wouldn't. He'd like to see her is what he'd like. He'd like to see her naked.

The thought is sudden and sweet, and he allows it to soak into him until he feels like a pancake drenched in syrup. Naked is not something he's allowed himself to dwell on when it comes to Jane. His mind has wandered there, of course, but on a short leash. There has been so little hope, and there remains little hope—no hope at all, in fact. But something has changed. A week ago, after chasing butterflies and sitting by the creek and eating Mrs. Hedquist's enchilada casserole baked in a Dutch oven and drinking a little tequila with Mr. Hedquist before bed, he was present in the tent when Jane mysteriously slipped out of her day clothes and into her nightclothes, and the transformation was enough to temporarily tie his tongue. It happened so quickly and without warning. After dinner he and Mr. Hedquist got to talking about the strange social habits of *Heterocephalus glaber*, the naked mole rat, an anomalous rodent if there ever was one, and there came Jane out of the shadows, wearing the most interesting pair of pajamas. A married woman wearing pajamas! Perhaps she only wore them camping. It was hard to tell in the lamplight, but they seemed to be covered with ducks. On closer examination, they *were* ducks. Wood ducks. *Aix sponsa*. Males. Since then, he has thought night and day about what lies beneath those pajamas. It excites him and embarrasses him. Sometimes he feels impatient and disgusted with himself. He feels like a spy. He's spying on her body and he feels it would be better—fairer and more reputable—to spy on her mind. But why? Her bottom reminds him of a ripe pear. Her breasts are plump, like two peaches, and her nipples, seen through her shirt that rainy day, point to the sky. Her mouth makes a little O of surprise when she laughs, as if laughing is new to her and unexpected. And her short dark hair swings when she runs. Forward and back it goes, like a sleek horse running. If a man finds beauty in a woman's body, what's the harm in it? If he wants to see her naked, wants to hold her and press his skin against hers and find his way inside her, what's the harm in imagining it? When there isn't the slightest chance in the world that it will happen, what's the harm?

He draws a breath, for all his imaginings have left him breathless. A loud knock startles him, and he tucks in his shirt, puts on his hat, returns body and mind to the role of Ranger Wigglesworth. It's the British couple. The wife, who stands ready to pound on the door again, is somewhat older than Jane, a tall, narrow woman with buck teeth, pink skin, and squinty eyes. She looks, in fact, surprisingly like a naked mole rat. The husband, a fat man who comes to her chin, holds up an imaginary bottle and glass and says, "Might we tempt you to join us after work, Mr. Wigglesworth? And your colleague Mr. Haas as well, if he's returned from his carousing?"

Ranger Wigglesworth searches for the right response to this invitation and finally settles on a tentative nod.

"Excellent!" cries Mr. Sayer. "A way to repay you for your assistance with our tent!"

His wife blinks but says nothing.

The husband says, "Until then, Mr. Wigglesworth. Of course you know where we are camped."

After they leave, Ranger Wigglesworth does garbage rounds, assists an elderly gentleman who has sprained an ankle while getting out of his car at Cape Royal, reunites a mother in the campground with her runaway son (who ran only as far as the outhouse), and checks on a report of a mountain lion roaming the parking lot of the Grand Canyon Lodge. Ranger Wigglesworth is well acquainted with this particular lion, a dog named Tuna, belonging to one of the busboys. He writes a note reminding the owner that pets must be kept on a leash, and attaches the note to the dog's collar. He returns to the station to find Warren Haas stretched out asleep on the kitchen table, and remembers what makes this man the ideal roommate: often gone, seldom sober, angelic in his cups. He shakes him and reminds him that in an hour he's scheduled to give a nature talk over at Grand Canyon Lodge. Haas turns a bleary eye on him and clutches his hand. "Do it for me, Wiggles."

"I can't. I've got to make a telephone call."

"You owe me. You and Huddleston. For a couple of beers."

"A beer for a beer, Haas. Don't be a jerk."

"Make your telephone call over there. For free. A girl named Lydia. Brown hair, big boobies. She works reception. Tell her I sent you."

Euell sighs. It isn't the first time Haas has sent him to one well-endowed Harvey Girl or another, but in Euell's experience, when Warren's name is mentioned, they seldom want to grant the favor requested. On the other hand, a telephone call free of charge? No grubbing for dimes in his pocket? His voice, then Jane's, unimpeded by time or money? It's worth a try. Maybe Lydia has kept her wits about her, or whatever it is a girl is required to keep in the presence of Warren's manly charms. (It's strange, he never thinks of Jane as a girl, or someone who's lost her wits even once.) He'll give the talk, go heavy on birds and mammals and leps, and light on land snails, which is Warren's field of expertise. When the dinner rush is over, he'll drop in on Hugh's latest love interest Betty and see how life with Casanova is treating her. If Hugh's been a good boy, Betty will wield her waitress clout to find Euell a plate of food, leftovers from the guests. If Hugh's been a jackass, well, alas. Before going back to the station he'll call Jane from the telephone at the lodge, where he won't be prey to Ranger Hemple's eavesdropping. To Haas he says, "Right. It's a deal."

"I knew you'd see the light. Remember," Haas winks at him. "Lydia with the boobs."

"You're an animal, Warren."

"Phylum Chordata, at your service."

"Phylum Mollusca is closer to the truth."

"Now, Wiggles. Don't insult the wee folk."

It isn't until after his talk, when he's dialing the Hedquists' number, that he remembers the malacologists. Doggone it! he thinks. All in all, it's been a most imperfect evening. His stomach is growling, evidence that life with Casanova is *not* going well today. He wishes he'd bought a Hershey bar. He wishes Hugh were not such a dolt. But he must concentrate. The telephone rings twice, and suddenly he wishes it would ring forever. He can't imagine why this seemed like a good idea. What if Jane answers? What if she doesn't? He hasn't thought it through. It's still ringing. He can hang up right now—she'll never know, no one will ever know. He can hang up and see if Haas has sobered up enough to go over to the campground and talk snails with Mr. and Mrs. Sayer. Perhaps drink something out of that imaginary bottle. He could use it. For courage.

Right now. The telephone continues to ring, and he finds himself wondering what kind of woman becomes a malacologist. A mannish kind of woman? Is Mrs. Sayer mannish? No, not exactly. She has long tubular breasts, a slim figure, a somewhat Byzantine face (he remembers Byzantium from an art course he took in college). The subject of a sacred painting, Mrs. Sayer. Madonna of the Buckteeth. But why is he thinking about the teeth of a woman he doesn't know, when he could be thinking about Jane? The telephone ringing in the Hedquists' house is causing his head to hurt. He imagines Jane in her wood-duck pajamas, hearing it and guessing it is he and deciding to let it ring. She rolls over in bed, pulls the pillow over her head. That does it. He'll give up. He'll never bother her again. And just as he moves the receiver away from his ear and begins to drop it back into the cradle he hears a distant voice say, "Hello?"

"Hello!" he shouts, pulling the receiver to his mouth again. Lydia, the melon-chested receptionist, casts him an admonishing look. "Hello," he says again, more calmly this time. And forgetting his manners, "I've wanted to call. It feels like forever since we talked in the meadow. I miss you. I shouldn't say that, but I do." The words tumble out of his mouth, they gush and tumble and suddenly he feels like a child, a cross between a child and a geyser, a child and Old Faithful. He doesn't stop to think because thinking will ruin it. "It feels like a dream. I feel like I'm floating in water. I may look the same, but I'm not. Inside I'm not."

"What do you mean?" she cries.

"I'd like to see you. I'd start running now and run all the way to see you if I knew you wanted me to."

"Oh, I do. I do want you to."

"It's downhill!" he laughs.

"Downhill? Where are you?"

"I can almost look across the canyon and see you."

"The canyon! Lowell, for heaven's sake. What are you doing here? It's Emery isn't it? He's gotten you involved. Oh, I knew it, I *knew* it! Those two ladies. The professors. Nothing but big snoops! Somehow they've dragged you back. You must be careful, *careful*, do you hear? Do you promise me? Say you do."

"I do," says Euell obediently, dumbfounded.

"Good," whispers Mrs. Hedquist. "Now, don't forget how I've waited for you. You know how I feel about you."

"Yes," says Euell.

"You haven't changed, have you?"

"No."

"But you said inside you're not the same."

"I said that?"

"My dark and handsome ranger boy," whispers Mrs. Hedquist. "When the fuss is over, we'll see each other. We'll— oh, they're here, darling. Oliver and Jane are here. I must go. I'll tell you about Jane later. Morris's wife. She's fallen, as we all do. She has a beau! He looks like you. I'm quite taken with him. And so amused by their predicament. They honestly think they're the first . . ."

She laughs softly and hangs up. Euell stares at the receiver, then replaces it in the cradle. He walks out into the night, which is overcast. The stars are visible only through a gauzy layer of clouds. He is confused, upset, and angry with himself for once more pretending to be who he is not, though this time he hasn't the faintest idea who he is not, some fellow by the name of Lowell. Which sounds like Euell, it's true, but that doesn't solve the matter. A dark and handsome fellow, at least. Someone worth impersonating. Is it possible to impersonate an unknown person? He was guilty once of impersonating Hugh (it seems like years ago that Jane, or rather Mrs. Merkle, lost her purse), but even then there was no premeditation. He was led to that particular falsehood like a cow in a chute. He was tricked. And he's being tricked again. Or so he feels as he makes his way to the ranger station, hoping to find Warren Haas upright. Because right now more than anything—certainly more than love—he needs the company of someone who likes to drink and likes to talk and can do both at the same time all night long and still wake up in the morning and think life is worth living. That would be Haas. God bless Haas.

The Second Law of
Thermodynamics

J ane Merkle cannot understand why he doesn't call. Does
he not think of her? Tomorrow Morris will arrive and
that will be the end of her freedom. Though perhaps
she's lost her freedom already. Perhaps one's freedom ends
when love arrives.

Oliver, meanwhile, has invited her to pin butterflies, and
the strange process so engulfs her, it's the only thing that
takes her mind away from Euell. Just this morning she pinned
up thirteen Schellbach's fritillaries, captured a week ago at
Kanabownits Spring, yet in the delicate spreading and pinning
of the wings—and the antennae, which Oliver insisted on—she
never once fell into nostalgic reminiscence or felt poetry leap to
mind. No tragic songs of sitting beside her handsome ranger in
the meadow. No. The *Speyeria atlantis schellbachi*, as she has

learned to call them, seemed to draw her down to the pinning board, draw her down into their caramel browns—their velvet wings still in death, yet rich in beauty, alive. And she lay with them, pinned and happy. Still. So still. Free from desire and love and not-love. A butterfly herself.

But there is nothing left to pin, a situation that ought to please Oliver, who has never had an extra pair of hands, especially hands as capable as hers. But it alarms him instead. He makes quite a fuss. They must get out and collect, for goodness' sake! The season is flying by (as well as a fair number of Nabokov's satyr, with its two pretty little eyespots). He suggests an early morning outing. "But Morris is coming," says Jane. She is standing in his study, leafing through Holland's *The Butterfly Book*. She feels quite lost, and yet quite found in the mute, colorful pages.

"Morris?" asks Oliver.

"Yes. My husband," she says, and starts to laugh.

"I remember, my dear. But when is he coming?"

"Tomorrow."

"Drat it all. We'll go the day after. Or the day after that. We'll drag him along. And if that's not—"

"Oliver," she says suddenly, the book a pleasant, anchoring weight in her hands. "What would you do?"

"What would I do?"

"If you were married to Morris. If you were me."

"If I were you. Yes, I see." He rubs his chin, his throat, his chest.

"It doesn't matter," she says, dropping her eyes.

"Oh yes, my dear. It does. It matters very much. That you ask me, that's what matters. My answer, of course, is only inadequate."

"Don't feel you have to—"

"I don't feel I have to anything. I would *like* to give you a helpful answer. It would please me very much. However, I'm not sure I can. I'm not you, you see. Well, I'm you and I'm not. I mean I . . . Well, I've been on both sides of it, haven't I?"

"I don't know!" cries Jane.

"Well, I have. On Morris's side and on what we will call yours. I too had a . . . a temptation once. It was years ago, when I was a bit more dapper and feeling my oats and generally worth a thing or two—"

"Oliver." Jane touches his arm.

"No," he says quietly. "Let me finish. I would be honored to tell you." He draws a breath. "We have been married for a very long time, Dotty and I, but not forever. And there was a time when we were so recently married we both felt . . . we felt in a kind of limbo. Neither here nor there. With each other but not of each other, if you follow me. For many pairs this time is a hopeful time, but for us it was . . . it caused . . . irritation. We chewed at each other. I think we were trying to discover what it might feel like to be free again, rid of the mate. Of course I stood a very real chance of being devoured, being the male—that is, if Dorothy and I happened to be spiders."

"Which you weren't," says Jane.

"No. It's somewhat irrelevant. But a different perspective can be useful, don't you think? Anyway, we felt like sailors on a sinking ship at a time when many in our situation seemed to feel like cocaptains. We were right and they were wrong, as it turns out. Second law of thermodynamics: everything goes to hell over time. The ship will go down; it is always sinking; it is only chance that keeps it afloat. Captains are irrelevant. So are sailors for that matter. We'd had enough of standing helpless on deck, gawking at a failing enterprise. Our instincts told us to jump for the lifeboats, and we did." He clears his throat. "My lifeboat was a young lady named Isabelle Finch. She was a friend of mine long before I met Dotty. We were schoolmates. Our names were alphabetically close so each year we sat next to each other, until a boy called Grumann joined our class. I think we both resented him. I know I did."

"But why didn't you know you loved her, way back when?"

"I did know it. I knew it every day when I walked into the classroom and walked to my desk and sat down without looking at her."

"Oliver! That's too strange!"

"You were never a boy," he laughs. "Terribly awkward, all that stuff, for a boy. And I was hopelessly unpopular—the odd duck. It was pure humiliation to like a girl."

"I don't believe it. You weren't unpopular."

"I'm afraid I was. Yes indeed. I was considered beyond the pale. My hero was John Wesley Powell, for one thing, and for another, I was mad about butterflies."

"So you forgot about her, then Dotty came along."

"Something like that, but not quite like that. She wasn't forgotten; she was left behind. Dotty came along, we married, we stood at the rail of our sinking ship until our feet got wet, then we jumped."

"You jumped to her. To Isabelle Finch."

"For a time, yes."

"But did you save yourself, Oliver?"

He smiles. "One thing we didn't consider was that lifeboats are subject to the second law of thermodynamics, too."

"Of course," says Jane, soberly.

"We might have waited a little, my dear. Until the water came to our knees. Perhaps that's what I would advise. Wait for the water to rise to the knee, then jump, knowing that the vessel of your salvation is but a diminutive version of the vessel of your destruction." He taps his head. "Keep that in mind."

The next day Jane and Dotty drive to Flagstaff to meet the train. The snow has melted off the mountain, except for a few white patches in the high gullies. The sight of all that bare gray rock stretching up into the gathering thunderheads puts Jane in a somber mood. She and Dotty talk very little.

Morris is waiting for them when they arrive. "Unheard of!" cries Dotty. "How in the world could you be early?" She gives her brother a dry kiss on the cheek. Jane kisses him also and stands beside him and pats his arm. She looks up at him as he talks to Dotty and is distracted by something she's never seen before: he has hair in his ear. Quite a nest of it. She moves to the other side and sees a nest in that ear as well. Her heart sinks. Yet she feels a softening toward him, a pity. Why, he's an old man! With hair growing in his ears! Suddenly she understands how grateful he must be to be with her, to have her as his young wife. Pure gratitude. It softens her and repels her at the same time.

That night in bed he wants to touch her and she lets him, though she feels no impulse in that direction herself. She pretends he is a bear, a bear who wants to mate with her but means her no harm. Though it is clumsy mating with a bear. He pushes hard. He gasps and grips her flanks, and she feels like a deer brought down. He pumps and grinds against her until she wonders how he can not notice that she is utterly still: she is still and dead as a deer. She is prey. She doesn't struggle. Maybe he likes that. She feels him driving recklessly up into her, pushing the inside of her aside, forgetting she's a woman, not a bear like him. Before he finishes she digs her nails into the soft flesh of his shoulders, to hurt him. He flinches. She can feel his startled penis flinch and miss a beat, and it gives her pleasure that even so far along in his excitement she can stop him with a touch.

"Thank you," he gasps, afterward. He goes into the bathroom to wash up, and she curls in the bed and feels what it feels like to be a large blank space.

In the morning he is merry, almost jolly, and she sees that this too is gratitude. At breakfast Oliver announces an expedition below the rim, to Santa Maria Spring. "We'll leave tomorrow morning in the dark, hole up during the day, and walk out in the evening. Jane and I are after *Cyllopsis pyracmon nabokovi*, Nabokov's satyr, and anything else we can find, of course. Would you care to join us, Morris? Give you a net and show you how to use it is what we'll do."

"Oh," says Morris. "I'll give it some thought. Dotty, are you part of this outing?"

"I'm outing-ed out," Dotty replies. "But why don't you go? You can walk down a little ways and walk right back up if it feels too much for you."

"I'm sure it won't feel too much for me. Good grief!"

"Take a little nap at Hermit's Rest if you need to. You've been on a train for two days."

"Yes, but I don't feel one bit tired. Though I ought to." He winks at Jane.

"The air is thin," says Dotty. "And it's hot."

"Yes, yes. I know."

"The last time you were here you were light-headed and almost fainted on us."

"I was hungry."

"Speaking of which, you look like you've dropped a little weight. Doesn't he, Jane?"

Jane hasn't the faintest idea whether weight has been dropped or gained. She notices eyes and lips and teeth and shoes but not weight. And to drop weight is a different matter than to lose it, isn't it? More accurate, really, because a person almost always comes back and picks it up again. "Yes," she says, lifting her breakfast plate from the table and reaching for Morris's. "He's never been fond of my cooking, Dotty, but look what happens when he's without it!"

"Oliver's the same," clucks Dotty.

"Oliver is not the same," says Oliver. "Oliver has never lost a pound in his life."

"I ate quite well," says Morris suddenly. "Catherine took care of me on weekdays, and on weekends I heated up her casseroles and cooked a little something for Martin."

"Martin?" asks Oliver. "Who's Martin?"

"His dog," says Jane. "He died."

"Oh, of course," says Oliver. "I do apologize, Morris. I didn't realize he was a cooked-for animal. I forgot."

"He liked his meat," says Morris. "I'm quite good at meat, if I say so myself. Beef was his favorite. Lightly fried. He was awfully good about pork too. Though chicken . . . chicken he wouldn't give the time of day to. I suppose that's no surprise."

"No," Oliver agrees. "We're all with Martin on that one, wouldn't you say, Dotty?"

Dotty ignores the question and asks, "But who is Catherine?"

"A temporary woman," says Morris.

"And in a more permanent state," asks Oliver, "what can we assume her to be?"

There is an awkward silence. "I would just like to say," says Dotty, "I think it's wonderful when a human being can feel warmly toward an animal. Moose was very fond of this dog. It shows a large heart on his part."

"He was easy to love," says Morris, frowning.

"There," she says. "You've gotten that off your chest."

Morris stands up from the table and volunteers to do the dishes. He will wash, Dotty will dry, and Jane will make a list and go to the store. Later she'll make tomorrow's sandwiches and Oliver will throw some nets in the car. It is, for some reason, a lighthearted day, a day in which she doesn't worry and wonder, a day when the tasks before her seem interesting and useful, beginning with the shopping list: milk, cheese, chops, sardines, rye bread for Morris. "Syrup?" she asks, sitting at the kitchen table. "Shouldn't we have a little syrup?"

"Candy bars," says Oliver, walking through.

"Lettuce?" she asks.

"There's plenty of lettuce in the garden," says Dotty. "We need Brillo pads."

"And succotash," says Morris.

"Succotash!" cries Jane. "What a silly old word. Say it five times fast, Morris. Come on. See if you can."

He looks at her strangely. "Suc-co-tash," he begins slowly, as if he were pronouncing the word for a foreigner. "Suc-co-tash, suc-co-tash, suc-co-tash, suc-co-tash."

"Oh, you're no fun," she laughs. "Fast!"

"Dearest, I—"

"No, Morris. No excuses."

"It's a joke, is it?"

"It's not a joke; it's a challenge."

"I don't want to . . . I don't want a challenge, not right this moment, darling. I don't mean to be a—"

"Spoilsport, Morris. Don't be. Give it a try."

He seems perplexed beyond expression. He appeals to Dotty, but her attention is suddenly riveted on the dish towel. His hands in the soapy wash water, his back to Jane, he attempts to say *succotash* five times fast. He fails. He tries again. Fails again. Tries once more and comes out with an unruly garble that resembles an obscenity. "Excuse me," he says quietly.

The kitchen is silent. Oliver walks through again. "Liverwurst," he suggests, "unless you don't like liverwurst, Morris."

"I do. I'm fond of liverwurst. Thank you."

The word *liverwurst* appears in the wake of Jane's pen and suddenly she feels ashamed. She remembers the happiness of her first encounter with Euell in the store, the feeling of being lifted on wings. Liverwurst was what they spoke of. Liverwurst! And now the soddenness of her relations with Morris, as if they are struggling to lift a heavy, waterlogged carpet. She's been unkind. She's humiliated him. How can it be? When she first met Morris, hadn't she felt the same lift around her heart, the feeling of flying through air? If not on wings, then on the woven threads of the magic carpet she believed carried them both? And now the whole endeavor lies in a soggy heap between them, and Morris is simply who he is, and she is too, and nothing will come of old resentments. His love for her has always been in question. She puts down her pen and says softly, "Forgive me."

"Yes, yes," he says, keeping his back to her. "I'm feeling under the weather is all. It's Martin, I'm afraid. There's not one thing that will bring him back."

After that there's nothing to do but get on her bicycle and ride out into the clean air. When she returns from shopping, a car she has never seen before sits in front of the house. She doesn't know one kind of car from another, but it's green. She sets her packages in the kitchen, wondering where everyone has gone. The house seems empty and quiet. She walks down the hall and stops before her bedroom door, which is closed for some reason. Oliver's voice comes to her faintly, and she continues on to the Hedquists' room where she finds him and Dotty and the doctor from the clinic, whose name she can't remember, standing around the bed. In the bed—or on it—lies Morris, looking pink and puffy, so little like the Morris she left behind one hour ago that she wonders, suddenly, whether it is truly he. "Morris?" she whispers.

He raises a weak hand to her and waves.

Dotty turns in surprise. "Oh, Jane, thank goodness you're here! Something terrible has happened!"

"Dotty, please," says Oliver. "Come in, Jane. Sit right down. You know Dr. Ruffey, don't you?"

The doctor, a long lean man with a bloodhound's face and delicate wire-rimmed glasses, extends a hand to her. The hand is heavy and very white. His palm is surprisingly fleshy. She feels like a woman in an open-air market, receiving a cod from a fishmonger. The doctor says, though she hasn't asked (she doesn't know what to ask), "Yes, he's coming around quite nicely."

"Gave us an awful fright," says Dotty.

"What exactly—" Jane begins.

"Bee sting," says Oliver.

"Your husband seems to be allergic to bees," adds the doctor.

"Which we all knew," says Dotty. "But did he take any precautions? No, of course not."

"Oh," says Jane, sitting down heavily on the other bed. She looks at Morris, who seems to have fallen asleep. "Where did he get stung?"

"On the foot," says Oliver. "He must have stepped on the culprit right there in your bedroom. He came running out—"

"He was panicked," Dotty whispers.

"We called Dr. Ruffey and—"

"Absolutely panicked. His skin was red and itchy. And bumpy. It's still a little bumpy."

Jane leans forward to take a closer look at the patient, to assess his bumpiness. "He's awfully pink."

"The high color may last a little while," says the doctor. "Let him sleep, and when he wakes up he should be good as new." He closes his black bag and bows. "Good-bye, Mrs. Merkle. Oliver. Dorothy. If there's a turn for the worse, Mrs. Merkle, don't hesitate to give me a jingle."

Jane nods dumbly, remembering that she is, in fact, Mrs. Merkle. *Mrs. Merkle.* How odd it sounds in the mouth of this man who's come to save the life of her husband. Her husband, Mr. Merkle.

"Well," sighs Dotty, after he's gone. "I think that's enough excitement for one day."

"But our expedition!" cries Jane. "He won't want to miss our expedition."

"He may be in tip-top shape by tomorrow," says Oliver. "We'll see. By the way, I closed the door to your bedroom, Jane. I have a feeling Morris's bee was not the only member of the family Apidae to take advantage of our hospitality."

"We'll have to destroy them," says Dotty firmly. "We can't have our lives taken over by bees."

"I know that, dear. But at the moment we have no evidence of a nest."

"We do," says Jane, reluctantly, then wishes she had said nothing at all. For suddenly the buzzing in the walls, in her walls, is dear to her, of the utmost importance, the sound of a life that's hers alone, hers and the bees', a secret life. "At least I think we do."

"We do?" asks Oliver.

"I've heard them."

She leads him into her room and they stand beside the bed and wait. Dotty comes in from making lunch and waits with them. The bees make no sound, and Jane imagines them waiting too. Dotty says, "Three perfectly good liverwurst sandwiches are going to waste on the kitchen table. I don't know about you two, but I'm going to eat one of them."

Later that afternoon Jane is stretched out on her bed (Morris is still asleep in the Hedquists' room), luxuriating in the cool solitude, about to shut her eyes for a short nap. Suddenly the wall starts to vibrate, ever so slightly, a tremor, and she tries to remember what to do in the event of an earthquake. Earthquakes are not unheard of at the South Rim, but she can't for the life of her remember if she should run out into an open place or find a root cellar. The tremor stops. She's afraid it will start again—she's read about aftershocks—and it does. She sits up, intending to wake Morris and leave the house, when she recognizes the hum. The bees! The wall is alive with bees! She sighs and lies back down again, knowing she must alert the Hedquists. But what an energetic sound they make, tending to their honey or whatever it is they tend to in their short lives. She'd like to join them. She'd like to work hard, hurry here and there, go out, come in, crush and push, make music with her body. What a life that would be, what an utterly useful and satisfying life. A life—a work—that must die prematurely, because of Morris. Morris, who sells life insurance.

That does it. Her mind is made up. She marches into the kitchen to announce that she and Morris will take a room at the hotel until he leaves. The bees can go about their business unmolested. But to her surprise, Dotty has already thought the matter through, and her solution is remarkable. "Here we are," she says, "miles from anywhere but rich in rangers. Goodness, Jane, every other person you meet is someone who knows birds and bears and flowers and what have you. Squirrels and butterflies. Not to mention bees, Jane. Bees. Isn't there someone you can think of who knows how to smoke out a nest of bees? He could come on his day off."

"Smoke them out?" asks Jane, feeling stupid with astonishment.

"Encourage them to live elsewhere. It can't be difficult, it's done all the time, but a young entomologist would be our best bet, I think."

"Well, yes," Jane stammers, "but Oliver's here."

"Oliver," says Dotty, "is an old entomologist."

A Bullet to the Head

From eight until five, seven days a week, Gavia Immer, the switchboard operator for Grand Canyon Village, hides her long, useless legs under her desk. Her hands fly, plugging and unplugging, her vocal chords gather and shake: "Hello. Oh, it's you, Dotty. I'll connect you. Just one minute please . . . Ethyl! How was your trip back east? New York, you say? Your Preston has the most adorable manners! I'm afraid Dotty Hedquist is on the line. No no, it doesn't sound serious. It never really is. With Dotty I mean. Well, nice to talk to you, hon. I'll put you through."

She's a robust woman with bushy white hair, a somewhat thick waist, thick white arms, and iron fingers. She's never been married, eats lunch at her desk, and has learned out of necessity to control her bladder. When not in use, her wheelchair sits in a corner of the communications room, which is itself no larger than a large closet. She has no window to look out of. Four beige walls enclose her. And yet she feels she sees everything, sees through her ears, and has for the twenty years she's ruled the switchboard. The pitch of a voice, its timbre—these are the clues that shape stories, give weight and girth to speculation. Rumors offend her. She has little use for gossip. Her imagination may seem like a wild animal that leads her down mossy paths, fords spring rivers in flood, and chases cows, but in fact it's accurate.

On this particular August morning she's putting the park superintendent through to the secretary of the interior in Washington, D.C. "What do you think?" asks Dr. Bryant, his voice crackling in her earphones. "Should I break the ice with the naked cow joke or the one about the rubber Chihuahua?"

"Neither," says Gavia Immer, firmly. "Trust me, hon. Washington's not ready for that. And besides, the secretary's a very busy man. Not to say you aren't. But he's *busy* busy, if you know what I mean."

"*Busy* busy? You mean a busybody?"

"Very funny."

"Admit it. I'm one of the funniest people I know."

What Narcissism Means to Me, by H. C. Bryant, thinks Gavia Immer. "Hold please. Yes, go ahead, Dr. Bryant. The secretary's on the line. *Remember, no jokes,*" she whispers.

"Jokes?" asks a voice behind her, scaring her half out of her chair. She turns to see Elzada Clover beaming with satisfaction. "I've actually managed to sneak up on you, Gavvy. I can't believe it. Aren't you the ears of Grand Canyon?"

"Getting old, hon. Ears getting waxy."

"Oh, boloney."

"Did you know that's spelled with a *g*?"

"It's a city in Italy."

"City in Italy! You can't fool me."

"It is, Gavvy."

"Then how'd it make its way into my lunch?"

"The city gives its name to the sausage."

"The sausage I've got in my sandwich?"

"That's right."

"You know, Professor, I don't know what I'd do without you, I truly don't. You come in, scare the living daylights out of me, and deliver a lecture on the geography of Italy, all in less than a minute."

"It wasn't the geography of Italy, Gavvy. It was Italian culture and cuisine."

"Okay, okay. See? I would've flunked the course. Culture and cuisine," she shakes her head. "You ought to get a real job, Professor. Give up that teaching and come work with me, what do you say?"

Just then a light on the switchboard blinks. It's the superintendent, trying to call Washington again. "But you just called Washington, hon. I think once is enough, don't you? Oh, you want the president this time." She rolls her eyes. "Sure, sure. If there's a direct line to the White House, hon, I'll find it. I'll do my best. Hold, please." To Elzada Clover she says, "H. C., he doesn't understand it's Washington he's calling, not his mother in Butterball, New Jersey."

"He's not from New Jersey, is he?"

"It's a for-instance, Professor. And no. Obviously he's not from New Jersey. I'm from New Jersey. A little place like this, you couldn't have two from the nation's armpit or there'd be an atomic war. Anyway, you can't just dial a number and end up with the president on the line. Hello," she says into the mouthpiece. "Oh, hello. Is this the Mr. Truman who's president of the United States? It is. Well, that's good luck. Dr. H. C. Bryant, superintendent of Grand Canyon National Park, would like to speak with you."

Elzada Clover smiles and shakes her head. "Gavia Immer, you're a genius."

"Who would've thunk it? The pee-resident. You want to sit down, Professor? Sit down." She points to the wheelchair. "It's not comfortable, but it won't kill you."

Elzada sits and looks around. "You need some artwork in here. Spruce up these walls a bit."

"I hate art."

"How can you hate art? No one hates art."

Gavia Immer ignores the question. She slips off the headset and swivels her chair to face Elzada. "Am I ever glad you came. Something fishy's going on. It's not just . . . you know . . . the thing in the . . . in Mr. Kolb's . . ."

"Garage."

"Right. It's this other thing. These telephone calls. He's been calling her, but where in the heck is he calling from? Heaven?"

"Who, Gavvy? Who's calling?"

Gavia Immer sighs. "She calls him Lowell."

"She, who?"

"Dotty Hedquist."

"And this is Lowell Dunhill, you imagine?"

"I happen to have a perfectly good imagination, Professor, but that's not what I'm talking about. This is fact, plain and simple."

"But surely there's more than one Lowell in the world. Isn't it possible Mrs. Hedquist knows someone named Lowell who isn't *that* Lowell?"

"No," she says firmly. "It's not the slightest bit possible."

Elzada laughs. More accurately, she snorts. A derisive snort. If there's one thing in the world a switchboard operator cannot tolerate, it's derisive snorting, and Gavia Immer is no exception. But she likes Elzada. They're like sisters. They met a dozen years ago and only see each other once a decade, but they talk on the telephone, and Elzada's told her things she's never told anyone, and Gavia's done the same. So she's patient. She merely says, "I can tell you don't believe me, Professor, but you don't know the story of Dotty and Lowell. That business was before your time, and you won't find it in a book. A reader like you, it's got to be in a book or you won't believe it."

The switchboard blinks and Gavia slips on her headset and goes to work. It's Josefina Delgadillo, the butcher's wife, calling around to ask if anyone among the stouter ladies of the village has a white dress that might fit her daughter, Lulu, who's getting married. Poor Lulu's on her way to motherhood. She ordered her wedding dress in Flagstaff, but when she went to pick it up yesterday, it was already too small. "She growing," laments Josefina. "By the time the wedding come she big and fat like a calabaza!"

Gavia Immer covers the mouthpiece and whispers to Elzada, "What's a calabaza? A pig?"

"A dumpling, I think."

Gavia nods. "I promise you, Josefina, she won't look like a dumpling. The wedding's only a week away. Yes, of course. Well, it's been a long time since I needed a white dress, but I might have a cream-colored one. With pansies on it. Oh, I see. It has to be white. Well, if you can't find one anywhere else, we can always try the Clorox trick. I don't know about the pansies, but the rest would be white all right. Yes, yes. White as the driven snow. Very virginal. No, nothing. Just talking to myself. Good luck to you! *¡Buena suerte!*"

"Your Spanish sounds very convincing," observes Elzada.

"Do you really think so?"

"At least I knew it wasn't English."

"Any time you want a lesson in how to give a real compliment, Professor, ask me," Gavia Immer says, scowling. "In the meantime, I'll tell you this. You're stubborn and you think like a scientist. If you weren't and you didn't, you'd understand that what I'm trying to tell you about Lowell Dunhill is impossible but true. He's alive, Professor. The man who died thirteen years ago, he's alive. I don't know how he is, but he is. And he and Dorothy Hedquist, who believed no one in the world knew about their love affair, they've been in touch all these years with telephone calls placed late at night, after certain amounts of alcohol have been consumed—"

"Wait!" Elzada holds up her hand. "How many calls are we speaking of?"

"Close to thirty."

"In thirteen years?"

Gavia Immer nods. "They were very rare at first. One a year. Usually Mr. Dunhill—"

"Hearsay," snaps Elzada.

"All right, Professor, 'the man called Lowell,' if you prefer that. Usually 'the man called Lowell' exhibited signs of inebriation—slurred words, repeated endearments—"

"What kind of endearments?"

"Honestly, I don't remember. Lovey-dovey names. I think he called her Birdie for some reason. And once, at least once, he called her Dodo Bird. But the point is, the calls were few and far between for many years, and then suddenly, in the past few months, there's been a flurry of them—"

"How many?"

"Approximately thirty minus thirteen. That'd be seventeen. It's as if he's waited all this time for things to blow over."

"He's waited, you mean, for his death to blow over?"

"Exactly."

"But why?" asks Elzada.

"Why, indeed, Professor! That's what you have to find out!"

"Does she ever call him?"

"No. I have a feeling he moves around. Maybe he's a man on the run. She lives in the same house, at the same telephone number. That makes it easy for him."

"And Mr. Hedquist has no suspicions?"

"I can't say. The only thing I know for a fact is that Oliver would rather eat soap than answer a telephone."

Elzada begins at once to pace the small room. On her third lap she comes to stand beside Gavia Immer. "It's not possible," she says. "It's simply not possible that this Lowell is that Lowell. That Lowell is dead. I saw him myself."

The switchboard operator's hand flies to her mouth and she gasps—something a woman of her profession is trained not to do. "Never display emotion," warns the handbook. "Create a persona and vocal presentation as close to machine quality as can be achieved." Gavia Immer has never excelled at sounding like a machine, but she has become used to acting with a machine's composure. For a long minute she sits and stares into the air.

"Why didn't I know this?" she finally asks, then answers her own question. "Because you didn't tell me."

"No one knows, Gavvy. Except Lois and Emery. We hardly knew each other, you and I. It was a confusing time. I didn't set out to see the body. I don't like dead things—unless they're plants. But one thing led to another, and the evening became somewhat unpredictable, and before I knew it that little wrangler—I forget his name—Italian fellow . . ."

"Amadeo."

"Precisely. Amadeo. He found the body, I believe, down at the river, and brought it up. Anyway, he got it in his head it was vital I take a look at the remains, and it was only at that point I understood he had something to show me. And quite a something it was, Gavvy. It was, I'm certain, the reason the matter was never brought to the police. And Lowell Dunhill didn't seem to have a family, so no one came forward to demand an autopsy or investigation of any kind. Didn't you find that strange? An unclaimed body? An unrecorded death at Grand Canyon? I thought it very strange."

"People said it was because of the love affair. *Discretion* was the word that went around. Dotty Hedquist was a married woman, and everyone's always liked Oliver. They wanted to protect him."

"But surely a married woman's affairs are subject to the same scrutiny as everyone else's. That's the law of the land."

"Not this land, Professor. Not here at Grand Canyon National Park. But you haven't told me," says Gavia Immer, impatiently. "What was it?"

"What was what?"

"What did Amadeo show you?"

Elzada begins to pace again, head lowered, hands behind her back. "A few days later the body vanished. I didn't know that, of course, because by then I had left the South Rim and was back on the river with Nevills, grateful to leave all that nasty business behind. But I heard about it later, and it all sounded very mysterious. And now Emery's got a skeleton in his garage, but the latest word is it's not Lowell Dunhill because the Kolb skeleton has a distinctive feature, a cause of death that doesn't match Dunhill's death. And that feature is . . . ?"

"Well, it's strictly hush-hush," whispers Gavia Immer, "but I've heard there's a bullet hole in the skull."

"That's right. At the base of the skull. Right here." Elzada places her hand at the back of her head. "A difficult place to shoot yourself, no? You'd go for the temple, wouldn't you?"

"I honestly can't say, Professor. I've never given it much thought."

"You would. You'd go for the temple. *But*, if you were going to kill someone, you'd most likely have them stand facing away from you while you shot them in the back of the head."

"I suppose you don't want to have to look a person in the eye while that kind of thing's going on."

"No, you don't. So the fellow in Emery's garage," Elzada continues. "Do we think he was murdered, or did he kill himself?"

"This is a quiz. I don't like quizzes. He was murdered plain as dirt."

"I agree. He was murdered. And Lowell Dunhill was . . . ?"

"That's easy. He died of unrequited love. Jumped in the river and drowned."

"So the story goes. But what if I were to tell you that I saw with my own eyes a bullet hole in the back of Dunhill's skull—"

"No!" cries Gavia Immer.

"And that was what the wrangler wanted to show me."

"It couldn't be!"

"It was a small hole, easy to overlook, especially given the deteriorating condition of the flesh and the superficial evidence of drowning. I don't know much about guns or pistols, but my guess is it was done by someone who knew what they were doing, at close range. I'd also guess its placement happens to match precisely the hole in the skull of the skeleton in the Kolb garage. I'm not convinced that makes Emery a murderer. In fact, it seems to argue against it. Who would be so foolish as to kill a man and hide the body on the premises? It was planted there, Gavvy. I'm sure of it. But by whom and for what reason, I just don't know. And Emery doesn't know either—I'd bet a dollar on it. He'd rather go to jail than cooperate with the Park Service. He's been at war with them for a long time."

The switchboard blinks, but Gavia Immer ignores it. She looks at Elzada, at her friend the professor, at her dark curly hair, without a streak of gray, and the glasses that make her look wide-eyed and intelligent. All those hours on the telephone. It's different from being in the same room with her. She wonders how well she knows her after all. There may be vast tracts of land inside her where no explorer has ever set foot and never will. The Elzada Clover Wilderness. And she, Gavia Immer, has set off naively into this territory, roped to her chair, whistling "Old Hundredth." No food, no water, no matches. A fool, in short. On the other hand, who isn't more than they appear to be? She herself, in placid moments, forgets entirely that her legs are thin as two straws and useless. She's at heart an energetic walker and the gal who kept them up all night laughing. So who do you trust? The person on the inside or the person on the outside?

"We need a strategy, Gavvy," says Elzada. "At times like this I ask myself, 'What would Inspector Roderick Alleyn do?'"

"Inspector Roderick Alleyn lives in a book, Professor."

"But a book must imitate life."

"Life's hard to imitate. At least in New Jersey, and here at Grand Canyon. The person who killed Lowell Dunhill, if in fact he's dead—"

"What do you mean!" cries Elzada. "Haven't I convinced you of that?"

"There's still this fellow on the telephone, Professor."

"I'll tell you what you do next time he calls, Gavvy. You eavesdrop, do you hear me? You discard the operator's code of ethics, put it aside for the sake of the greater good, and you *listen in*, Gavvy! Do you understand? Find out who this imposter is and what kind of trick he's playing on Mrs. Hedquist. Meanwhile, we won't breathe a word of this to anyone else. It's no one's business but our own."

"It's not our own," says Gavia Immer crossly. "It's Kolb's. It's his garage got the skeleton in it, not mine."

"There's been a murder, and you're in a position to help solve it."

"All right," sighs Gavia Immer, wrinkling her brow. "All right. But I'm no sleuth."

"Leave the sleuthing to me."

"I've got two talents, Professor, and you're welcome to both of them. I can run a switchboard, and if I keep away from Saltines, I can whistle pretty good."

"We won't need the whistling, Gavvy."

"I'm just telling you."

"We're looking for a murderer and a motive, and we need your ears."

"You got 'em." Gavia Immer nods. "What else?"

"We've got to get Emery to talk."

"I can't help you with that, but I know who can. Edith."

"Edith?"

"Edith Chase. At the post office. She was, let's say, close to the Kolbs. Emery's brother Ellsworth in particular. They were what I think you'd call an item. Oh, this was years ago."

"Edith Chase." Elzada nods. "She doesn't strike me as much of a talker."

"Oh, she can flap her lips with the best of them." The switchboard suddenly comes alive, blinking in three different places. "Excuse me, Professor. I got calls coming in. It's that darn H. C. again, and Josefina. You know what I ought to do? I ought to put *her* through to Washington and let *him* fuss about Lulu Delgadillo's dress. They've got the wrong jobs, those two. I could fix a few things around here. But wait just a minute. Who's this other one? It's the Hedquist line. Let's see what mischief Dotty's up to . . . Hello, this is the operator. Why, certainly, Mrs. Merkle. I'll see what I can do for you." She covers the mouthpiece and grumbles, "But don't hold your breath, missy." She frowns at Elzada. "It's the sister-in-law, wanting to get in touch with Mr. Wigglesworth, and she asks me would I happen to know where he is right now. What do they think? I've got a crystal ball?"

"You do, Gavvy." Elzada points to the switchboard. "You've got better than a crystal ball. You've got technology."

Anax Junius

Euell wakes in a cold sweat from the same dream he has dreamt all week. A giant slug with the face of Mrs. Sayer, the malacologist, crawls up the side of his bed and across his helpless body, coating him—smothering him—in a thick, malodorous slime.

In the kitchen Roger Hemple is brewing a pot of coffee. "Morning, Euell."

"Morning." He nods and shuffles to the table.

"Who's the lucky dame, buddy? You had quite a night of it."

"I did?"

"Moaning and mumbling all night long. Having your way with the ladies, I figured."

"Mollusks," Euell replies. "Having their way with me. *Limax maximus*, if you want to know the truth. How about some of that coffee, Roger."

Euell has four days off and the only thing he's certain of is that he doesn't want to spend them here, talking to Hemple. He drinks his coffee, showers, dresses in dungarees and a clean white T-shirt, grabs his butterfly net, and heads out to his truck. It always feels strange to him to be out of uniform. He feels directionless and mortal—though the net acts as a kind of compass. At Jacob Lake he stops to buy a box of doughnuts, then the road comes to a T and he can put it off no longer: left to Utah or right to . . . ? He won't allow himself to think about her. Instead, as he turns east, he thinks about Ivy Sayer and her husband Ethan, whose company he'd shared a few nights ago. "From Norwich," they told him, "rhyming with *porridge*." When Euell confessed he didn't know his geography, Ethan drew a map of England in the air and pointed to what he called "the left hip."

"Well, it's the right hip, isn't it," Ivy insisted.

"It depends which way the old girl's facing," said her husband. "Looking at us, it's her left."

Euell nodded politely, though he wasn't much interested in England's hips. He couldn't rid his mind of the evening's earlier event, his bewildering telephone conversation with Mrs. Hedquist. He hadn't found Haas, though he'd searched in and under every bed in the ranger station. In the end he'd gone alone to the campground, where the Sayers were playing checkers by firelight and drinking out of a flask.

Ethan Sayer brought a camp stool from the tent while Ivy related the history of the tent, including the fact that it went with them on safari and was mauled by elephants. Euell sat between them, which doubled the time he spent with the flask. It was straight gin and went right to his head. He hadn't eaten since lunchtime. At some point Ivy Sayer brought him a plate of crackers, cheese, and sardines, and he remembers balancing the small meal gratefully on his knees.

Bumping along the road past the new Cliff Dwellers Lodge, the accommodations at Vermilion Cliffs, and the lodge and service station at Marble Canyon—a three-jeweled necklace of food, drink, and slumpy beds—he fears he made a fool of himself that night, but he can't remember how or the extent of it. He does recall, late in the evening, a dramatic reading by Ethan Sayer from Pilsbry's *Land Mollusca of North America*. The stout little man stood by the fire, one hand tucked into his coat, looking very much like another stout little man, a certain ambitious and highly successful French general. He'd all but committed to memory several passages about the mating rituals of *Limax maximus*, and he delivered them like poetry to Euell's astonished ears.

Afterward, Ivy Sayer put her hand on Euell's knee. "The terms of courtship are often more depraved than delicate, Mr. Wigglesworth. You've found that out for yourself, I imagine." She smiled at him, a chilly smile full of teeth, and he nodded dumbly.

He finds himself now on the short stretch of road to Lee's Ferry, an unpremeditated detour, perfectly pleasant, if a little hot. The butterflies will be flying, and after he chases a few he can soak in the Colorado River. Past the peach and pear orchards of the Lonely Dell Ranch, he crosses the Paria, only a braided trickle of a tributary today. The road follows the base of the cliff, down to the landing, where the water is high and muddy red. A dozen Boy Scouts drag their inflatable rafts onto the shore. Odd-looking craft, Euell decides, descendents of hippopotami. The more familiar creatures lie at the other end of the landing. Three wooden boats—cataract boats, he's heard them called, with a blunt stern and a pretty point at the bow, "Mexican Hat Expeditions" painted on their sides.

It's a good day for lycaenids—marine blues in abundance—and queens, drawn to seep willow and climbing milkweed. In an hour Euell collects three of everything he sees and heads upstream to swim in an eddy. He pulls off his T-shirt, looks around to make sure he's alone, then kicks off his sweaty dungarees. He's taken to not wearing underwear, and suddenly buck naked, aware of the sun's heat and the hot wind's arousing touch, he stands for a minute, feeling an intense pleasure in the day. The pleasure of the hunter and the physical, sensual pleasure of living in his own body.

The water is warm and silty. He swims a few strokes downstream, against the pull of the eddy, then turns and lets the current carry him up again. He climbs out onto a flat rock and lies on his back, looking at the cliffs above him, the line where rock meets sky. He closes his eyes, and when he opens them again a dragonfly, a green darner, has come to land on a seep willow branch by his left hand. He raises his hand slowly, millimeter by millimeter, until he's almost there, then with a sudden sweep he closes his fingers around the creature and lets out a cry of happiness. "*Anax junius!*" He sits up, then springs to his feet, waving his hand in the air, and in this blessed state of unself-conscious joy he is spied by two women who have wandered from the landing in search of a swimming opportunity of their own.

Hidden from view by a stand of arrowweed, Elzada Clover

and Lois Cutter are surprised but unembarrassed by the nude young man, dancing on his rock. His Latin is perfectly clear to them, as is his utter satisfaction in having caught his prey with his naked hand. The rest of his nakedness, as far as Elzada is concerned, is his own business. But Lois can't help but comment, "Why, he looks like Bill!"

"Bill who?"

"From the Nevills expedition."

"I thought you said you paid no attention to Bill Gibson's looks."

"I didn't much. But enough to know that this gentleman resembles him. Don't you see the resemblance, Elzie?"

"Only with his clothes off."

"Oh, pish! What would you know about Bill Gibson with his clothes off?"

"I'll tell you who he looks like. From the neck up, he looks like a young Lowell Dunhill."

Lois yawns and covers her mouth. "I never laid eyes on Lowell Dunhill. And neither did you. Not alive."

The ladies continue upstream unnoticed, take their clad swim, and return to the landing where half a dozen canyoneers are loading three cataract boats with the requisite gear for an expedition: canned goods, tents, bedrolls, cook pots, wash buckets, lanterns, life jackets, and several large jugs of whiskey. The young man who does or doesn't resemble Lowell Dunhill is nowhere to be seen. A truck, apparently his, has vanished from the parking area as well.

In the Belly of the Edith

"What bothers me," says Lois Jotter Cutter, who sits with her feet in a pan of warm water and Epsom salts, to which she has added a teaspoon of ginger, "is that two of the most brilliant men our civilization has recently produced should argue like children over something so mundane as the size of their gray matter."

"It wasn't an argument," Elzada points out. "It was a wager. And the gray matter in question wasn't simply a bit of sludge in the skull cavity. It was what they'd lived their lives with: their brains."

"Which they'd temporarily lost the use of, quite obviously."

"No. They believed, or were perhaps parodying the belief held by others at the time, that a larger brain equaled a smarter man. Fashionable Victorian discrimination is what it was. Proof that big-noggined Caucasians were mentally superior to the darker races. To be posthumously more intelligent than your closest rival apparently meant a great deal to John Wesley Powell and Edward Cope. Why? I don't know."

"They were underemployed!" cries Lois. "Too much time on their hands. They should have been put to work!"

"Oh, I think they worked hard enough, probably for twenty men. As I see it, it wasn't so much a contest of gray matter as a battle of egos. As old men near the end of their lives, they have less to fight with. Teeth and claws are gone. What's left, dear girl, but language and self-importance?"

"Good Lord, Elzie, what a dreary thought!"

"But we aren't old men and never will be. So cheer up, Mrs. Cutter. How are those feet of yours?"

"Ruined."

"I'm not surprised. It was a great sight, though, to see you clambering up those Vermilion Cliffs."

"I wasn't clambering, I was scampering."

"Wearing yourself out is what you were doing. But wasn't it lovely in the shade at the Lonely Dell. And what a crop of peaches!"

"It reminded me of home," says Lois wistfully.

Elzada hesitates. "Maybe home is where you need to be."

"But our work isn't done! The mystery isn't solved!"

"Perhaps there's something more important than work, Mrs. Cutter."

Lois looks puzzled. "Why, Elzie. There's never been before. And besides, what I've uncovered about the Skłodowska Institute . . . It's intriguing, like watching a photograph develop in the mix. Slowly the picture grows. Owen Dunhill was the founder and only member."

"Owen you say. Not Lowell?"

"It could be a pseudonym."

"Or a relative," Elzada suggests. "But if he had any relatives, why didn't they make a fuss about his disappearance?"

"That's another thing. The records only go as far as 1938."

"When Lowell Dunhill died. And after that?"

"Nothing. The institute disappears."

A sizzle of fine, hard rain spatters the window, and shortly the two women leave the hotel, sharing an umbrella. They make their slow way through the village to mail a postcard to Ellsworth Kolb. Lois's feet are puffy and sore, but she's eager for the outing. They walk at a sloth's pace. All of a sudden she stops and says, "Who won, Elzie?"

"Who won what?"

"The wager. Mr. Cope or Mr. Powell? You never got to the end of the story."

"Ah," laughs Elzada. "It ended in death, of course, for Mr. Powell and Mr. Cope. And when all was measured and done with, the larger brain was Mr. Powell's."

"And what did he win?"

"The chance to be enshrined in the Smithsonian in a pickle jar."

"His brain?"

"His brain."

The post office is a small stone building with window boxes of red geraniums. Elzada can't help but think sweet alyssum or even plain old pansies might have been a better choice. So many of her experiments involve geraniums, she's come to see them as the rats of the plant world. And besides, they smell of old bandages.

Lois steps across the threshold, but Elzada puts a hand on her arm and draws her back. "Let's wait," she whispers.

"In the rain?"

"Stand under the umbrella."

Through a window Elzada sees a woman shaped like a rutabaga, arguing with the postmistress. She recognizes Ramona Stark, the clerk at the store. "Now Josefina'll be here any minute, and you let her in, Edith! She's enough worked up about this wedding! You let her in!"

"I won't, Ramona. Not after five. That's one minute from now. She has one minute."

"The wedding's in three days, Edith!"

"That's none of my business. If Mr. and Mrs. Delgadillo have waited this long to send out invitations, they can certainly wait until tomorrow at half past eight when I open."

"Don't say it's not your business, Edith! Of course it's your business, and I'll tell you why! That little girl—"

"She's hardly a little girl, Ramona. She's twenty-three."

"The girl, Edith, the daughter, she's—" Ramona Stark straightens up and pats her bulging belly.

"She isn't!"

Ramona Stark nods solemnly.

"Who did it?" whispers the postmistress.

Ramona shakes her head. "A boy!"

"I do understand *that*, Ramona. What boy?"

"No idea!" She pokes a finger in the air. "Maybe you'll find out and tell *me*!"

"Well, isn't his name on the wedding invitation?"

"Maybe yes, maybe no, Edith! The one who's on the invitation, he's the fella gonna marry her, that's all I know!"

With that, Ramona Stark turns and leaves the post office, brushing past the two ladies with a satisfied smile. She's wearing what Elzada has heard referred to as a muumuu, which makes her look like she's been swallowed by a pale blue balloon.

The postmistress, Edith Chase, is a wrinkled prune of a woman with the pale, powdery skin of a government drone who spends her life indoors. She's wearing what appears to be a tweed blazer in the middle of summer. She lacks the shopping gene, thinks Elzada. Edith Chase gazes skeptically at the two ladies and shrugs her narrow shoulders. "The U.S. Government would like me to close in less than one minute. What the government wants, the government gets. I serve the government."

"We're here to mail a postcard," says Elzada brightly. "It should take no longer than a minute." She has a sudden, unwanted vision of the postmistress at home, eating an overdone omelet for dinner and drinking rum out of a jug.

Edith Chase whacks her stamp pad and says, "You're the professors, aren't you? Friends of Mr. Kolb's, right?"

"We're old friends."

She smiles oddly and leans forward across the counter. Her face is close to Elzada's. It's the color of fish flesh. "He hated me," she hisses. "He has good reason to now, but back then he didn't. If anyone got close to Ellsworth they had to reckon with Emery. But he's in the thick of it, isn't he? His chickens came home to roost."

"If you're talking about what's in his garage," says Lois, "you won't convince anyone he's guilty."

"Guilty of what?" laughs the postmistress.

"Of murder."

"I hope he's above murder, but it's hard to know with Emery. It's not your average Joe keeps a skeleton in his garage."

"He didn't keep it," says Lois hotly. "He found it."

"He didn't find it; he put it there. There's no other logical explanation. If a man, a body, is hidden in a boat in a—"

"Hidden? What do you mean, hidden?" Elzada interrupts. The temperature in the post office seems to have risen.

"Stashed below the deck of the *Edith*."

Elzada nods. "His old boat. From the 1911 expedition. But how do you know that?"

"Everyone knows it."

"It's the first I've heard of it. Wrapped in a canvas sheet in a closet is what people say."

"Well, people are wrong. It was in the belly of the *Edith*, down in the dark where no one would ever know about it, no one but Emery himself."

"So let me get this straight," says Lois. "Emery steals a smelly old body, puts it in his boat, and forgets about it for thirteen years. Then one day he wants to do a little work on the *Edith* and he finds a skeleton. 'That's odd,' he thinks, 'where did that come from?' and he tells someone who tells someone, and the trouble begins."

"It makes him look innocent, doesn't it?"

"Without a brain in his head is more like it," says Elzada.

"Like Powell and Cope!" snorts Lois.

"I take it you've never smelled a rotting corpse." The postmistress smiles. "If a body is fresh, there's little choice but to hide it on your own premises and keep the doors shut tight."

"I'll remember that," says Elzada, "but the problem is this: Mr. Emery Kolb was nowhere near the South Rim on the evening Mr. Dunhill's body disappeared. He was on the river with us."

Edith Chase regards her carefully. "Of course you'd remember that detail, though few people do. In the end it means nothing." She laughs abruptly. "That's what accomplices are for."

"Well, we won't keep you," says Elzada, consulting her watch. "It's one minute after five, and there's no getting around the government. We've mailed our postcard, and now it's home to our hotel. My friend Lois here has sore feet," she adds, "and I'm in the middle of an excellent whodunit."

The postmistress scowls. "So you're a mystery buff."

"Ngaio Marsh is my great weakness. Have you a weakness, Miss Chase?"

The postmistress looks surprised. She picks a piece of lint from her sleeve and says coolly, "I'm a reader of romances."

The rain has stopped and the air is almost chilly as they make their way back to the hotel. Lois leans heavily on Elzada's arm. "I know you're pleased," she says. "I think you've got another piece of the puzzle. What is it, Elzie?"

"Did you notice I mentioned Mr. Dunhill by name?"

"Yes, you said, 'on the evening Mr. Dunhill's body disappeared.'"

"That's right. And our postmistress didn't question the fact that it was Dunhill."

"Why should she? You don't either."

"Ah, but everyone else in the village does. Because now they know the skeleton in Emery's garage has a bullet hole in the base of the skull, which isn't consistent with the fact that Lowell Dunhill drowned in the river."

"But he didn't!" cries Lois. "We know that!"

"Yes, but Edith Chase shouldn't know that, should she? Only you and I and Emery and Amadeo knew it. And now Gavia Immer. How does Edith Chase know?"

They've reached the steps of the hotel, and looking up at the impressive edifice Elzada says, "I must admit, malicious intent is something for which the study of plants has left me unprepared. Every year I suggest to my department a course in plant psychopathology, a study of all the ways a good plant can go bad. Don't you think it would inject a bit of humor into poor old academia and expand some minds in the process? Everyone knows the Venus flytrap, Loie, but what about the other villains that sting and paralyze their pollinators or trap them in goo? And parasites are always scheming to alter the behavior of their host. Who's to say a mild-mannered currant bush might not suddenly sprout horns and a tail, or a cliff rose turn inky black and venomous?"

"Oh come, Elzie," Lois protests. "That's fiction, not science."

"And don't you think mutation narrows the gap between the two?"

They climb the steps and Elzada says, "Have you ever noticed there's not a guest room in this hotel that looks out over the canyon?"

"How very odd."

"It was designed that way, to get people out of their rooms."

The Monarch Census

Oliver Hedquist is losing patience with his brother-in-law, Morris. First the bee sting, then a series of irregular bowel movements have kept the man in bed—Oliver's bed—for three days, and each day he insists that in one more he'll be fit to go 'awandering,' as he calls it. Meanwhile the *Cyllopsis pyracmon nabokovi* are three days closer to their inevitable mortal fates and he, Oliver Hedquist, hasn't had the opportunity to wrap his net around a single one of them.

He is confident there is a solution. After a light supper of chipped beef on toast, he retreats to his study and sits before his old friend, his desk, drumming his fingers on the ink-stained oak. While there is no real reason to wait for Morris's recovery, he feels obligated to honor his brother-in-law's interest, feigned or not, in joining the outing to Santa Maria Spring. Yet he gets the distinct feeling that the man, having gone to bed, may never get up again. An inconvenience, for one thing, as it forces Oliver to sleep on the living room sofa, a faithful old relic to be sure, but uncomfortable as the day is long. He is quite sure Morris has no idea what torture it is to an entomologist to note the passing of each summer day—each summer hour—in which no attempt is made to capture invertebrates. Morris's line of business is different in that way. Any day is a good day for life insurance.

Perhaps Dotty should speak to him. Or Jane. No, not Jane. There seems to be too much freight in the married situation at the moment. No need to add a boxcar carrying a circus elephant. Oliver himself would give the man a good talking to, but he doesn't want to excite ugly feelings between them. He's a houseguest after all, and Dotty's only brother, and Jane's husband. Jane is a houseguest too, he realizes, though he hasn't thought of her in those terms since the day she came to roost in the spare bedroom.

The clamor of the telephone interrupts his thoughts. Dotty knocks on his door and pokes her head in. "It's for you, Oliver. Good heavens, why are you sitting in the dark?"

"It's no more dark in here than I'm General Dwight D. Eisenhower," he replies.

"That woman," she snorts, "has the most childish hair."

"What woman?"

"That Mamie Eisenhower, his wife. Now come to the telephone, please. It's his excellency, Dr. Bryant."

In the eleven years he's served as superintendent of Grand Canyon National Park, H. C. Bryant has never learned to be comfortable with the wives. Oliver suspects he's cowed by their efficiency, as are so many of his sex. He himself has often wondered why Ethyl Schellbach isn't running the park. He's had more than a few frank talks with Ethyl, and recently become aware of her great gift for managing information. She's masterful at putting one at ease at times when one should be most alarmed. Besides, with Ethyl running the park, H. C. would be free to pursue his very worthwhile avocation: chasing butterflies.

He lifts the receiver and Bryant cuts to the heart of the matter, bypassing pleasantries. He'd like to borrow one man and one net for a week or two of training, starting immediately. Could Hedquist recommend an individual interested in the monarch census, preferably a mature volunteer?

"Must this individual be experienced?" asks Oliver.

"No no!" says Bryant cheerfully. "Absolutely no experience necessary. He'll have all the training he needs by census time. That's why we start early. It would be useful, however, if he knew how to make his own lunch and that kind of thing. So many of our older volunteers have been undertrained, domestically, and to be away from their wives for regular stretches of time . . . Well, frankly, it does them good, Hedquist, but when it comes to foraging and all that . . ."

"Foraging?"

"Well, shifting for themselves."

"They'll be living outdoors?"

"No no. We'll return them in the evening. They can sleep in their own beds. We'll be working around the village and in the vicinity of Rowe Well. The details are up to Ranger Wigglesworth. He's organizing us this year."

"Ah," says Oliver. "Would a woman, then, be, let's say, appropriate?"

"Appropriate for what?"

"An appropriate volunteer."

The superintendent thinks for a moment. "My guess is no. But why? Have you a woman?"

"I do," says Oliver with satisfaction. "But I'm more than happy to keep her for myself."

There's an awkward silence. Finally Bryant says, "Well, I'm glad we spoke, Hedquist. Put it in your hat, will you?"

"In my hat?"

"Chew on it. And if you think of anyone, do let me know, will you?"

"I will," Oliver agrees. "In fact— What about allergies, Superintendent? Say a man had an allergy to bee stings. Would that disqualify him?"

"I can't imagine why. We'll be working with butterflies, not bees."

"Right," says Oliver gleefully. "I believe I have just the man for you."

"Splendid! Have him here in my office by eight o'clock tomorrow morning. Can you do that? And Hedquist, he's to bring his own lunch."

The next morning, Oliver pries Morris out of bed as agreed upon the night before. Jane has made two tuna fish sandwiches and placed them, along with a pickle, in the only bag she can find, a large grocery bag from Babbitt's. The size of it disturbs Morris, who has never before eaten lunch out of a bag. He'd prefer something smaller, more clandestine. "I feel like a horse with a great big sack of oats."

"Don't be silly," says Jane, and Dotty adds, "You'll be happy to have your sack of oats come lunchtime."

Oliver walks his brother-in-law to the superintendent's office, where a group of eight able-bodied men of all ages is already assembled, brown bags in hand. He introduces Morris to the three men he knows, including Bryant, who is in extremely good humor. Ranger Wigglesworth is nowhere in sight. Afterward, he says his good-byes and walks home. In his study he makes a list of what he and Jane will need for their expedition below the rim, which they are finally free to embark upon tomorrow at the crack of dawn. Funny about Morris. He seemed delighted at the opportunity to join up, as he called it, as if the monarch census were a call to arms. And yet the prospect of a stroll down the Hermit Trail laid him flat. Ah, well. The afflictions a man can conjure are surely as numerous as the ghosts that plague him, though Oliver himself is not much of a believer in ghosts.

His window faces east and catches the long, thin morning shadows of ponderosa pines. The light and shadow fall in bars across the road, and as he watches, a bicycle appears, as if in an old flickering movie. He recognizes the rider right away. Young Wigglesworth. Some business about the monarch census, no doubt. Moments later the doorbell rings. He goes to answer it, but Jane, running in her bare feet down the hall, beats him to it. She turns to him with a look of triumph. "I'll get it, Oliver. He's here to see me."

It is not his intention to eavesdrop, but by now it's an old and unbreakable habit, a requirement of his marriage. A certain fluttery energy plagues his chest as he stands with the door of his study cracked open so he might better hear the conversation down the hall. As far as he can tell, Wigglesworth has practiced his elocution since the last time he came to visit.

"I could kill Huddleston," says the ranger. "I'd like to wring his neck and throw him in a vat of boiling oil."

"Oh!" laughs Jane. "But that would kill him twice!"

"Twice might not be enough."

"Good heavens, what's he done? Don't tell me he's been impersonating you."

"Worse than that. Harboring information."

"What sort of information?"

"About your bees," says Wigglesworth forcefully.

"But you've come about the bees, haven't you?"

"Jiminy Christmas! I would have come sooner."

"Oh, well," says Jane. "They're still here. I had a conversation with Hugh and he simply forgot to tell you. But now he has, and here you are. I'm . . . ," she hesitates, "happy."

The ranger says something Oliver can't make out. Jane responds with an audible sigh. Wigglesworth says, "And he wasn't the one to tell me anyway. It was his girl, Betty."

"But he promised he would!"

"So I'd like to kill him."

"It seems only fair. I'll help you. Oh, but Euell, I can't. Today Oliver and I are getting ready for a trip, and tomorrow we'll be at Santa Maria Spring, and then . . . then of course you'll be gone again."

"I won't be. That's what I came to tell you. Dr. Bryant put me in charge of this year's monarch census. For the next two weeks we'll be training volunteers, so I'll be staying here and I can move your bees."

"My goodness," she says thoughtfully. "You'll meet Morris."

"Morris?"

"My husband. He's one of your volunteers."

"Your husband? I thought he died."

"Died! Heavens no. He was stung by a bee, that's all."

"I'm sorry, I—"

"Morris dead? How on earth . . . ?"

"Hugh told me."

"Hugh!"

"He called him Martin."

"Martin! But the dog is—"

"He said he died. He didn't say when. I thought maybe that was why you never spoke about him. I had no idea you . . . I would never have . . . I'm at a loss, Jane. I don't know what to say. I feel a bit led on by you. There. I've said it."

Oliver leans his head against the door frame and waits. Finally Jane says, "If you've never been married, you can't understand the desire not to be. From now on I'll try to conduct myself like a married woman, but I'm going to fail, Euell. Sooner or later, I can promise you, Mrs. Morris Merkle is going to fail."

It seems to be the end of the conversation. Oliver turns to the window to watch Wigglesworth pick up his bicycle (it's fallen to the ground), throw a leg over it, and pedal stiffly away. He seems like a different man from the young man who came to call on the widow Merkle just minutes before. How quickly love can be shattered. With a gesture, a look, a word, the dream of belonging to someone is tossed away. The weightless dream that feels golden and lusciously sweet. Now it weighs heavy and burns like vinegar. And despite what they say, only rarely does such disappointment move a man to poetry. More often it dulls the appetite, increases wakefulness, and inspires long pointless walks. It takes hold of the mind and won't let go, and all a man can do—or a woman—is endure the hours until it runs its course, when the simple absence of the aggravation has a golden, luscious sweetness of its own.

Vespids Under Her Veil

The bride is dressed in a blinding white gown covered with faded pansies. The faint scent of Clorox trails behind her like a bridal train. She wears a tulle veil anchored to her short dark hair with a sequined crown. One of the rangers has made her a bouquet of bunchgrass and black-eyed susans, something Ethyl Schellbach finds unusual and charming.

The church is overflowing and hot as hinges. The entire village is here—except the postmistress, Edith Chase, who doesn't like crowds. Before the ceremony, as people waited and grew irritable, there were rumors that there was no bridegroom, that he hadn't been chosen, that there was a list and poor Lulu hadn't yet found the boy who would agree to marry her. Well, it was fiddle-faddle, mean-spirited fiddle-faddle. Not unheard of in Grand Canyon Village, as Ethyl well knows, but still no way to act as guests at the Delgadillo's only daughter's wedding. The bridegroom is, in fact, a perfectly nice-looking young man by the name of Jones, C. O. Jones. From Williams, right down the road. Everyone, including his parents—a tall, slim pair of ranchers—calls him C. O. The passable looks come from the mother, Ethyl notices. The father, with his slicked-back hair and prominent teeth, resembles a prairie dog.

Not that looks mean a thing. Well, they certainly don't mean everything. Even if her Louie weren't the handsome man he is, she wouldn't trade his looks for all the gold in China—nor for Spencer Tracy, for that matter, who proposed to her so many years ago. She pats her husband's knee, remembering her own wedding day, while at the altar the newlyweds linger in some confusion about what to do next. Finally they turn and start their slow walk back, the boy looking terrified, as if the church is a pirate ship and the aisle a red-carpeted plank.

After the couple passes, Ethyl squeezes out, for she's agreed to hurry ahead to the reception, which on Lulu's insistence will be held outside the Bright Angel Lodge. The Canyon Songbird, as Ethyl is affectionately called, will serenade the wedding party and guests as they make their way to the rim, where Lulu, though she hasn't told her mother, will toss her bouquet into the canyon as a warning to other girls.

The clouds are building as Ethyl Schellbach starts to sing. Oliver Hedquist cannot help but notice a lone Grand Canyon ringlet fluttering around the wedding cake and finally coming to rest on the edge of a large glass bowl full of Catholic punch. Catholic with a capital *C*, unfortunately, meaning little chance for intoxication. Luckily he anticipated the problem and brought his own solution, tucked in his pocket in a silver flask, which he has consulted from time to time during the day. It is well past ringlet season, so the butterfly on the punch bowl is a record breaker and ought to be collected. Oliver didn't think to bring his net, but he's wearing an old straw hat. He approaches the bowl, like a tiger his prey—or a tiger beetle, an even more impressive predator—and with a deft flick of his wrist, swiftly, so as not to call attention to himself, he sweeps the air directly above the butterfly and . . . misses. Though his smelly old hat lands directly in the punch bowl.

Jane Merkle wishes her husband looked a little more like Oliver, or at least tanned up nicely the way Oliver does. But apparently Morris still has the power to attract women of a certain age. His age, she realizes. She'll bet her bottom dollar that's Dr. Elzada Clover he's talking to. There's something familiar about her. Jane wonders if they've met somewhere. Goodness knows she's heard enough about her from Dotty and Oliver and Morris too, who's run across her at the hotel, where he's sensibly taken a room in order to escape the Hedquists' bees.

At first Jane assumed she must go with him, and for one night she did. But she found herself unsuited to hotel life, the stiff sheets and fat pillows, the tiny soaps that delighted Morris but made her feel like Gulliver among the Lilliputians. And the fact that just beyond one's door lay public life, and along with it a scrutiny that made her feel uncomfortable and guilty. She felt she'd been exiled—from the Hedquists' house and her now-familiar life—simply for wanting to keep the company of a man who wasn't her husband. Her flirtation with Euell was wrong, impossible, and therefore misleading, but was it more than an error in judgment? It was not—nor, she realized, had Dotty and Oliver asked her to go. They had, in fact, asked her to stay, she and Morris both. If young Wigglesworth, as they called him, wasn't available to smoke out the bees, surely someone else was. But Morris seemed relieved at the prospect of quitting his sister's home, and Jane, his dutiful wife, marched into exile with him.

In a hotel her husband was a different man. They had never stayed at a hotel together, not in five years of marriage. In their room he became less agreeable than usual, picking fights over little things like whether to wear one's shoes indoors or the correct positioning of the shower curtain, which went inside the tub rather than outside, as any nincompoop knew. And in public, in the lobby and dining room, to Jane's astonishment he became a man who guffawed. So overnight she developed a rash on a part of her body he would never ask to see, an allergy to the bedclothes. Publicly laundered sheets and towels were the culprit. What choice was there but to return to Dotty and Oliver's, which of course didn't mean she and Morris wouldn't spend time together when he wasn't busy learning how to tag butterflies for the monarch census. He seemed momentarily downcast, then back to his old agreeable self. It was a shame, he assured her, to sacrifice domestic life for the sake of one's allergies, but bees or bedclothes, allergies could kill you. And, thought Jane uncharitably, domestic life could not?

He looks now to be a man enjoying his freedom. Against the backdrop of a building thunderstorm, he bends his head close to Miss Clover's. Something he says makes the lady professor smile, then throw her head back with laughter, which seems unusually coarse for a woman of Miss Clover's caliber. Perhaps it's one of his off-color jokes. Jane hopes not. But what can they possibly find to talk about? What lies at the intersection of desert plants and life insurance? She steps closer. The laughing has stopped, and she hears Morris say something she will never forget: "I loved him like a son—no, more than a son, because I wouldn't trust a son to love me back." Martin, of course. They're discussing Martin, and in the next breath an individual of similar proportions, also deceased, whom the botanist refers to as Scabiosa Spanky Pants.

A collie, Jane decides. Miss Clover looks like a woman who would own a collie. Or perhaps even raise collies in her spare time. She herself could never own a collie—all that hair, and their general shape, which resembles a love seat. She's not sure any dog would suit her, but certainly not a collie. Anyway, she's tired of watching her husband converse charmingly with a woman old enough to be his wife. She hasn't said hello to Euell yet, though she's seen him. She's kept her eye on him all day. They haven't spoken since . . . that terrible encounter at the house. She acted so poorly! But so did he!

Across the lawn Oliver Hedquist has misplaced his hat. He's looked in the punch bowl—for the third time—and searched the heads of the other guests, male and female. For it would suit a lady, that hat of his. It's a sexless thing in its old age. Gavia Immer has something similar but she swears it's hers, and it's not smelly enough to be his, and besides, it's got a spray of coreopsis tucked in the hatband. He goes to sit down in the shade and wait for the bride to cut the cake. It's too damn hot for a shotgun wedding, and soon it's going to rain. But there's

Wigglesworth. "Wigglesworth!" he calls out. "Over here, Wigglesworth! Come talk to me." The young man approaches, wearing his uniform and looking quite dashing. "Wigglesworth," scowls Oliver, shaking a finger at him. "You're too damn polite!"

"Yes, sir."

"You've got to learn to disobey!"

"I know it, sir. Yes. Thank you for telling me."

"Oh, you're hopeless, Wigglesworth."

"I know it."

"Is there one damn thing you don't know, son?"

"Well, of course there is. Well, yes, I mean . . . yes. Yes, there is."

"What what what?"

"I'm not sure, sir."

"You're completely hopeless."

"I mean, I'm not sure I can tell you, sir."

"Oliver. Call me Oliver."

"Oliver, sir. I'm not sure I can—"

"Oh, for heaven's sake, Wigglesworth, of course you can. It's about Jane. I love Jane too. You can tell me anything about Jane. Your secret is safe with me."

"Th . . . thank you, sir."

"Oliver."

"Yes, okay. Oliver."

"She's a married woman, isn't she?"

"Is that a question, sir?"

Oliver Hedquist laughs. "There's marriage and there's marriage, Wigglesworth."

"Well, I don't know, sir. I guess so. To be honest, it's not something I know much about."

"One day you'll know too much about it. But right now I'll tell you. What makes one person married is not what makes another married. These two, for example. Lulu and her beau. What makes them married is sitting in her stomach."

"Her stomach, sir?"

"Well, not literally her stomach, Wigglesworth. Where babies come from. You do know where babies come from?"

"Yes, sir. Since I was four. My mother told me."

"Well, good for her."

"Where were you and Mrs. Hedquist married, sir?"

"Right at the hip!"

"The hip?"

"The trouble with you, Wigglesworth, is you lack a sense of humor."

"I know it. I've been told that. Thank you."

"And you're too polite."

"Yes, you said that."

"I'll say it again. You're too damn polite."

"I agree with you. But there's nothing I can do about it. And anyway, where I grew up it was . . . it was good to be polite. People liked that."

"To hell with what other people think or like."

"Well, that's easy for you to say, sir, if you don't mind me saying so, because you're old. You don't have a whole life ahead of you. You've lived your life already and you can do or say what you please. No one's going to stop you. Or fire you. Or marry the other fellow. I wish I were you, sir. I really do. I put on this uniform and I feel like a . . . a . . ."

"A turd caught in a tube."

"Well, I don't know about that. Well, yes . . . I guess so. Yes. A . . . a turd. Squeezed into a narrow tube."

"That's it."

"And it all looks good from the outside—"

"To hell with the outside. Have a sip of this, boy."

"Oh, I couldn't, sir."

"You lily liver! Have some."

"But I'm in uniform, sir."

"Drink up, Wigglesworth. That's an *order*."

It seems to Ethyl Schellbach that Oliver Hedquist is assaulting Euell Wigglesworth over by the wedding cake. This is just the kind of behavior weddings are famous for, and Oliver too, when he's in his cups. A hard rain is beginning to fall on the North Rim as she makes her way through the jumble of guests to find the bride. Lulu is leaning on the arm of her new husband, who is staring starry-eyed at Lulu's cousin Consuelo, the maid of honor. They'll sort it out, Ethyl reminds herself. This may, in fact, be the newlyweds' first date. "It's time," she tells Lulu.

"Time?" asks the girl.

"Yes," says Ethyl sharply. "It does in fact exist. You'll know that all too well when the baby arrives." She points to the rain falling on the North Rim. "The cake, Lulu. People are hungry and the men are beginning to fight."

"The cake?" Lulu repeats.

"It's time to *cut* it!" Ethyl barks in exasperation. Lulu is her goddaughter, and she feels in some way she's failed the girl.

A cry goes up as the bride and groom clasp hands and sink the knife into the crisp white frosting. "Isn't it lovely?" Dotty Hedquist whispers to Jane. "Five tiers. Yours, I remember, was three. Or two, was it?"

"Four," Jane replies.

"A delicious cake," says Dotty contritely.

The cake is passed around on thick white plates. There aren't enough forks, and Lulu's cousin Consuelo starts to eat with her hands. Suddenly she approaches the bride, pushes yellow cake into Lulu's mouth, smears frosting in the bride-groom's hair, and steps back, laughing. "Oh dear," says Dotty. "Here we go."

The bride moves forward, determined and resilient. She cuts a large piece of cake and hurls it at her cousin. "Ethyl taught her to throw," says Dotty.

"She has quite an arm," says Jane.

"I was never involved in sports of any kind."

"Not Ping-Pong?"

"Well, Ping-Pong. That's not a sport."

"I'd say it is. It takes timing and a certain angle and momentum."

Dotty stifles a laugh. "That sounds more like you-know-what to me."

Jane gapes at her sister-in-law, as if a pink frog has just jumped out of her throat.

"Oh, don't be such a prude, Jane. Have a little fun. Life isn't half as serious as you think it is. Now I'd better go find Oliver and drag him home. He's potted." She calls over her shoulder, "Tell that brother of mine to dance with you. Otherwise, divorce him!"

Such an ugly word, *divorce*. Especially at a wedding. Jane looks for Morris and sees he's still bending the ear of the lady botanist. The sun is hot despite the clouds that boil across the North Rim, trailing long gray fringes of rain. The bride stands beside her ruined cake, laughing, her tiara skewed, her tulle veil floating around her face. She seems happy, Jane notices with surprise. She doesn't remember being happy on her wedding day. Relieved and nervous, yes, and aware of the strange animal odor coming from her own body. But happy was something else, for another time. She didn't expect it that day and wasn't disappointed by its absence. Though Morris seemed happy, and all day he was very good to her.

As Jane watches, Lulu Delgadillo dips a champagne glass into the punch bowl and lifts it to her lips. Then with a sudden grimace, she flings it at her new husband. "Get away from me!" she screams. "Consuelo, get it away!" She bats the air with one hand and flaps her veil with the other. Her cousin waves her hands and cries, "Shoo! Shoo!" The bridegroom picks up the cake knife and moves slowly toward his bride, swatting at the air around him as if he is clearing a path with a machete. "Yellow jackets!" cries someone in the crowd. "No, they're bumblebees," decides a myopic gentleman Jane has never seen before. He must be on the groom's side. He looks like a foot doctor or a dentist. "Bumblebees?" says another. "Those aren't bumblebees. Bumblebees are cute and hairy, and they make a buzzy noise." "Yellow jackets. I'm telling you!" "Stay calm!" "Only the females sting!" "Run!" Then a voice, reasonable and reassuring, like a rubber boat in a lightning storm at sea. The familiar sound of it causes Jane to turn, and she sees Euell Wigglesworth threading his way through the crowd. He holds his hat high in the air and squeezes forward, calling to the newlyweds, "I'm an entomologist, folks. Coming through . . . Excuse me . . . May I get by you, ma'am? Thank you . . . thank you, sir . . . I'm an entomologist . . . coming through." He nods at the bridegroom. "Mr. Jones, that knife's not going to do us a whole lot of good." He approaches the bride and instructs her to stand still.

"I can't," she says, and starts to cry. "There's bees everywhere. They're in my hair. They're everywhere."

"They're not bees, ma'am," says Euell Wigglesworth. "They're wasps. Same order, different family. And you've got a few caught in your veil, that's all. Bend your head down. Let me take a look. Nope. None in your hair."

"He called you ma'am," giggles Consuelo.

"If I could take a look under your veil, Mrs. Jones, I could tell you just what we've got here."

"Mrs. Jones!" whoops Consuelo.

"I'll tell you why. They look like paper wasps imitating yellow jackets, and if I could collect them I'd get rid of them for you and brighten up your day—it's meant to be a happy day, isn't it?—and I'd brighten up mine because I'd learn a little more about what these amazing vespids can do. Would you let me do that?"

Mrs. Lulu Delgadillo Jones nods solemnly and stands very

still. The crowd is quiet, watching as Euell slips his hands lightly under the veil, as Jane has seen him do dozens of times, reaching inside his butterfly net. The bride catches her breath as the young ranger sweeps the wasps—there are two or three of them—into a glass and covers it with a napkin. He's so close, their clothes must be touching. Their faces are almost touching. Jane expects to see him lift the veil and kiss her—they're that close, and he's a dreamy, handsome man, and it's her wedding day. Yet he gives off no feeling of romance. He's businesslike and courteous, Jane can see it in the way he moves. This relieves her and disappoints her at the same time. And she doesn't know why it matters anyway, what Euell Wigglesworth does or doesn't do on this day. She only knows that suddenly she feels too hot all over her body and she wants to get out, to get away, to push through the crowd and find a place to be alone and look down into the canyon and perhaps, though her shoes aren't right for it, walk a short way in, to feel its grandeur and its protection, though from what she doesn't know. Her feelings boil up inside her like the clouds on the opposite rim. She's proud of him and torn with a feeling she's experienced before, and she knows what it is: it's jealousy. She doesn't want to be Mrs. Jane Merkle, age twenty-five, going on fifty. She wants to be Lulu, with vespids under her veil.

It starts to rain, a few fat drops falling like stones. She remembers that day in the woods with Euell, how she had drawn his attention to her and wallowed in it like warm mud, then become frightened and pushed it away. All that afternoon she'd wanted him to kiss her. She led him under the canopy of a pine tree—it smelled of butterscotch, almost sickly sweet—and waited there in the rain for the kiss, and when it didn't come she felt relieved and at the same time furious at him. She felt like a river in flood, boiling and free and certain to destroy everything in its hurtling path to the delta. And yet not free. Because the other part of her wanted tenderness, the slow lap of quiet water, the current gathering and flattening beneath a cliff where sharp-winged birds skimmed her shining surface. She had watched the Mississippi, walked along it many an afternoon while the meat was marinating, and she realizes now she misses it. That is all she misses, the moods of the river. And this other river is far away, a mile beneath her feet, a tan thread in a many-shaded cloth stitched by an accomplished seamstress who knows how to hide her stitches. It is hard to glimpse, this river. People speak as if it is there, and certainly it is, but it ducks and turns and hides—though sometimes it roars—and the greater part of it is all the stories told about it, like a gallivanting uncle who lives on another continent, where he wrestles wildebeests and walks among elephants and captures the world's smallest antelope with his bare hands. A man who remains exactly the age of the young man in the faded photograph, who happens to be him. A man by his absence frozen in time, until all that is left of him, the only life left of him long after his death, though he is not allowed to die, is story. It is so with the river for Jane. She feels cheated of the source, like a woman who has never seen a garden, who admires a bouquet. The whole canyon before her is the work of the river. And the wind and the rain. And time, of course. But the river. This river. It comes to her suddenly that all she needs to do is ask, and Euell will take her there.

A Botanist's Breakfast

Morris Merkle takes a swing at a big, fat bright yellow butterfly. He thought this would be hard—he was told it was somewhat difficult—but instead, how easy it is! Nothing to it, nothing at all! For days he worried he'd be a clumsy oaf when it came to the actual catching of the things, but here, one swing of the silky little net and he's hauled in a customer—or at least he thinks he has. For suddenly, to his astonishment, the net that felt like his friend seems to be quite empty. What in the dickens happened to the crafty bugger? He searches the grass around him for an injured butterfly, wondering if they hobble or wobble or limp. He even searches the heavens. He looks away at a patch of prickly purple thistles and his heart leaps, and sinks, for there, with its face stuck in a flower, is the beast—or perhaps it's a different one. He gives chase but the thing has an unsportsmanlike head start and sails away with a few heavy flaps of its wings and disappears into the woods, leaving him huffing and puffing and uttering profanities but determined to do better next time.

Lunch is a great relief. The grocery sack that so embarrassed him on his first day of work has become a symbol of hope and respite. He's fond of its large, brown, cleanly creased surfaces. It reminds him of a freshly ironed shirt. Each morning Dotty or Jane packs his sandwiches and fruit into a brand-new sack, which in the evening, after work, he discards. Even this ritual gives him pleasure: the ringing out of the old bag and bringing in of the new. The puffy sound of the bag as it drops into the trash can, whose lid opens and closes by stepping on a pedal. These are things he's never taken notice of before—like butterflies— and in the discovery of life's details he feels a renewal.

He wonders if he's becoming more religious. He remembers the first time he discovered a tick on Martin, an actual tick crawling through the fur behind the dog's left ear. He'd never seen a tick before and was afraid of it at first, but finally from somewhere came the courage to pick it off. To pick it off and bring it to Jane, who drowned it in kerosene. After that he noticed ticks everywhere and was no longer bothered by them, even when they blew up with blood and dropped off the dog and rolled around like peas on the floor. It was a transformation similar to the transformation caused in him by carrying his lunch in a sack. Or chasing butterflies. Or living on his own (except for meals) at the hotel.

Or perhaps love's the culprit. He hopes not, because it wouldn't do, would it, to feel the amorous tug and have to fend it off? In recent decades he's not been much of a one for amorous tugs, though he certainly felt a nibble when he first met Jane. He's inexperienced, there's no getting around it, but he finds himself acting like a schoolboy whenever Miss Elzada Clover enters the hotel dining room, where now and then—and more often now, because he knows her schedule—he takes his breakfast before running off to Dotty's to pick up his lunch. If he's not mistaken, she, Miss Clover, seems quite enthusiastic about his presence. He tries to arrive first, to claim the table next to the most desirable table, and after ordering his two poached eggs and coffee, he reads—or tries to read—the paper, glancing surreptitiously toward the dining room door. When she arrives, she is always alone. Her companion, the other lady, seems to be a late sleeper or, perhaps, not a breakfast aficionado. Miss Clover always wears the same clothes—a man's shirt and a pair of clean, pressed trousers that remind him of his lunch sack—and she moves comfortably and automatically to the most desirable table and immediately sets her reading material in front of her. With a brief yet heartfelt greeting, such as "Good morning," she commences her perusal of manuscripts or notes jotted on legal pads, and one recent morning she hefted an enormous reference book, something to do with flowers no doubt, onto the table and dove in. And he has his paper, so altogether it's quite pleasant.

Once or twice he's taken a stab at conversation, but it seems Miss Clover isn't much of a morning conversationalist. He would say she was a woman of few words, but at the wedding reception she did more than hold up her end of things, divulging the entire short history of Spanky, her collie. This indicates to him that afternoons are best for her, so he's decided to invite her to tea. This decision alarms and excites him at the same time, though he tells himself it's no more than a friendly gesture, and the West is a friendly place. He and Miss Clover hail from midwestern cities settled by Scandinavians, Slavs, and malcontents, but here on the edge of the world, on the edge of a crack in the earth too grand to conceive of if one is not standing beside it, gazing across and down, a different kind of humanity is called for, the kind that reaches out to say hello.

He has a growing list of topics he thinks might interest her, and every night in bed he adds to it. Dogs, dog breeds, dog food and exercise are the obvious subjects of choice, but there might be something to say about midwestern cooking, trees of the Midwest, trees in general, and butterflies. Hopefully she knows something about butterflies. He's not sure what he knows about them except that they keep vanishing as if through a hole in his net. And today, in a short lesson from Ranger Wigglesworth, the young man in charge of the monarch census, he learned that butterflies and plants are "interdependent." He finds it compelling, yet horribly embarrassing, to imagine himself as the butterfly and Miss Clover the plant.

To his great relief a conversational opportunity arises the very next morning, which happens to be the morning after the capture of his first bona fide butterfly. The very butterfly that eluded his net and flapped away into the woods circled back again and came to rest on one of the purple thistles, where Morris swept it up, or rather plunked the net down on it, smashing the specimen somewhat in his hasty joy. But never mind. He got it. And though there was considerably less fanfare than he hoped surrounding the event, Ranger Wigglesworth, a taciturn young man if there ever was one, identified the broken creature as a tiger swallowtail. "Good catch," was all he said.

At breakfast, still feeling somewhat elated, his mind is elsewhere and he makes the silly mistake of sitting at the wrong table. It doesn't dawn on him until he sees Miss Clover crossing the dining room. Her face wears an odd expression, the look one might give a fellow driver who happens to be traveling on the wrong side of the road. He rises from his chair—or rather her chair—to apologize and correct the situation. "I'm terribly sorry," he begins.

"Oh, my goodness, Mr. . . . ."

"Morris."

"Ah, yes. Mr. Morris. We are creatures of habit, it's true, but a little mix-up of our daily routine keeps our brains active, our minds sharp." She gives a little wave of her hand. "Think nothing of it. Please." And she sits at *his* usual table. Instead of her botany tome, she has brought a slim novel to read. A paperback, of all things. A detective story.

He can't think what possesses him, but he hears himself say, "Do you read, Miss Clover?" He immediately regrets it.

She looks patiently at him. "I do, Mr. Morris. Do you read?"

"I'm . . . well, of course. Yes. I do, in fact. The paper. My habit," he shrugs.

"And a sensible habit it is. More sensible than murder mysteries." She leans toward him and whispers, "I'm afraid I'm at the mercy of Ngaio Marsh. Always have been."

He can't make sense of that confession, but says instead, "I see you've ordered the same breakfast I have."

"Toast. Is that what you had?"

"Yes, I've just finished it. See?" He holds up his plate. "Nothing but crumbs."

"There's the evidence." She smiles. A beautiful, encouraging smile. "I suppose toast in the morning is common enough."

"Oh, it's common," he says quickly, "no doubt about that. But don't you find the common clues are often the most . . . uncommon ones?"

"Well, now that's something I haven't ever given a thought to. Are you a sleuth of sorts, Mr. Morris?"

"No no. Heavens no!" he laughs. "Just an observer of human nature."

"One and the same, I say. I wonder." She taps her right forefinger lightly against the rim of her saucer. "Perhaps I might borrow your ear for a moment. I'm trying to work out a puzzle, but I can't seem to make the pieces fit."

"You've looked on the floor?"

"The floor?"

"When Jane does puzzles, half the puzzle is on the table and the other half on the floor."

"Jane?"

"My wife. She stays with the Hedquists and I stay here. Rashes," he adds. "Allergic to the bedcovers. A better arrangement for both of us in the end."

"Ah."

"The first piece is the most important one," says Morris, from a well of wisdom about puzzles he didn't know he possessed. "It's often right in front of your nose. Like that toast there. It may take a form quite similar to toast. By which I mean it may look unremarkable."

"Toastlike."

"If one is in the realm of toast."

"And if one is in the realm of, let's say, mistaken identities, skeletons in the closet, what might that first piece look like, Mr. Morris?"

"Well, it's fairly obvious, isn't it? It would look like bone, Miss Clover."

"Bone." She nods. "Of course. Why that's it! We must have a look at the bone. The structure itself may speak to us. Or to someone who knew him well, who knew him as a living man. Though not as well as Mrs. Hed—" She draws a breath. "How foolish of me to leave that stone unturned."

"What stone?

"To not insist upon a look at the evidence."

"The evidence?"

"Sadly, I've become dimmer with age, like an old lamp whose genie has gone on to greener pastures."

"I don't believe that," says Morris gallantly. "I find you most intelligent and—"

"Thank you," she says, rising to her feet. "And now there's someone and something I must pay a visit to. You've been most helpful, Mr. Morris. I certainly hope I haven't bored you. Good luck in your butterfly hunting." And she is gone.

He watches her until he can see her no more. He wishes he had a net large enough to capture her.

A Slow Walk Home

To her sister-in-law she tells a little white lie, but to Morris she says nothing at all because he hasn't noticed: her wedding band is gone. She can't remember when she last wore it, or where she put it when she took it off. Instead she wears the turquoise ring, the ring that brought Euell Wigglesworth to her door—though he was Hugh then, and she was Mrs. Merkle.

She still is, of course, though her name, Jane, feels like the essence of who she is. Jane. She likes the simple, regular sound of it, the single syllable that doesn't tax the mouth. A month and a half have passed since she stepped off the train and breathed the western air and laughed at the snow high on the mountain above Flagstaff. She feels as if her life has passed from one country to another, one continent to another, and she has trailed along behind it. Dotty has begun to watch her more closely, which is why the subject of the wedding band arose. Jane was washing the dishes and Dotty, who was drying, suddenly said, "You're not wearing your wedding ring."

"Of course not. Not in soapy water."

"But you wear that other ring."

"Oh, it's nothing! It cost me a dollar. It means nothing. And it's tight. A bit tight. It won't slip off and go down the drain. That happened to my friend Helena with her engagement ring. They called the plumber and he looked wherever plumbers look, but he never found it."

"You can bet your bottom dollar he found it," said Dotty knowingly. "You have to keep an eye on your plumber, as your friend should know."

"Oh. Well, I never thought of theft."

"Theft is one of the major contributors to society's ills. In fact, you'll never believe what I heard today. Babbitt Brothers was broken into."

"Again?"

"But this time the culprit was apprehended." After a pause, Dotty suggested, "Ask me who it was."

"Who was it?"

"You'll never guess."

"I'm not trying to guess," said Jane with annoyance.

"It wasn't wild Indians after all. It was . . . it was someone you know, someone we all know. She didn't have to pick the locks or break the windows because . . . ?"

"Because she came down the chimney."

"What chimney?"

"I don't know. Who was it, Dotty? I give up."

"You can't give up."

"I most certainly can. I can and I do. Why is this sink not draining properly?"

"Probably a mouse pelt."

"A mouse pelt?"

"One of Oliver's projects. He skins them next to the sink and sometimes the pelt goes down. They're slippery."

"Goodness," said Jane with a shiver, untying her apron. She longed to be in her room, lying on her bed, with a cool cloth over her eyes.

"Mrs. Jicama," said Dotty.

"Mrs. Jicama?"

"Ramona Stark, at Babbitt Brothers. She's the culprit. She's been stealing from the store for years. It seems she's a . . . Oh, what do you call it when someone takes things? All kinds of things. Things they don't need—or even want."

Jane was perplexed. "A carpetbagger?"

"No no. That's not it. A something-maniac."

"Pyromaniac?"

"No, the other one."

"Nymphomaniac."

Dotty shook her head. "We'll ask Oliver. Anyway, they'll be looking for a new cashier and I thought I . . . well, it does get lonely sometimes, now that Oliver's retired. It seems I'm lonelier with him than without him. That's terrible to say, isn't it?"

"Not if it's true."

"I think a little time away from the home is what every woman needs."

"Why not go on a trip? Go somewhere you've always wanted to go, somewhere nobody knows you, where you're free, free to be any kind of Dotty you like."

"Oh, but I couldn't." She gave a quick, breathless laugh. "I couldn't leave Oliver. What would he eat?"

"He'll eat what I cook," said Jane firmly, "he and Morris both, whether they like it or not. All you have to do is decide where to go and go there."

Dotty smiled a curious smile. "I wonder what you'll think of me, Jane, when I tell you I've already decided. I have a friend in Los Angeles, someone I've known for years. I think I'll take the train over and see him. Or rather her," she said quickly.

Jane pressed her lips together and nodded. "Your secret is safe with me."

Since then Jane has felt a physical impatience that keeps her moving restlessly about all day, and awake at night. Her limbs—especially her legs—tug at her, as if they're on a journey of their own. Twice she has a dream of standing in front of her house in St. Louis, under a large golden halo that threatens to fall and crush her. After sending Dotty off, the impatience is replaced by a lassitude that keeps her in bed until noontime.

At night she makes Morris's lunch and leaves it on the kitchen table for him. Breakfast and most dinners he takes at the hotel. Their exchanges are cordial, but empty, which adds to her lethargy. It seems without Dotty her marriage is a loose bundle of sticks, not a dwelling place. At meals Oliver tries to make conversation, but Jane is barely interested. Even books, one of her favorite subjects, fails to engage her. Her brother-in-law suggests she take a crack at the Russians, those bards of darkness and foul moods, but to her dismay she cannot read more than a few pages without feeling boredom well up in her. She buys *Life* magazine and plods through it as if it were a long, complicated novel.

Then one evening, after Morris drops in for a leathery little dinner of pork chops, says his good-byes, and goes back to the hotel, Oliver too excuses himself and Jane is left alone. She feels like a horse waiting to be saddled. She feels no direction, no compulsion to do anything or go anywhere. She doesn't even have the yearning to read. She stands up. Standing, the kitchen looks different to her. Larger. More frank, as if the space could and would speak to her truthfully. She glances at her reflection in the window and what she sees saddens her. There, ghostly transparent, is Mrs. Jane Merkle, Mrs. Jane Yarborough Merkle, whose only error thus far in life is to have mistaken love for freedom and marriage for love. Flawless otherwise, there she stands, a female of good heart, willing to give it her best shot. She looks away, at the table full of dishes, wondering whose life it is she thinks she's leading, as if life itself is a blind horse.

A sudden movement beyond the window startles her, and she looks up again. Out in the yard a man crosses behind her reflection, as if passing through her, and she opens her mouth to scream but sees it's Euell. He waves at her. The gesture seems ludicrous and wonderful. She points toward the front of the house and mouths, "I'll come out."

She closes the door behind herself and steps out into a darkness deep and black. She doesn't know where he is but hears him breathing—shallow, rapid breaths that tell her he's scared and excited. She senses his body, the warmth of it nearby, then his smell. She has no compulsion to speak. She has never walked out into the dark this way. It's wrong and right. His smell is strong and good. How does she know it's his? Suddenly he says her name. Jane. The one word, and he pulls her to him. The scent of the pines. Butterscotch. Mixed with a rainlike sensation, the way he touches the bare skin of her arm above the elbow, as if his fingers are smoothing a rhythm into her flesh. His dry hands, a little chapped but so welcome there on her arm, and then his face, closer than she's ever been to it, and the sudden drop of his lips onto hers, startling and heavy at first, but soft, like the meat of an orange.

Hardly a word passes between them. Her name. His name. They move away from the house and she draws him down to sit beside her on the damp needles. His lips brush her ear, her neck, her collarbone. She turns away from him, lifts her blouse up over her head, feels the cool night on her skin. He sighs, inhales deeply. She feels him watching her, smells his smell, like barrels of gunpowder. Suddenly he reaches and catches her to him, pushes the cup of her bra aside and puts his mouth to her breast, groaning softly and pulling at her nipple. It startles her. He nudges her nipple with his tongue, rolls it between his teeth, and she almost cries out.

He lifts his head. His face is close to hers and she can see his half-closed eyes, his soft, childlike mouth. "Don't ever let me do something that doesn't make you happy, Jane. I would hate myself."

She has never heard an utterance like this before, and quickly, before she can turn away, she starts to cry in front of him. He takes her blouse and drapes it across her shoulders, and takes her hand and pats it. She puts her head against his arm and says, "I've missed you. I've missed you so." It's a strange thing to say. But he says, "I know, I know," and she believes he does know. She closes her eyes to drink in the feeling, which is shaped like a large white sail. The air is cool, even cold. She slips on her blouse and whispers that it's time for her to go in, and he asks if he may walk her home. "But home is only a few steps away," she laughs.

He puts his finger to her lips and she can taste him, a salty, bitter taste. "We'll walk slowly."

The Week's Mail

Ellsworth Kolb is the proud owner of a Zenith television whose eerie glow causes his neighbors to believe he is visited nightly by the Holy Ghost. He has little use for the Holy Ghost, though being a free thinker he doesn't begrudge the family next door their supernatural beliefs. Still, it puzzles him, how a septuagenarian bachelor like himself can inspire such fantasies. Obviously his neighbors, like most people in the world, have never been dragged to the bottom of a muddy river and left to wonder which way is up.

The television lives at the foot of his bed in his house in Los Angeles. After brushing his teeth and putting on his pajamas, he settles in to watch it. Tonight it's a cowboy movie, a shoot-'em-up filmed in Hollywood against a backdrop painted to look like the Arizona desert. The cacti are too tall, and the Indians are poorly disguised gringos, but Ellsworth Kolb enjoys it. It reminds him of the old days at Grand Canyon, and some of his adventures there with his brother, Emery. There's a lovely girl in it who reminds him of Edith Chase, though she's a good deal prettier than Edith, and more forgiving. It rekindles his desire to see her, though regrettably, if his math is accurate, she's no longer a girl in her twenties.

The sudden desire for a glass of milk propels him from his bed. Milk and gingersnaps are what he's after. He stands at the kitchen sink, eating the cookies, slowly drinking the milk, dreamily recalling Edith Chase's form, in particular her soft, bouncy breasts. He erases from his mind her prominent chin and sharply pointed nose, her tendency toward tweed and tightly laced shoes. He brings his concentration to bear on her fluffy, cloudlike bosom. Is it possible time and gravity have changed that particular area of her body? He is suddenly curious, though familiarity with the cruelty of aging tells him yes, of course, those little pillows are gone. He finds this over-whelmingly sad. He's missed his chance, hasn't he? And she's missed hers. She was a ripe plum of a girl back then and now . . . now . . . ?

To distract himself from grim thoughts, he sits down at the kitchen table and shuffles a pile of the week's mail. There, by extraordinary coincidence, he comes across a postcard, one of his own photographs of the winter canyon: Zoroaster Temple, like a great head hooded with snow. He holds the card for a mo-ment, regarding the scene as if he's standing on the rim, looking out over the canyon itself. Turning it over he reads the short message from Elzada Clover: "Have tried to reach you by tele-phone. Call me. Lois and I are lodged at El Tovar."

It's all he needs. He's never liked telephones. The South Rim is only a short journey away. The thought of standing on the edge again, marveling at the towering buttes clothed in yellowing summer light, and in the evening watching the crimson blush rising from the river like a ruddy tide running before the shadows . . . His heart beats too fast, suddenly. He puts his hand to his chest to hold it back. Then without giving himself a chance for second thoughts, he gets in the car, backs into the road, and drives east in his pajamas.

By the time he crosses the Colorado River at Needles, California, just upstream from the ruins of the great port of La Paz (which once connected the Grand Canyon State to the sea—to the world!), the night is over and the desert sun beats down ferociously on the roof of the car, creating within him a vegetable-like quality of thought. A certain insubstantial woolliness overcomes him. It's time to pull off the highway and sleep. And sleep he does, for an hour or two, with dreams refreshing as dank cellars.

On his way again, he considers the fact that he's an old man who's set out across the desert in heavy pajamas, and at some point soon he must enter the public realm and fill the car with gas. From there his mind moves on to transportation, the building of highways, engineering in general, and the building of dams. Upstream the mighty Boulder Dam and its reservoir, Lake Mead, are just the beginning of it. Now the damn bureaucrats are determined to put a great big chunk of Grand Canyon underwater. And other sinuous recesses as well. The Glen, Marble, Dinosaur—all soon to sink beneath the surface of a man-made sea, where pikeminnows and humpback chub nibble the bones of boatmen, and skin divers gawk at canyons, arches, monuments (to nature's folly!) that never will see the light of day again, never will sing again. Rainbow Bridge. Music Temple.

Friday, September 8, 1911. He remembers the day like it was yesterday—or the day before. He and his brother Emery stood on the banks of the Green River and christened their boats *Edith* and *Defiance*. They were Galloway boats, shallow hulled, with a covered deck and lapstrake sides, built in Racine, Wisconsin, far from the sea. But seaworthy they were, and the sister boats brought the brothers Kolb down the Green River to the confluence where the Colorado was born, and on through Cataract, Glen, Marble, and Grand—canyons with their own personalities, their living natures. One, with its drops and falls, would tear you to pieces, while the next rocked you in a sweet cradle of easy water, smooth sandstone beauty. Days without time, when mortal danger lay only an arm's length away, followed by lazy drying-out days ashore when every bone in the body cursed water's hardness (as hard as iron it was). Mud, silt, sand everywhere: in their cameras, bedrolls, in the food at night. As he lay down to sleep, Ellsworth never failed to thank the river for another day alive.

Now days have passed—about forty years' worth—and the rain begins to fall in loud *rat-a-tat-tats* on the windshield. The tires soon kick up plumes of water and the road's a river. He knows what he ought to do: row ashore, tie to a willow, and wait out the storm. But where in Sam Hill is he? Ash Fork? A dazzling cow town. Fella on the porch of the one-hole saloon gives a two-finger wave and hauls back to spit in a pail. A dozen horses stream across the road, their soggy manes plastered against their necks, ears flattened, eyes blinded by rain. Through an open gate, into a pasture they run. They stare at him, a man in a machine, sliding down a paved river in the rain.

Billy Bones

For forty-five years he has lived suspended in air, the great chasm below the floorboards so familiar he could tell you how the shadows lie on any given day at any given hour. A man who looks through a porthole and sees not sea but land, for that is where his camera points—at ancient monuments, sky islands dusted with snow or draped with cloud, a line of terrified riders astride their balky mules, descending steeply into what seems like nothingness. Or Harvey Girls arriving by train, and notable figures—Theodore Roosevelt among them—posing on the porch of El Tovar. His brother Ellsworth lining the *Edith* and *Defiance* through furious rapids, patching the boats, breaking up river ice, cooking up grub or that intolerable brew he called coffee.

Most days Emery Kolb feels like a sane man living on the edge of a miracle. He clings to it, his nails dug in. Below is the realm of raptors and Anasazi ghosts, disenchanted prospectors and dead conquistadores. Foolhardy, he knows, to come to the canyon to wring something from her, drag something out of her, sell her downriver, but thousands have tried and failed, and his failure too will come. As it is, the perfect photograph eludes him, like a fleet-footed muse. He cannot fully capture the essence of what he sees, and he lives with this the way a man lives with a high-spirited wife.

Recently, the messy business of the body has made it impossible for him to work, and he wishes he had done what his good sense begged him to do: leave that bundle of bones right where he found it, in the belly of his old boat. But the *Edith* wasn't built to be a coffin. She was made to run the river, to feel the waves along her lapstrake sides. She'd been living too long in a garage, with a stowaway aboard—some Noah or Jonah or a modern Moses. Emery knew his Bible well enough to be misled, for hadn't pharaoh's daughter found the bulrush babe and got herself a place in history? Yes, while he, Idiot Kolb, came across a human skeleton and suffered threats of arrest! He feels crabby and cantankerous. Let them send an alligator in after him, he'll wrestle it to the floor. But meanwhile no one, *no one* will set foot on his premises. He sits up day and night in the cave of his garage, with its familiar smells, each board, each nail known to him, in a lawn chair with a comfortable pillow, a shotgun on his lap. It is in this position, and because of his long sabbatical from the actual shooting of the gun, that he finally almost commits murder.

The intruders are experienced, *that* he knows. They choose to break and enter at dusk, the monochromatic hour when form

and shadow are indistinguishable—a poor time for photogra-
phy, but an excellent time for an old man's nap. Which is exactly what Emery Kolb is occupied with when the side door of
the garage squeaks open (the hinge as good as a watchdog), and
a flashlight fairly blinds him as he sits straight up and calls out,
"Hands in the air, you bastards, or I'll shoot!"

"Oh dear," replies a lady's voice.

"For the love of Pete," cries a man, "put that thing down
before you kill someone!"

"Lower your light!" Emery orders. His hands are shaking.
He was right in the middle of a dream about river otters.

"You're a damn fool," grumbles the man, "but I'd be a
greater fool to lower my light. We used to hunt deer this way,
remember?"

"Come forward!" barks Emery. "Show yourselves or I'll
blast you to high heaven!"

"If someone's got a gun, they often intend to use it," the
lady points out. "Emery Kolb, we're—"

The sound of his name startles him. And his blindness.
And the fact that there's another one outside, maybe a whole
gang of them—he can hear them moving and whispering and
knocking on the garage door. His finger jumps. He'll admit he
hasn't used a weapon since he used to shoot at tin cans with his
brother Ellsworth. He has no intention of using this firearm,
despite what the lady says. He just wishes that fellow would
lower the damn light—or snap the picture. At the thought of it,
his finger acts on its own and squeezes the shutter, and the gun,
belching smoke and powder and an ungodly noise, kicks him in

the shoulder and knocks him out of his chair. He lands flat on his back on the cement floor, and the first thing that seems unusual is the silence. He doesn't feel dead, though the possibility crosses his mind.

He wakes up in a muddled state, with a lady hovering over him in the dim light of the garage. He immediately rules out the possibility of heaven because she's dressed in trousers and has no wings. It is, in fact, a person known to him: Elzada Clover, his old friend. "Who did I kill?" he asks. He feels he can trust her.

"Not Lowell Dunhill, I hope."

"Now, why would I do that?" He frowns and reaches for her hand. "It's good to see you again, Elzada."

"That comes as a surprise," she says evenly. "A man who just tried to shoot me."

"I was aiming at the other fellow, the one with the light. I didn't hit him, did I?"

"I'm sure he'll tell you himself."

"He's still here, is he? I hope he's in better shape than I am."

"You'll live," she says without emotion.

"Ah, you're a tough old boot, Elzada. Just remember who saved your derriere."

"My life is what you saved, reaching into the river to fish me out below Upset Rapid."

"Aw, Nevills would've grabbed you if I hadn't. He liked you, that Nevills did."

"Enough to save me from drowning. But you were the one who did it, and I'll never forget it. That's the second reason I'm here."

"What's the first?"

"You asked for me, apparently, though you haven't done one thing to make my job easy. I've tried to defend you, Emery, but it's no use when you continue to do everything in your power to incriminate yourself—"

"Incriminate? I just keep my mouth shut."

"And shoot at people." Elzada sighs and shakes her head. "I'd like to go home. I miss my plants. But I need to examine the cause of all this trouble before I give up and pack my bags."

"You're looking at him," says Emery without remorse.

She smiles despite herself. "Not you, though I'm happy to report your self-importance hasn't suffered one bit. It's Billy Bones I'm here to see. I brought Gavia Immer with me, and someone else."

"The fellow I tried to pop off?"

"That's right."

"I didn't mean anything by it. It's not even my gun. But you have no idea how they've been after me. A man has his property and at some point he's got to defend it."

"I hear you're in possession of a skeleton," says the fellow, coming up behind Elzada Clover. "Is that what you're calling your property? If so, I guess it's my property too. Or did you steal my share of this place when I wasn't looking? I can't quite remember how that all fell out?"

He's a normal-looking fellow but for the fact that he's dressed in his pajamas. The light is poor and Emery's still seeing shooting stars from his fall. He tries to sit up but lies back down again. "Who is it? Who are you?"

"Who is it? Why, you're worse off than I thought. Who do you think it is?"

"Not my brother Ellsworth."

"The very same, brother Emery. That's my gun you almost got me with. I never thought I'd meet the barrel end of it."

"Well, what the hell are you doing here?" cries Emery. "Help me up, will you? If you hadn't shone that light in my eyes I wouldn't have tried to kill you. What are you dressed in those pajamas for? All those movie stars out there, they go around in their pajamas?"

"At night they do."

Emery grins and shakes his head. "You were never any damn good."

"Meet my brother, the murderer," says Ellsworth with a snort.

"Don't believe everything you hear. Unless you hear it from me."

From the back of the garage Gavia Immer announces, "I can see it from here, Professor. I believe I've found what we're looking for." She wheels herself forward. "Where I come from in New Jersey, we call that a skeleton."

"Don't touch it," warns Emery.

"We're only going to take a closer look at it," she assures him.

"It's laid out on the tool table back there just like I found it in the boat. Every bone, just like I found it, and a body has more bones than you want to know about, Miss Immer, in places you've never thought of before, like a great big puzzle. Go ahead. Ask me how I did it."

"I know how you did it," says Ellsworth. He brings his hands to his face and clicks an imaginary picture.

"You photographed it!" cries Elzada. "But how did you get below the deck?"

"I pulled the deck right off."

"Dry rot'll ruin a boat quicker than wet," Ellsworth says, nodding.

"I've been intending to do it for years. That's how I came across the thing to begin with."

"It was planted there," says Gavia.

"Of course it was planted there."

"By someone who expected it would never be found."

"Or more likely by someone who knew it *would* be found. By me. Many years later. When I finally went to work on my old boat."

"But who would that be?" asks Elzada.

"I can think of two people who had it in for me. It could be one of them or someone else entirely."

"For heaven's sake, Emery! Who?"

"One of them's standing right here. My brother, Ellsworth. We started quarreling thirty years ago and never seemed to quit. He knew better than anyone how long it would be before I got around to fixing up the *Edith*. I always said I was going to, but I never did. He knew that."

"The whole town knew it," says Ellsworth with a laugh. "You're just trying to get my goat."

"I'm just pointing out the facts."

"Your side of the facts, maybe. My side is different. I left the state in 1924 and never came back. Not even to plant a body in your boat. Though I wish I had, seeing how peeved it gets you."

"Peeved? Who's peeved?"

"You're peeved."

"I'm not peeved."

"I think you are."

"Gentlemen," says Elzada Clover. "Please." She turns to Emery. "You said there were two people who had it in for you. Who was the other?"

"The other one," says Emery slowly, "is someone I have a feeling about, but only a feeling. Add to that the fact that the old boat carries her name, and to hide a body in it would be her kind of humor, as well as a clue. She reads romances, and I believe those books are known to warp the mind."

"Edith?" asks Elzada. "Edith who?"

"Edith Chase is who he's talking about," says Ellsworth. "A girl we once knew."

"The postmistress? What on earth would be her motive for murder? Or yours, Ellsworth? We have to have a motive."

"Not for murder, necessarily," Emery reminds her, "but for hiding a body."

"But why would someone hide a body someone else killed? It doesn't make sense. And as far as I understand, he had no enemies. He was well liked by everyone. There was, of course, the business of his involvement with Mrs. Hedquist, but Mr. Hedquist hardly fits the picture of the vengeful husband. I can't imagine him putting a gun to Dunhill's head."

"Dunhill?" asks Emery. "What does Dunhill have to do with it?"

"Lowell Dunhill," says Elzada. "Isn't that who we're speaking of? The man whose remains are back there on your table?"

"Oh, that's not Dunhill. There's no question of that."

"But the bullet hole, Emery."

"It's there, right where you reported it to be, that night on the river when you took me and Lois into your confidence. Right at the base of the skull, Elzada. This is who you saw. This is the body Amadeo dragged up from the river. But it isn't Lowell Dunhill. It never was. You couldn't have noticed it then because the fellow was wrapped in a sheet, and before that he'd shot the rapids and banged himself up pretty well and twisted some limbs. But if you look at him now, you can see it plain as can be. Lowell Dunhill was a southpaw. He was teased for it; it was part of his charm. But this fellow, on the left side, he couldn't pick up a pencil to write with. And if you don't mind me saying so, in the lover-boy category, he wouldn't be much of a contender. The man has a withered arm, Elzada. The bones are half-size. He's all crippled up. Go and see for yourself."

"What did I tell you, Professor?" says Gavia Immer with a satisfied smile. "Lowell Dunhill's alive, because apparently he's not dead."

The Miracle of Travel

Union Station in Los Angeles, with its tiled floors and walls, with its high windows and wooden ceilings, its echoing bustle and crush of human life, and vendors selling sandwiches and cheap charm bracelets, and people from other countries wearing what look like sheets with towels around their heads, and children spilling out of blankets laid across cushioned benches, and babies swaddled in colorful cloths, and strange languages ringing like the sound of cicadas, and rows of palm trees teeming with parrots and doves—why, it all makes Dotty Hedquist dizzy and she has to sit down. Right there on one of the benches, next to the babies. It reminds her of Morocco, where she's never been, and Rome, where she imagines the pope walking around in scarlet slippers and a high gold hat, touching his holy staff to the little children and mumbling a prayer to keep them safe. She feels like a pilgrim, and she's frightened. She hasn't told Lowell she's coming. She hasn't seen him in close to a year. She was hoping he'd call, as he frequently does now, late at night, with the sound of a restaurant or street traffic behind him, but he didn't. She has the address of his sister-in-law in Santa Monica, which isn't far from Los Angeles, and she intends to go there as soon as her dizziness passes. He's told her over and over again it isn't safe to come to him, he'll come to her, and in fact for the past thirteen years they've met in the middle—in a hunter's lodge in the Sierra Nevada, in a quaint bungalow in Death Valley, in a motel run by Arabs in Needles, and in a number of other places that bear no trace of his life or hers. Plain gray walls, bland food, and a diet of love—and cigarettes. She even smokes a little herself when she's with him. As she sees it, she isn't coming to him but to his sister-in-law's. A cup of tea and a Danish might pep her up.

How in the world do all these people fit inside the trains? she wonders. She pays the vendor and thanks him and sits on her luggage to drink a very nasty-looking cup of tea. Very black. The kind that takes the lining of your stomach and rolls it like a rug and forces it upward into your throat. The Danish is stale and filled with crusty cheese. But isn't travel a miracle? It makes infidelity so easy. Here she is, in the city of Los Angeles, eating a rather poor breakfast, but soon to be in Lowell's arms, and only hours ago she ate her supper in Flagstaff, at the Howard Johnson's, where Oliver, dear old Oliver, ordered his usual fried clams. She hardly slept a wink on the train, aware of every jolt, but the ghastly tea and Danish have refreshed her, and she carries her suitcase out to the curb to find a taxicab.

Number 424 Ashland Avenue is a green clapboard house

with a wide front porch and a large square window facing the street. It sits on top of a hill, in the shade of a tree. Dotty asks the driver what kind of tree it is, and he tells her it's a eucalyptus. She climbs the steps to the porch, lugging her suitcase. Suddenly she wishes she'd packed more economically: a change of clothes and her bathroom things and a magazine. But she can't very well leave it all behind, so up it comes with a bump and a plunk. She stands on the porch, realizing to her dismay that she's forgotten Lowell's sister-in-law's name. She's married to his brother, Owen. That's right. But her name? Gloria? Vivian? Violet? Oh, it might as well be Mesopotamia. Well, there's only one thing to do, and that's ask. She leans forward and places her finger on the bell and presses lightly. From inside the house she hears a sound like a calf bleating, then the sound of footsteps shuffling toward her across what she imagines to be a solid oak floor.

The door is heavier than it appears. It swings open slowly to reveal a woman much younger than Dotty, with startling white hair. It's cut just above her shoulders and frames a pleasant round face. Her skin is the color of walnuts. She's wearing a yellow housecoat and no shoes, and no makeup to speak of. She peers at Dotty with some confusion and says, "You are very early, no? We have it in the back. You come around and look." She starts to close the door but Dotty says, "No, I'm terribly sorry, but I must not be who you think I am. I'm not here to see anything at all."

"No?"

"No, you see, I'm—"

"Maybe you want something you don't need."

"I beg your pardon?"

"We sell not just the hideaway bed. A nice electric mixer, all new. Picture frames. My husband's camera. He don't want to sell it, but what we gonna do? Honey!" she calls over her shoulder. "*Viejo*. We got a visitor. A lady. You wait," she says to Dotty. "I go in and see if he's dressed. Sometimes he don't want to get up and come to the door in his pj's."

From within Dotty hears muffled voices—the sister-in-law and a voice that must be Owen's. She glances through the open door and sees a large shadowy living room without a single piece of furniture in it. Beyond that a dining room with only a card table and two folding chairs. Hard times have fallen upon the Owen Dunhill family, it seems. She hears the sister-in-law returning. The yellow housecoat hangs open, revealing a pink nightgown covered with tiny blue noodles. The sister-in-law rests her cheek against the back of the door. For a moment she simply looks at Dotty, and it's then Dotty notices the milky cataracts covering both her eyes. The sister-in-law holds the door handle and lifts her left foot and rests it against her right knee. She's a hefty woman, short and square. Her feet are large and flat. She isn't a ballerina by any means. Her chin juts forward and her head tilts slightly, as if straining to hear. But she seems comfortable standing there on one leg, cooling her face against the door. This puts Dotty at ease as well, and she says, "I'm terribly sorry to bother you this early in the morning, but I'm looking for Lowell Dunhill."

The woman's face sags, as if pulled from below. Her white hair slants forward. "Wait one minute," she says, returning her foot to the floor. "I get my husband."

From inside comes the unpleasant smell of garlic and cigarette smoke. The voices are scarcely audible, whispering angrily. Dotty waits on the porch. Somewhere a loud clock ticks the seconds. She sits on her suitcase and looks out at the street. Was it foolish to come? At home right now Oliver is making his breakfast, a BLT, and Jane is packing a sandwich for Morris, though her heart isn't in it. A dutiful sandwich, Dotty knows, a kind she is very familiar with. She packed them for years when Oliver carried his lunch to work. A slice of resentment and a great big chunk of irritation, with mustard or mayonnaise, on white bread. She wishes now she'd been more patient, that she'd been able to be more kind.

A car goes by and she realizes she can just stand up and walk away. Her body's in Santa Monica, but her mind's in her kitchen at home. She leaves her suitcase on the porch and starts down the steps, not knowing where she's headed but allowing her legs to lead the way. They take her around the side of the house where the Dunhills' fat black dog woofs at her from behind a picket fence. She opens the gate and steps through, as easy as that, and the dog retrieves a tennis ball from the dirt and presses it into her hand and woofs excitedly. She throws the ball as far as she can, though she never did learn how to handle a ball properly. The dog chases it into the backyard, which is mostly bare, with trees along the edge. The strangest trees she's ever seen. Banana trees, the fruit bright green and growing upside down. A whole tree of avocados. The back of the house is shadier than the front, and the paint is peeling. Outside the back door a stone patio is strewn with the extraneous contents of the Dunhills' life. A stack of firewood, a hideaway bed and mattress, a lumpy sofa, a hi-fi, stacks of records, a bowling ball, a box of women's shoes, jigsaw puzzles, kitchen bowls and utensils. Why, what on earth could have happened to the unfortunate couple? This certainly isn't the moment to press them for news of Lowell. She decides she will turn right around and leave, without saying good-bye, without disturbing them further. But then the electric mixer catches her eye—a KitchenAid, the very best—and next to it, three good-as-new Oxford-cloth shirts, still in the package, one white and two blue. Dotty glares at them and they seem to glare back. Her gift to Lowell all those years ago. Somehow they've ended up here. Dotty of course has the rest of them, her keepsake from that terrible time when she thought he was dead, when she stood in his cabin desperately needing some part of her lost lover to take with her. And then a few months later the telephone rang and there he was, at his brother's house in California. What confusion. She didn't believe it at first. She thought she was talking to a dead man, a ghost. And then the terrible secrecy. For if Emery Kolb had found out his intended victim was alive, he would have tried to kill him all over again. But as it is, Emery suspects nothing. Dotty has this from Amadeo, who has ways of knowing things without appearing to know anything at all.

The dog comes and drops the ball in front of her. Such a smelly dog. She wishes it would go away. It stands there looking up at her, panting and dripping saliva. The air thickens as the fog comes in. The yard suddenly smells of dog doo and rotting foliage. Her head swims. The three pristine shirts seem to mock her. She should take them, it's as simple as that. Add them to the useless freight in her suitcase. She can't bear the idea of some stranger, some scavenger come to pick the bones of Owen Dunhill's misfortune, paying a nickel apiece and walking away with them. They were intended for Lowell, to clothe his body, and if not his, her own.

He comes to the door and stands in the shadow, looking out at the fog. Then he notices her. He turns his shoulder and she sees him from behind as he's moving into the house, and she calls to him, "Owen? It's me, Dotty. Lowell's friend. Dorothy Hedquist."

"*¡Aiyee!* What I tell you!" cries the sister-in-law, pushing past him onto the patio. An Aztec is what she is. A blind, jungle Mexican, padding around Owen Dunhill's house in her large bare feet. She should be wearing a serape, carrying a machete and a basket of bananas on her head.

"I'm sorry to—" Dotty begins.

"No," he calls out. "Please. It's not what you think it is."

"Think it is?"

The sister-in-law stumbles across the yard, crying and shaking her hands in the air, beating her chest with her fists. He says her name sharply—"Gracia!"—and she starts to wail.

"I'll come back," says Dotty. "I didn't mean to—"

He steps out onto the patio, and the dog picks up the ball and lumbers over and drops it at his feet. At the familiar sight of him, Dotty sinks down onto her knees. Her throat feels dry, her tongue catches behind her teeth. And yet it makes a kind of sense to her. The shirts, the camera he doesn't want to sell. He's here. Of course he's here. "And your brother?" she whispers. "Where is *he*? Where's Owen?"

"Dotty, I can explain everything."

Wits and Teeth

Euell Wigglesworth is thinking of going away.

"Going away sounds asinine," says Hugh Huddleston, sitting at his friend's table, eating the last piece of chocolate cake. "Don't go away."

"She's not free, Hugh. The dog died, not the husband, you idiot."

"Stop pacing. You're making me nervous. Have some cake."

"She's married to someone old enough to be her father. And he can't catch butterflies worth a damn."

"Maybe he is her father. Don't look at me that way. A fatherly type. It may not be a hop-in-the-sack kind of marriage. They may not indulge in sexual congress ever, at all."

"How can you tell?"

"*I* can't tell," says Hugh wearily, "but you can, by the way she kisses you. She does kiss you, doesn't she?" Euell nods solemnly. "Kiss her again is my advice. As often as you can. And once for me."

After a game of backgammon, which Euell wins, Hugh goes back to his borrowed bed in the cowboy dorm for a late afternoon nap. Euell is restless. His house is too small, yet the rest of the world seems too big, like a pair of baggy trousers he's forced to put on when he steps out the door, a costume that makes him feel ridiculous. For no reason he suddenly thinks of Ethan and Ivy Sayer, the British malacologists. He imagines their life in a tent, on safari, the African savanna overrun with herds of giant land snails, and Ivy with her binoculars, exclaiming at the number of species while Ethan scribbles excitedly in his field book. An odd couple, but they seemed happy together. He tries to imagine living a life like that with Jane, and it's all too easy. She knows practically nothing about insects or the natural world, but she seems eager to learn and a good worker and experienced in ways he is not. But what is he thinking? She has a husband. Someone she appears to spend no time with, he reminds himself, and with whom she shares few interests, and possibly no physical relations. What if he, Euell, were simply to provide her with a choice? What if he were to pursue her—cautiously at first, spaciously, then closing in, running her flank, like a wolf she might offer an invitation to with her body?

It's all new, exciting, and dreadful to him. What if the invitation doesn't come? He can make it come. Didn't she take off her blouse for him? Without a word she was naked in front of him. Or practically naked. It amazed him and amazes him still, the softness of her breasts, as soft as silt. He can draw her in, draw her close with the names of butterflies and dragonflies, Lepidoptera and Odonata: red-spotted purples, hoary commas, cloudless sulphurs, *Libellula saturata*. The names of grasses, romantic names: the gramas, *Bouteloua*. Songbirds, bees—tales of the fall nuptial flights of *Bombus*. And *Limax maximus*, giant slugs whose mating rituals are the stuff of poetry. He must get his hands on a copy of Pilsbry's *Land Mollusca of North America*, last seen in Ethan Sayer's possession. To hunt down a woman he needs tools and ammunition; he needs time, endurance, his own sharp wits and teeth. And he needs Pilsbry. But where can he find that definitive book about slug love? One name comes to him: Louis Schellbach.

The chief park naturalist isn't home, but Mrs. Schellbach answers the door. At her feet the little tyrant Reginald, who has a reputation for ankle nipping. Ranger Wigglesworth has discovered the best way to deal with a pug is to treat it like a tourist—a cross between a tourist and a badger. He greets Mrs. Schellbach, then Reggie, inquiring about the health and happiness of each. He is unfailingly polite, as he is with park visitors, yet he keeps his feet planted outside the door, declining the invitation to come in.

Mrs. Schellbach is quite certain the South Rim library now houses her husband's mollusk tomes, including Pilsbry, a book she seems familiar with because she smiles knowingly at Euell's request and raises her eyebrows. "Shall I tell him you came by and what you were looking for?"

"Oh, that's not necessary," he assures her. He thanks her and leaves, blushing furiously. Idiot! he scolds himself. You're acting like a girl! But the truth is, all his life he's watched insects *in copula*, and birds and wild animals mating. He's as comfortable talking about spider genitalia and odonate claspers and variations in penile shafts of certain land snails as he is the weather. It's occurred to him, of course, that someday he too will be part of the mad flash and dazzle of wings, the secretion of pheromones, the swelling of throat and scrotum to attract the female. And of course he knows that the color patterns of butterfly wings, the scent and diminutive size of male black widows, the dance of hornbills, and the chest pounding of gorillas are all designed to keep the genes afloat, to leave a legacy, to create life after death, evolutionary immortality. But somehow, even when he was in love with Sally Domani, and his friends, Douggie Warren and the rest, had already entered the race, he held back. He observed. His heart wandered here and there, but there was no girl he wanted to fight for. His antlers were small and soft and unscarred. There was no one he wanted to give up his youth for. But Jane. He says her name aloud. Jane. He thinks of holding her to him, her breasts, her belly, smooth as chalk. Under the stars, with the far sound of the river rushing over rocks. A soft place to lie, and the darkness hiding them from the eyes of the world, and her hands exploring him where no hands have been, and her faint cries, and his. To the river then! He hurries along the road to the library, feeling bold and determined.

Confession

In his wife's absence, Oliver Hedquist has tried to become a man worthy of her return. He cooks simple meals and keeps the kitchen counters clean, the dishes washed, the floor reasonably unsticky. He washes the clothes and even replaces a button on one of Dotty's blouses. In the evening he picks tomatoes and tarragon from the garden. He feels, at this time, not like a bachelor as he supposed he would, but like a tree in late winter waiting for the first urge of new life to usher from its limbs. He feels like a man set down suddenly in a deciduous world, a world of loss, of empty boughs and gray stillness from which color and flower and fruit will erupt, and emptiness again. It is the first time he has considered the absolute necessity of change, including death. He has known it, of course, as an entomologist knows such things, but he has not felt it beneath his skin, which he imagines now as the skin of a palo verde or the smooth bark of a sycamore.

One morning while eating his breakfast alone, feeling suddenly sodden and bored by the heavy taste of the bacon in his BLT, Oliver scribbles something in Spanish, a phrase that appears in his mind like words on a billboard: "Por algunos, la belleza es en la caeda." He's not aware of having thought it, and he doesn't know exactly what it means. He gets up and goes to the sink and consults Dotty's conversational Spanish book, which Morris at one point took an interest in but has now forgotten, just as he has forgotten that dishes rarely wash themselves. He finds no *caeda*, but comes across *caedizo*, meaning "deciduous." It doesn't seem like a terribly useful word, the way *toilet* and *train station* are useful. He can't imagine ever relying on the word *deciduous* in a foreign country. But there it is. *Caedizo*, or *caediza* if the flora involved is feminine. Perhaps Spain has a famously beautiful autumn, when talking about the trees is quite as necessary as asking for the ladies' room. It's possible. He himself has traveled so little. It is certainly possible. "Por algunos, la belleza es en la caediza." For some, beauty is in deciduousness.

His days are spent like a fisherman, hauling in his catch in the long hours of sunlight and repairing his nets in the evening. The currant bushes tear them up, but he can't help himself, swinging for vespids and new species of *Bombus*, and one late afternoon a remarkable little clear-winged sphinx moth nectaring on the columbine. He feels the summer ebbing, notices the increase of monarchs and California sisters, and because of this he rises earlier each morning and sets out along the rim or below it, taking his net, a canteen, and a candy bar.

One day he invites Jane to come along. Since Dotty left, the poor girl has lapsed into a gloomy self-satisfaction, as if repressing a secret joy. He senses the cause and would like to occupy her with a more hopeful project than Ranger Wigglesworth. Not that he doesn't like the fellow—he likes him tremendously. But there are limits to such relations, and the last to know it, or to admit it, are those involved. He would like to bring her out a little, back to where she once was. Or rather, not back, but forward. She has never in her life been free. He knows that, though when she stepped off the train two months ago, she appeared curious and open, unencumbered by luggage and willing to take the worst of Morris with the best. There was a freshness about her, an aliveness, but it fell short of freedom because it was dependent on novelty. On new places and customs, new clothes, new food. And now, Oliver sees, a new love.

He does not quarrel with his sister-in-law's method. Her choice is the unextraordinary choice of anyone who confuses the moment's happiness with true freedom. But he feels obliged to remind her—only remind her—that from time to time she used to avail herself of him. He wishes to offer again his services as a doddery old fellow of limited wisdom, whose affection for her nonetheless knows no bounds.

He opens the conversation at breakfast, though Jane no longer eats breakfast, at least not with him. Still, she has coffee, which requires her to scurry in and out of the kitchen, lured by the smell, and her timing seems to put her there when Oliver's mouth is full of crunchy toast and bacon and drippy tomato. He nods and chews, and by the time his palate's clear she's filled her cup and set sail for foreign shores, usually the privacy of her bedroom. Though once or twice he's seen her standing in the garden, staring intently at the neat, flourishing rows, as if taking the pulse of the featherlike carrot tops and the lettuce going to seed, trying to work something out in her mind as she sips her coffee in the cool morning air. She's become mysterious, a quality he's not fond of, though he senses in her case it's a necessary step to becoming her own species of butterfly.

This time he does not let her get away. He's made himself some oatmeal and swallows it efficiently. He's had quite enough of BLTs. "Do you think it's strong enough?" he asks. Jane is filling her cup. She looks at him as if she's met him somewhere but can't recall his name.

"Strong enough?"

"The coffee."

"I haven't tasted it yet."

"Well, taste it and tell me."

"It's usually perfect."

"Today it seems feeble. Like an old man's coffee. Try it."

With a sigh, she tastes her coffee. "It's perfect."

"Less bite than usual?"

"A little." She holds up her thumb and forefinger, indicating the smallest amount.

"So it's not quite perfect."

"No, it is. It's perfect."

"Not if it's missing its bite. It can't be both flawed and perfect, Jane." He looks at her, hoping she's had enough of him.

"What's got into you today, Oliver? All of a sudden you're worried about the coffee?"

"With good reason, my dear. It's not up to snuff."

She starts to walk away, then turns in the doorway and smiles, not at him but at the prospect of being free of him. "Tomorrow I'll make the coffee. I promise."

"That's a splendid offer. And will you make the oatmeal as well? Or do you know what I'd like? I'd like corned beef hash with a poached egg on top. With some fried potatoes. Dotty never allows me the potatoes, because as she points out, the hash itself is half potato, but I'd still like some on the side, fried up in butter. Doesn't that sound good? Oh, you'd be an angel, Jane, if you'd do breakfast every now and then. It's a sad affair when I make it myself. I don't really enjoy cooking, and I'm a frightful cook." He looks directly at her. "She left me in your hands."

He watches her closely and sees that she's been stung, and he continues, "With coffee it's all luck, pure dumb luck. A cow could make a decent cup of coffee. You see," he laughs, "today I'm not even up to a cow. But who would want to be a cow, really? It's a rotten life. Eat, eat, eat, if you call all that roughage food, and all that masticating eating, and then you're squeezed into a little chute that leads to a little box on wheels and taken to a strange place full of the anxious smells and cries of animals like yourself, and then you're struck dumb and killed. By a stranger," he adds inconsequentially. "Yes. By a stranger."

"Why, Oliver, that's a horrid story. Why do I care about being a cow?"

"You probably don't. But you should. Or you should at least consider the fact that behind even the simplest thing, such as a well-cooked steak, lies a story, a story made up of stories, and the more we know of the life of that thing, of its past, the more complicated becomes its simplicity."

"Really, Oliver, I don't follow you today. I thought we were talking about coffee, and now we're on to steak."

"Which in turn might lead to a stroll in the woods or to Ranger Wigglesworth, for that matter."

"Euell?" says Jane, truly puzzled. "What does this have to do with Euell?"

"He's the object of your affection, silly girl, and therefore a subject both complicated and simple. Now shush. There's no point in denying it. It's there for all the world to see—except Morris, of course. I believe he's quite blind to the matter. He loves you, but in a way that suits him more than you, perhaps. I don't know, and I've no interest in meddling; it's just that married love tends to be blind. I was quite like Morris at one point in my life. I walked around with my head in a bag because I was too conceited to show my hurt and humiliation. It's terrible with your head in a bag. You knock yourself out all the time, running into walls, falling over things. You can imagine."

"I must admit I'm mystified," says Jane, shifting out of the doorway, into the kitchen again. She sets her coffee beside the sink and crosses her arms, as if she intends to scold Oliver.

"Nothing mystifying about it, really. Either you're in over your head or you're not. You choose, Jane. Perhaps you've already chosen."

She drops her arms. "Chosen what?" Her voice shakes a bit.

"To run away with him or not. Simple, isn't it? And look how complicated!"

"I don't understand you. I'm not running away with anyone."

"You certainly have in your thoughts."

"Why, what do you mean? What are you saying? Oliver Hedquist, you have no right to—"

"Now now," he laughs, conscious of his role as the pesky mosquito. "Keep your protests for another time, Mrs. Merkle. You may need them. Why not give me the benefit of the doubt—all your many doubts—and accept the fact that I know you a little. I've observed you, as if you were just another cloudless sulphur. I'm well trained in observation, Jane, which gives me a distinct edge over those who deal in life insurance, the requirements of that field being that the agent first assess the aliveness of the client, and second, decide whether the client will someday die."

He is distinctly aware of wandering from his point, but Jane brings him back. "Oliver," she says quietly. Her demeanor has changed. She has dropped her helmet and chest plate and sheathed her sword. "I once asked you what you would do if you were me, and you advised me not to jump ship until the water rose to my knees. But what I've come to understand is that when we were married my husband and I boarded different vessels. Mine seems to be sinking while his stays happily afloat, so even the act of jumping is a solitary matter, not a shared one. You and Dotty sailed together for a while before the . . . the wreck."

"We did, and have sailed together since."

"With a period of time when your interests went in different directions. Your interests and your affections. Is that right?"

"I think of it," says Oliver thoughtfully, "as a whaling expedition. The mother ship launches the whaleboats—the size of lifeboats, you see, but with a very different mission—and these small craft chase about quite independent of the mother ship—"

"Let's call it the relation ship!" cries Jane.

"You're a clever girl. Yes. The relation ship. The little boats go on about their business, and in the end the whale is brought in. The mother ship takes it on board, stows the meat and oil, and this is how the project is accomplished. The larger, sturdier vessel carries the small and swift ones. They work together. The whaleboats have no existence without the whaling ship that carries them out to hunt, and no purpose without the great ship's hold to store the whale and carry it home to market. The one cannot succeed without the other. And in the end the ship goes home full, and the men receive their pay, which we might say is the point of a marriage as well."

"Do you mean," asks Jane, "that two people should embark on their own adventures in order to live soundly together?"

"Adventures? Certainly!"

"Including those of the . . . well . . . I don't know how to—"

"Flesh," says Oliver, simply.

"Yes. That's what I mean."

"Should or shouldn't, it makes no difference, because it happens just the same. Our love affairs move away from the containing vessel, because that's the nature of things, but give them enough time and they'll return. They must. They're not meant for the open sea but for short bursts of excited activity. And what they bring back from their wild romp is a boon to the expedition, not to mention fresh food for the crew."

"But, Oliver! This isn't a whaling expedition. It only resembles one. The . . . protocol surrounding a marriage is different. Don't I know it!" cries Jane, pacing back and forth. "I feel it every day, the restraint imposed from without. At least on a woman. Such harsh restrictions! Some days I know I must leave Morris. It's inevitable. We're hardly suited to one another. We've never been. I pushed for it. I longed to be married. He held back." She stops and looks at Oliver. "He was right to hold back. He had been in love before and knew what it meant. He was engaged to be married. Perhaps with me he hoped . . . He thought . . . We do share a fondness for each other and an earnest desire for the other's happiness, a happiness we cannot provide. I think about you and Dotty and how you've managed to cling to each other over all these years and—"

"*Cling* is a rather terrible word for it."

"Yes, I know. *Cleave.*"

"Too biblical."

"Oh, for heaven's sake, use whatever word you want."

"We've had a romp or two and survived them."

"Yes, that's my point. And I, who have had no romps, am impatient to leave him. It doesn't seem right. To leave him, I mean. It seems," she looks at the floor, "ugly. And something I'd regret."

When finally she raises her head, he sees the old Jane. "I know," he says at last. "I know."

"I'm not much of a wife."

"It's not much of a job. Taking care of poor benighted dinosaurs like me and Morris. It's thankless work. Being a mother, now that's different. I don't know why women put up with husbands. Someday they'll find a way around us."

"But until then, what are we to do?"

He sighs. "Spend enough time outdoors."

"Oh, Oliver, that's ridiculous advice."

"Did you ever meet anyone who spent too much time outdoors?"

"No," she laughs.

"Well, there you are."

She brings her cup of coffee to the table and sits down. "I must tell you. I don't see anyone, Euell or anyone else, as the solution to my marriage or my happiness."

"You're wiser about the smaller boats than I was."

"They're not just love affairs, these small boats."

"No no. They're anything we love."

Jane is quiet, thinking. "I haven't yet found that love brings me freedom."

"You're still young."

"Young," she laughs. "I feel very old." She holds her hands in front of her for a moment, then rests them on the table. "Do you think Dotty, as a woman, sees things the same way you do?"

"How could she? As you say, she's a woman. But I won't

speak for Dotty. I can't. And I doubt she'll speak for herself. She never has to me."

"You've never discussed the . . . the hunt for the whale?"

"Not in so many words, no."

"So the romps you speak of may in fact be trials to her, Oliver."

He laughs sharply and shakes his head. "No. No, they aren't, I'm afraid." He draws a breath. "You see, the truth is I've been forced to adopt a philosophical position about these things because Dotty seems to feel so differently about them. The whaling analogy is, as you point out, only that. It falls short of reality, or at least my reality, and apparently yours, but it's very close to Dotty's. I am," he pauses, as if to give himself a last chance to stay silent, "in a difficult and somewhat compromised position with her as my wife. I married my beloved, but she married . . . She married me, Jane. Just me. Someone, something, but not quite enough. And so I wait for her, and I try not to interfere, and I have my pleasures. Bugs." He smiles. "Of course in these situations it helps to have obsessions, things we can be proud of in order to shore ourselves up for the personal humiliations."

"The romps have been a trial to *you!*" cries Jane. "Her romps."

"Yet I can see the point of them. I've been persuaded they do us good. Without them she would have left long ago. I'm sure of it. And they've made me honest," he adds.

"But how can you be honest, Oliver, if you and Dotty never speak about it?"

"Not in words, my dear, but we practice that old-fashioned

form of frankness known as reading between the lines. And action too, one's actions. Never underestimate them. They're as revealing as the words of children. Oh, there are all kinds of ways. You know, if you've lived beside someone for thirty years, you have a sense of their mind before the thoughts turn to language on their tongue. It's what marriage has to recommend it."

He hasn't meant to overwhelm the girl, but it's better she know the truth. Seeing her pretty face with its wide green eyes (until this moment he could swear they were blue) and the new wrinkle of confusion riding between her brows, he feels a tenderness for her that translates into confession.

"How much do you know?" he asks.

"Know?"

"About her lover."

The word distresses the girl. She shakes her head.

"It's all right, Jane," he says kindly. "If you know, there's no need to tell you."

She looks about her, then finally rests her eyes on the table. "I know she had a letter from someone called Deo. The spelling was poor and I couldn't imagine Dotty having . . . You know. But they met. In . . . in the mule barn."

He nods. "Ah, of course. Her informant."

"Yes, there was something about getting information. Mr. Kolb. I think his name was mentioned."

"You needn't worry," says Oliver with a smile. "I won't ask how you happened to overhear this little exchange." She starts to protest but he holds up his hand. "I understand perfectly.

Secrets breed secrecy. I've done some things I never imagined myself capable of. And worse, I felt justified in doing them. I've lied to my wife, Jane."

"Oh, Oliver, surely she's lied to you."

"That excuses nothing. It makes it all the more intolerable." He stands up suddenly and walks to the sink. "My plan was to lure you out of the house today with a net in your hands. I quite miss our collecting together."

"I do too."

"The purple hairstreaks are flying."

"So I've heard."

"You have? Ah, of course you have." He waits for the unpleasant feeling of jealousy to pass. "I hope, if you continue with Mr. Wigglesworth, you'll make that part of your adventure with him."

"I'd like it to be my adventure with you too, Oliver."

"You would?"

"Yes. Don't you know that?"

"I'm old and dull, Jane."

"You're nothing of the sort. You're a legend, in fact. Anyone who's seen you with a net, as I have, leaping through the air—"

"Legends are by definition very old."

"Yes, that's true, but you have no idea how age impresses the young."

"You," he laughs, "you impress the young. A woman of twenty-five is quite an impressive creature to a young man of twenty-one."

"He's older than that," she says coolly.

"If you would care to join me for a quick run down to the first rest house, I'd be honored, Mrs. Merkle."

"Won't it be in the shade?"

"Ah, by the time we get there, maybe so. Shoshone Point, then. Easier on the knees."

"I'd like that," she says. "May I ask you something, Oliver? Will Dotty be coming home?"

He suddenly feels weary. "She'll come home. When she's had enough of the open sea, she'll come home. She likes to drown every now and then. Home is not a place for that."

"How do you . . . ? How do you manage it?"

"If you're asking how Morris will manage, I can't tell you. He seemed wrapped up in the dog. Maybe a new dog would be the answer. Of course there is no answer; there's just a kind of maneuvering around the central fact."

"It's you I'm interested in, not Morris."

"I hide in my work," he says bluntly. "That's what I do. And I inform myself of the events in progress without drawing Dotty's attention. She has no idea that I know. I know everything. I know a good deal more than she does, in fact. That's been rewarding, though it's an unpleasant reward, like chewing on an old chicken drumstick, all gristle and stringy dark meat."

"It sounds dreadful."

"Dreadful for me would be to do nothing."

"Have you ever considered interfering?"

"Interfering? You mean preventing her from feeling drawn to the fellow?"

"From seeing him."

"Ah, what good would that do but fan the flames? It's all very Bovaryesque. You've recently read that bodice ripper, Jane."

"Bodice ripper!" she laughs.

"There's nothing like guilt and interfering husbands to make one all the more fond of one's paramour. And besides," he says soberly, "I'm not in favor of eradicating love. Who says it can't occur outside the nuptial bed and bonds? It's bound to, you know. And the strength of a marriage, the shape of a marriage, especially a childless one, is determined by how these affairs of the heart are managed."

"But you're each managing alone, without the benefit of the other."

He returns to the table and sits down but finds he cannot stay still. "I'm waiting for her to come to me."

"And she's waiting for you to come to her! And meanwhile things are alluded to, yet not spoken of."

"Now look here, young lady. It's not as simple as all that. I don't see you running off to Morris and confessing you've fallen in love with a handsome young ranger. Or have I missed it? Is that why he's retreated to the hotel? Or is it just a feeling he has? A feeling of not being altogether welcome in your heart at the moment? If I were you, and I lived as you do in a glass house, I would put down my stone, Jane Merkle." He springs to his feet.

"Where are you going?"

"I'm going to get the nets ready."

Jane faces him with a look of excitement. "He isn't the only one, that man in the mule barn."

"What man in the mule barn?"

"Deo. She has another lover, doesn't she? In California."

Oliver frowns. "Amadeo has a wife in Italy to whom he is faithful, as far as I know. Dotty's business with him has never been romantic. He's her eyes and ears, her informant. He keeps her apprised of the situation as it unfolds."

"Situation? What situation?"

"The comings and goings, lies and evasions of the man who tried and failed to kill Lowell Dunhill, her lover."

"Who?" cries Jane. "Who is it, Oliver?"

He answers soberly, "Emery Kolb."

Carnal Business

Elzada Clover's Italian is rusty. A year ago she traveled in Tuscany, studying truffles, which left her with a good command of Italian fungal names and not much else. And before that, at the University of Michigan, she completed a Beginning Italian course designed for the traveler who desires to know where the bathroom is and whether the gnocchi are fresh, the wine local, and what time the bus leaves. This has given her just enough courage to approach Amadeo in his native tongue, which she feels is imperative.

She learned many things in her travels: how to drink strong coffee standing up, how to insult an Italian man by insulting his mother, and how to grease the palm with a few soldi. (She has a five-dollar bill in her pocket for just this purpose.) But most important, she learned that in *la bella lingua* secrets seem juicier, exaggerations ooze effortlessly from the mouth, and confidences are comfortably betrayed. Unlike English, which is spoken from the head by a well-groomed jury and judge, Italian roams here and there across the countryside, drinking and carousing. It's a carnal language, and her business is more or less carnal. The subject of her investigation died an unwanted death, and she has her suspicions as to the reason for that death. That *murder*, she reminds herself as she approaches the cowboy dorm.

The building itself has seen better days. It slumps on its stone foundation like a greenhorn in a saddle. The door is open but she hesitates, then enters the cool darkness within. Several narrow bunks line the walls, and to her surprise, as her eyes adjust, she sees that each bed is neatly made. Shirts, trousers, and jackets are hung up on pegs. Boots and shoes are lined up against the wall. There's a washstand in the corner. A dull mirror above it reflects the meager light of two small windows. This is quite unlike her picture of a tribe of men living together. She had expected an untidy cave.

"You do not knock?" asks a voice behind her.

She gives a yelp of surprise and whirls around, and there in the doorway is the man she has come to see. He's short and muscular in a stringy, catlike way. He wears a bandana around his neck. A greasy hat shades his face from the late-afternoon sun.

"I wait for you to come sooner," he says. He laughs sharply, and suddenly she's nervous. She thinks of the ease with which he tosses hay bales or carries two saddles at once or picks up a mule, for all she knows, and she wonders if it was a good idea to come alone. She searches for the Italian word for "afternoon" and scolds herself for not preparing her introduction ahead of time. *Buona sera*, she says to herself. "Good evening." That will have to do. But before she can speak, he pushes past her, his arm roughly brushing hers. He drops his hat on the nearest bunk and sits down heavily, though he is not a heavy man. Grunting, he removes one boot, then the other, then his socks, which are frightfully smelly. To her surprise he lies back on the bed and closes his eyes.

Her courage comes to her and she says, "Mi ricordi, signor?"

He opens one eye. "It's a long time we do not speak, but I don't forget you. You got some Italian now. Is nice."

Perhaps he really does intend to sleep. "Amadeo," she says urgently, "I need to talk to you before the others—"

"Calmati, signora." He waves his hand. "The others they no come. Two kids. Indians. They both name Butch. Good packers. And the other one. Junior. And now we got this Hugh. He got a woman somewhere. Lots of woman. He only come here to shave his face and shine his boots, that's it. I'm the papa, the *nonno*. I get 'em up in the morning and clean up the place when they go. They nice boys. But young. I gotta rest now. Now I lie on my bed and we talk. You like some whiskey?"

He rolls to his side and pulls a bottle from under his bunk. The effort seems to exhaust him, and she realizes he's an old man. He was old when she met him thirteen years ago. The light from the doorway illuminates his face, brown and weathered. He's tired and would like his whiskey, and drink is the great lubricator. It greases the wheels of impropriety and releases swarms of secrets. Soon enough he'll lapse into Italian like a horse given his head. His tongue will loosen and he'll run, as wild as any youth, and he won't stop until it's over. This is the race she came for, the sprint to the finish she hoped to inspire. All she has to do is keep up with him.

He waves the bottle in her direction, and she considers the custom of drinking with one's enemy. Is he her enemy? She thinks not, but one can never be sure. Stay alert, Elzada! she warns herself. A touch of whiskey, but only a touch. And only if he produces a glass.

A Serviceable Quilt

Oliver Hedquist answers the door, looking pale and older than Elzada remembers him to be. "Come in, come in," he says hurriedly. She crosses the threshold and he offers his hand, as if to pull her into a boat from a swim in a dangerous river. A handshake, she realizes too late, for by then he's turned and started his long walk to the kitchen.

"I'll make you some tea," he says, though he makes no move toward the kettle.

"Tea would be lovely, Mr. Hedquist." He stares at her blankly and she adds, "Why don't *I* make us some?"

"I've never cared for tea."

"Ah. I'll make it for myself then." She fills the kettle and sets it to boil, while he walks around the kitchen with small hurried steps. She's met him only once, at dinner at the Schellbachs', but tonight he looks like an entirely different man. His face that night was hopeful. His bones were well defined. Now there's a droop, a sag to his features. His mouth is somewhat collapsed.

"You've heard the rumors," he says.

"Many rumors, Mr. Hedquist. Was there a particular—"

"Oliver," he says sharply.

"Of course. Oliver." She hesitates. "Tell me something. What does this skeleton have to do with you?"

He draws a breath and turns to face her. "I'm in an awkward position. I've never told anyone, and I've struggled with whether or not to tell you."

"You needn't say a word, but my understanding is that's why you've asked me to come."

He drops his gaze. "There was a fellow by the name of Lowell Dunhill. A ranger here. He worked in the backcountry most of the time. I didn't know him well, but he was well thought of, especially after his death, thirteen years ago. His body washed up at Phantom Ranch and was found by a gentleman named Amadeo, who was and still is a wrangler here. He came across Dunhill and brought him out, and I happened to be there, and for reasons I don't need to go into, Louie Schellbach wanted the body at his house. While we were managing that, Louie alluded to the fact that the poor man had died of love."

"And exactly how did this person do that, according to Mr. Schellbach?"

"By throwing himself off a cliff, into the river. But for me the point was not the method of suicide, but the cause of it. For some time I had felt something from my wife, Dotty—a coolness toward me, a change of heart, but I hadn't gotten as far as putting a name or face to it. And still it took a while to put two and two together. She withdrew after his death. Her body seemed to shrink. Finally I understood she had lost her lover. And partly because he was no longer there to challenge me, I felt tender toward her, and she seemed to respond to this and came back to me. Briefly," he adds. "The kettle, Dr. Clover."

"Please," she says. "Call me Elzada." She moves to the stove and prepares her tea.

"During this time," he continues, "a strange thing happened. After it arrived in Schellbach's house, Dunhill's body was stolen and never seen again. A few months after that I noticed a change in Dotty. All of a sudden she perked up. She got over her tears. I was happy for her, of course, until I began to feel the old familiar distance, a wandering of her attentions. I tried to think nothing of it, but when it didn't go away, I became curious as to who had captured her imagination this time. I poked around and found myself quite suited to detective work. It satisfies my inquiring mind, and apparently I give off an air of being perpetually muddled, so no one guessed I was closely following my wife's affairs. There was the telephone, of course, which brought its own piece to the table. Mr. Dunhill called our house infrequently but called just the same. A bold move, I'd say. I certainly felt I had every right to listen in."

"I've been told you hate the telephone."

"Now you understand why." He moves to the sink and fills a glass with water. "It pained me, of course, that it was my wife, but a scientist learns to distance himself from the project at hand in order not to influence the data. I'll admit I was cold. I was terribly calm and cold. Quite serendipitously I enlisted the help of the little wrangler, Amadeo, and quickly learned that he was acting not only as my informant but Dotty's. She wanted him to keep an eye on Emery Kolb."

"For what reason?"

"I'll get to that. Meanwhile the situation worked well for me but poorly for Dotty, because of course she never suspected my suspicion, and Deo, for his part, encouraged by a small sum of money, never revealed it. Soon enough he told me the following story: Dunhill, or the man we called Dunhill, didn't die of drowning but of a bullet to the back of the head."

"I see," says Elzada, bringing her tea to the kitchen table. "Yet he came back to life."

"My dear wife was led to believe that Emery Kolb attempted to kill Lowell Dunhill but botched the job."

"But how could that be? It sounds like a third-rate mystery novel!"

Oliver ignores this. "At first she believed Mr. Dunhill dead, as we all did. Her grief was not fabricated. If it had been, I would have known it in a minute. She's a poor liar, and I'm not ashamed to say I take comfort in that." He looks away, out the window. "I think it was two or three months after the death that she received her first telephone call from Mr. Dunhill. It must have shocked her. Keep in mind, she never saw the body nor knew of the striking resemblance, so at least she wasn't puzzled by that, as I am. Anyway, the reason he gave for his continued stay on earth was this. He told her he and Emery Kolb came to blows over a camera. Then Kolb sent someone to kill him, but they got the wrong man, and he, Mr. Dunhill, thought it best to flee for his life before Kolb became aware of the mix-up and came after him again. Why Emery would trouble himself to murder Lowell Dunhill is beyond me, but Dotty wasn't of a mind to question. He'd returned from the dead, and that was undoubtedly foremost in her thoughts. But she took it upon herself to keep an eye on Emery after that, through the eyes and ears of Deo. It was important to her for Mr. Dunhill's sake but also for her own. Naturally, she didn't want her liaison with Dunhill to be known, but especially as it would expose him to Kolb, and her to Kolb, and me to Kolb as well. She became wilier, more intentional, more aware of the perils of setting out in a whaleboat across open waters."

"Whaleboat?" asks Elzada. "I wasn't aware there was a whaleboat involved."

"Never mind," says Oliver. "The point is, she tried to protect me."

"From a danger that didn't exist."

"What do you mean?"

Her tea is cool enough to drink. She sips it twice. "I suspect you've asked me here because you have your doubts, Oliver. We detectives depend on doubts, don't we? On intuitions. The stories told to us always hold an element of truth, but we sense the flaws and our curiosity compels us to deepen our search. You're not sure why an argument over a camera would lead one man to murder another, and you're right to question it. It's a flimsy motive. A fabricated one, by the way. It was fiction, and the author of this fiction, your wife's . . . paramour, was well acquainted with her gullibility. He counted on it." She looks down into her cup. "There's a great deal I could tell you. I don't know what you'd like to hear. Perhaps you're curious as to why the body you saw bore such a striking resemblance to Dunhill, if it wasn't Dunhill. The story is long. Another night, when it's not so late and we have time to—"

"No," he says firmly. "Dotty comes home in the morning."

"And you'd like to tell her?"

"She'd like to hear it from me."

"Well, then," says Elzada, "where shall we begin? Why not with our friend the wrangler? It was July, 1938, and I was staying at the El Tovar Hotel, where the Nevills expedition had come to rest for a few days. The attraction of clean sheets and hot water should not be underestimated after a month on the river and a long climb out of the canyon on the back of an ornery mule. We had heard of Mr. Dunhill's misfortune but were eager to get back to our field work and the outdoor life. That night, for reasons I will never understand, Amadeo took me into his confidence. He showed me the bullet hole you describe, and when we returned to the river the next day, I gave this information to Lois Jotter—Mrs. Cutter—and Emery Kolb, who joined our party. For me, until recently, that was the end of it. There was nothing I could or cared to do, and my life was quickly absorbed with collecting and teaching. But up on the rim, quite a drama was unfolding. The body was removed, as you mentioned. But before that, our wrangler, being an Italian, sensed the possibility of foul play—there was already the fact that a murder had been committed, rather than a suicide—and he made it his job to guard the body. I have it from him that he was there outside Schellbach's house that night when a man arrived on foot, dressed in dark clothes, with a hat shadowing his face, and entered Louie's study by means of the side door, which was inexplicably unlocked."

"My dear woman," says Oliver, coming to sit at the table, "there's no such thing as a lock here in the village. Except at Babbitt's, where they're only locking in the thieves."

"Yes, well the man entered. There are some gaps in Deo's narrative here, which indicate to me that he fell asleep."

"Asleep! At a time like that?"

"A whiskey sleep. And when he came to, a woman was making her way toward the same door. She hadn't attempted to disguise herself, a fact that clears her of premeditation, and it was easy enough to see it was the postmistress, Edith Chase."

"Oh?" says Oliver. "She's always struck me as being on the shifty side. I'm not surprised."

"Perhaps you aren't, but he was, and he crept up to the door. Inside, there was an angry exchange going on between the fellow and Miss Chase, who apparently came to see the body. The whole business was hushed up on the one hand, but rumors were flying on the other—just the kind of thing she enjoys. She arrived quite by accident at the right place at the wrong time, and her curiosity might have been the end of her if she hadn't done some fast talking. They struck an agreement, she and the fellow. She would help him remove the body and keep his secret—"

"What secret?"

"Patience. You'll see. If he would allow her to hide it in Emery Kolb's garage. She never liked Emery, for some reason. I suppose as a woman one couldn't like Emery and Ellsworth both. And Deo, who has a feeling for these things, assured me that as much as Miss Chase disliked Mr. Kolb, she was forever sweet on the fellow with whom she bargained. The intruder. Mr. Dunhill."

Oliver looks at her blankly. "I'm confused."

She moves to the window and looks out. At the edge of the garden a small green pumpkin shines. She turns to him and says, "The man you saw, the face of the dead fellow brought up from the river, that wasn't Lowell Dunhill, as you've guessed, though it looked exactly like him. It was his brother, Owen. His twin, though no one here knew he had a twin. I suspect even your wife doesn't know. Nor does she know that Owen is dead and Lowell killed him."

"Killed him!" cries Oliver. "What do you mean?"

"Killed him. Right here in Grand Canyon. Out in the back-country. Shot him with his Park Service pistol and disposed of the body in the river—hopefully never to be seen again. Though he knew, as any ranger knows, that as often as drowned men disappear, they just as regularly surface and take up shop in an eddy, or wash ashore. He couldn't neglect that possibility, and it occurred to him if that were the case, he would exchange places with the dead man. He would let you think he killed himself, a suicide."

"He warned Schellbach of such a possibility."

"He would leave Grand Canyon—he intended to anyway."

"I think it was Dotty who held him in place."

"For a time, yes. But someday he knew he would tiptoe away, as it were, and go to his brother's wife. It was she over whom they quarreled—fatally, for Owen. But that's another story altogether. I don't think he intended to kill his twin. I don't believe he was a bad man, Oliver. *Is.* Is a bad man. His brother, on the other hand, was contemptible."

"Lowell Dunhill a murderer!" cries Oliver in anguish. "I would never have let Dotty go to him!"

"I think he was caught by surprise, and certainly something terrible was said between the brothers. We'll never know. But it was not the first time. They had a history of disagreements. I imagine Lowell invited him here to smooth out their differences, which seemed to him possible in the outdoors."

Oliver sits quietly for a moment. He flattens his hands on the table and strokes the red and white checkered cloth. When he concentrates, his features become softer, as if trying to enfold this new idea, this new information. The news might harden him, but it hasn't yet. He seems puzzled, yet not surprised. He looks up. "How do you know all this?"

"Do you sew, Oliver?"

"Sew?"

She sits down and crosses her arms on the table. "Knowing is like sewing. Like sewing a quilt. Many people know a small part of the story I've told you, but I've been the one to sew it all together. It lay in pieces—one from Gavia Immer, one from Amadeo, and several, especially concerning the brother's wife, from Ethyl Schellbach, the Canyon Songbird." She laughs.

"The sweet voice hides a hungry ear—and, to be fair, a generous heart. Lowell confided in her as everyone does. I've been busy sewing. Not an elegant tapestry but a serviceable quilt."

She stands up suddenly, and Oliver asks, "Where are you going?"

"Home to bed, Mr. Hedquist. You may be in the bloom of youth, but I am not."

"But the rest of the story!"

"The rest of the story," she repeats. "What more is there?"

"Why did Mr. Dunhill come back to remove his brother's body?"

"Ah, of course. He realized that despite the poor condition of the flesh, after its journey through some frightful rapids, the bullet hole might be discovered, and he didn't want that. Making the body disappear, once it was acknowledged to be his, seemed the best solution. And unbeknownst to anyone until just the other day, Owen Dunhill was in possession of one remarkable feature that distinguished him from his twin brother—that is, a withered arm. Originally Dunhill must have thought that if the body surfaced, it would be in significant disarray and the arm might go unnoticed. On seeing the body that night, he changed his mind."

"So the brother went to Mr. Kolb's garage?"

"Where he lies still."

"The postmistress certainly had her fun."

"Her revenge," says Elzada.

"Love is the cause of so many misfortunes."

"Do you really think so?"

"Don't you?"

"I think we often blame things on love, when in fact the source of our spite and unhappiness lies elsewhere. Love is not something we understand. Science can't quantify it, and therefore it remains a mystery. We can shape it any way we wish. We give it life and definition as it suits us, and who's to contradict our version of a story that's essentially unknowable?"

"I've come to know it," says Oliver quietly. "A small parcel of it."

Elzada nods. "Yes, I believe you have."

Off Broadway

Dotty has tried not to think about the unpleasant events of the past week, though her mind wanders to her suitcase every now and then. She imagines the Aztec lugging it from the porch to the street, where it awaits the garbage truck. She sees Lowell watching silently from the front window, making no move to stem his wife's anger or salvage his mistress's belongings.

Meanwhile she is content to carry her life in a single shopping bag. It is freedom indeed. She thinks of Jane arriving from St. Louis, on this same train perhaps, though headed west not east, arriving with only the clothes on her back. She remembers the fun they had shopping, their moments of closeness while fitting her sister-in-law for a brand-new life. It makes her smile. Of course she herself doesn't need a brand-new life. She has Oliver, her old friend Oliver, and much of the time that's enough.

She gazes out the window of the train, savoring the journey

before her. She feels damp, slightly rotten, from her week of sightseeing along California's coastal highway. She has seen enough sea otters to satisfy her for the rest of her life. And redwoods—frightening edifices hardly in the category of tree. And Hearst's castle, and beaches with pounding surf, the ocean gray and cold, or blue and cold, and a fascinating park north of San Francisco where white deer sniffed the bumper of her rent-a-car while she was sleeping in it, for heaven's sake! It was her chance to ramble and roam, and she took it. Not in the way she imagined, with Lowell by her side. But it did not occur to her to feel sorry for herself. She was shocked and surprised and would soon feel unpleasant things, but in the time before the unpleasant things, she wanted only to feel free. And alive. She had given her heart to a dead man. She understood that now, and she intended to take it back. A man who hid his life was as good as dead, and all the blood and flesh and excuses in the world didn't make him alive again.

She can feel the hot breath of the desert coming closer, the cool wet tongue of the coast receding as the evening settles to the ground like a soft gray dew. She has no seatmate and stretches sideways. She pries off her shoes and drops them with a satisfying *clump clump* to the floor. In the morning she will see Oliver. They'll have breakfast at the Howard Johnson's, visit the hardware store, do their food shopping, and go home. Life will be ordinary again. She'll tell him about the sea otters lolling on their backs like human babies, and the young men riding the waves on boards the size of kitchen counters, and the wine served with every meal, and the abundance of green vegetables, and the large beetles attracted to her headlights at night. And perhaps someday, though she can't imagine it, she'll tell him the other story, for it occurs to her that until she does, she's a woman who is hiding her life, a woman as good as dead to him.

She rests her head against the window and decides not to think. She's gone through all her magazines, and it's too early to sleep, and the movement of the train is jarring. She feels like an infant in a cradle rocked by an angry nurse. She never had a nurse or a cradle. She slept in a dresser drawer. Her clothes were hand-me-downs and her dolls were made of sticks and rags, and her ambition was to sing and dance on Broadway, in New York City, where people dressed up just to go out and buy a bottle of milk. But instead she married Oliver. All these years it was Oliver who kept her from the stage. Oliver, with his plodding good nature, his scatterbrained charm, his need to be fed and tidied up after—he's the reason she wakes up in the morning and slops around in her housecoat and slippers and heads off to town with hardly a thought to her appearance. No makeup, no hairdo, no fashionable clothes. Why, it's terrible the way she's let herself go! Surely, in New York City she would make the effort. She might even have a little dog with a diamond-studded leash and its own outfits. She would carry it in her arms to the beauty parlor and dry cleaners, and she would wear stockings every day and felt hats with feathers and perhaps a boa. She would have men. Men would fall in love with her and woo her with flowers and chocolates and expensive meals in first-class restaurants. She would take taxis everywhere and learn how to tip, and her talent would be recognized and sought after, and she would refuse to appear anywhere without her male bodyguard, who was also her chauffeur and houseboy, and in the evening he cleaned the pool. But are there pools in New York City? Maybe she would move to Los Angeles. Yes, thinks Dotty, Hollywood. Beverly Hills. A large mansion with a gardener and servants, and perhaps Oliver might come on the weekends and drive her around in a convertible that would muss up her hair. But she wouldn't care. They'd laugh and travel north along the coastal highway and take in the beauty of the cliffs and the sea. They'd eat in an attractive inn on the water and watch the sunset and order coffee, then retire to their room and act young again, act young all night, and watch the sunrise and eat breakfast in bed: coffee and rolls and bacon. She looks at her watch. In a short while he will meet her at the station in Flagstaff. He will welcome her home. He will ask where she would like to have breakfast and she will say, "Oh, I can't think of any place I'd rather eat than Howard Johnson's." And because he has so hoped for this his face will light up, his old familiar face, and she will see his dearness and breathe the air and take in the early light on the mountain and know why she never had a life on Broadway. Why she's here with him instead, about to have a cup of bitter coffee and a plate of overcooked eggs and undercooked bacon, and why it makes no difference in the world what a person eats for breakfast as long as they're comfortable sitting in a booth with the one they've sworn themselves to. Not by the gold band on the fourth finger, but sworn through years of waking up and going to sleep, like two old dogs on the porch. It would not be right for one to wander off alone and never come back.

Don Juan's Hat

The two ladies have a train to catch, and the chief park naturalist wishes to leave time for questions. His questions. In an unofficial capacity, of course. So he arrives early and sends word upstairs with the bellhop and waits outside the hotel in the car.

Several minutes pass. Finally the bellhop returns. He's a new boy, obviously, and Louis Schellbach can't for the life of him understand why a respectable establishment like El Tovar puts its greenest employee at the gateway to its legendary hospitality. The young fellow sports wispy tufts of blond hair on cheeks and chin—he's obviously not acquainted with a razor—and a bright dot of ketchup adorns his upper lip. He leans against the car, one arm draped across the roof, and ducks his head into the window on the driver's side. His nose practically brushes Schellbach's eyelid. "They're doin' their hair," he says, grinning, and withdraws his person.

The message itself is almost as disturbing as the messenger, for time is running out and with it the opportunity for clearing up some of the finer points of what's come to be called the Dunhill Investigation. Too many Dunhills, as it turns out. The misses Clover and Jotter—or Cutter, or whoever she is—certainly got to the bottom of that. But as to this business of the dead man's wife, and her connection to that nebulous entity called the Skłodowska Institute, the investigation seems to have fallen short. And though it occupies only a distant corner of Shellbach's mind, which is occupied with so many other things, his wife Ethyl is consumed by it. Lowell Dunhill was sincere in his concern for his sister-in-law, according to Ethyl, but to what danger was she exposed? Schellbach believes it may all be simpler than anyone suspects. It wouldn't be the first time a man has fallen in love with his brother's wife and pushed his sibling over the edge to make room for his own desires.

He pulls the car ahead into a parking place and reaches for his hat, which rides beside him on the passenger seat. He places it on his head at a jaunty angle, adjusting it in the rearview mirror. The Bogart of Grand Canyon, he smiles to himself—a far cry from old Don Juan Schellbach, but a happier and more honest man. He extricates himself from the car and walks the few steps to the edge of Grand Canyon, where he stands looking down into the visible heat, marveling at the miracle of summer. An afternoon storm is building to the north, fat gray clouds moving like buxom queens. He loves this country, its seasons and weathers, its rituals of wind, fire, and rain. Out in it he can forget the tangles of paperwork and park administration that more and more define his job and cause in him thoughts of retirement, of days spent fishing for bluegills in White Mountain lakes. Recently he has been plagued by his old bedfellow, insomnia. He wakes in the night, his thoughts churning, and slips from the bed without disturbing Ethyl. He tiptoes to his study and sits facing the window, facing the darkness beyond which lies, or seems to lie, his own death. The death of many things. The death of gentlemen, of that he is certain. The death of Renaissance men and scientists at the helm of the national parks. The death of free nature as the world becomes more anaesthetized and sanitized, everything rule bound, the old dirt roads succumbing to pavement, deer and elk preyed upon by sightseers too out of breath to leave their cars. He imagines it in twenty years, a Grand Canyon National Park of traffic jams and roadside hot dogs, the occasional visitor tottering to the edge to gasp at nature's wonder. In thirty years perhaps there will be no need to come to the edge at all. Instead, a cushioned seat in a theater with a large screen, where the canyon stars in her own movie. The word *technology* comes to him, like a ghost clad in armor. In his lifetime he has seen the motorcar, the airplane, Boulder Dam. He has seen the atom bomb and two world wars. How easily the miracle of technology is tilted, bringing harm. Factories lure outdoor men indoors and promise freedom.

On those sleepless nights he turns from the window, feeling frightened at that look into the future where his two boys must venture beyond his and Ethyl's deaths, and to comfort himself he speaks to his hat, which rests on the desk in front of him. His dear old hat. Hat, he says (a fortune-teller addressing his crystal ball), I defer to you. You live in close proximity to my brain and know it better than I. But it occurs to me we are being left behind, that technology is leading us, that we have begun to lose its company and come instead under its control. Someday, in the lifetime of my boys, it will cease to mean mechanical parts governed by science in service to civilization. Instead, formulas and riddles decipherable to only a few. Where it goes, we'll have to follow, like soldiers in another man's army. It will rule our lives and subject our hearts to a loneliness, an isolation greater than you or I can imagine.

"Mr. Schellbach?" says a voice, startling him out of his reverie. "Excuse me, but the train is here, and Lois and I are ready to say our good-byes."

"Certainly," he replies, though certainty is the last thing he feels. "My car is at your service, Dr. Clover. Why don't we load up and travel the short distance in style?"

There is some confusion as to who will sit where. Dr. Clover finally takes her place beside him. He senses from her a weariness that was not present when he collected her and Mrs. Cutter from the train, and he guesses it is no small feat to leave one's field of expertise and venture through the tangled woods of mystery solving. "You're a clever detective," he addresses her. "I hope we won't be losing you to that nefarious profession."

"Nefarious, Mr. Schellbach? If so, a necessary evil. It certainly leads one into unsavory places. But so does digging in the ground, wouldn't you agree?"

"Especially if you don't like earthworms," adds Mrs. Cutter from the backseat.

"Eventually you'll come upon something that frightens you," continues Dr. Clover. "It may be an earthworm or an amulet. In our case it was fratricide."

"And something else," says Mrs. Cutter, leaning forward. "Tell him, Elzie."

"The Skłodowska Institute. Have you heard of it, Mr. Schellbach?"

"Yes, Ethyl is quite involved in that."

"Not involved," Mrs. Cutter puts in. "Involvement wasn't voluntary. It was the brother, Owen's, brainchild, and he had a very sick brain."

"It turns out that anyone can have an institute," says Dr. Clover. "You just give it a name and there it is. It's handy. It makes it easier to acquire illegal or controlled substances. Owen Dunhill wrote a charter and recorded it with Los Angeles County, and those records are public. If you're willing to live in the library, as Lois was, you can find them."

"The purpose of the institute was research," says Mrs. Cutter, "but Mr. Dunhill never indicated what kind of research he was doing. He couldn't have. He would have been arrested. It was Elzada who read between the lines."

"By reading the lines themselves."

"I don't understand," says Schellbach. His chest feels tight with anticipation.

"Madame Curie has long been a heroine of mine," says Dr. Clover. "I enjoy reading about her and in fact am reading an excellent biography at the moment."

"Dr. Clover, our time is short and I'll have to encourage you to come quickly to the point."

"I do understand, Mr. Schellbach. What I'm getting at is my discovery, in the pages of my book, that Madame Marie Curie was born Maria Skłodowska. The Skłodowska Institute that took her name was an affront to all she stood for as a researcher and human being. Its intent was diabolical, to say the least. Owen Dunhill was a brilliant but warped individual. He was interested, as are many of the agile minds of our time, in the effects of radiation on human beings. He had access to a laboratory, apparently, and experimented on human subjects, most of them from the lower rungs of the social ladder, who responded positively to his promise of food and lodging. One of these subjects eventually became his wife, a kind of slave, I imagine, and soon enough he released the others and worked solely with her. Her grasp of English was poor and her education nonexistent. We can deduce from Lowell's descriptions of her, told in confidence to an individual here at the park, that she suffered from radiation poisoning. She herself had no idea her husband was exposing her to high doses of an experimental substance—"

"But why?"

"As far as we can tell, in order to satisfy his own curiosity. He seemed to have no scientific credentials or to care much for them. If he left a record of his research, the data have never been found. He was a madman, Mr. Schellbach, a most persuasive sociopath. His brother, Lowell, was the only person who tried to stop him—with words for many years, then finally with a bullet. The latter, as you know, accomplished this end."

The chief park naturalist steers the car into the parking area beside the train. His heart is pounding. He has a feeling his wife is the source of much of the information he's just received, though he does not wish to ask. In the early days she and Lowell Dunhill went on long walks together, whenever the ranger wished to unburden his heart. Schellbach always assumed that heart to be full of Dotty Hedquist, but now he's not so sure. Possibly Ethyl tried to tell him what she herself had been told, but he had been busy, always too busy, to listen. He'd preferred the late-night company of his hat, and he'd failed her.

He cannot shake the heavy feeling but dutifully gets out of the car. He opens Mrs. Cutter's door. Dr. Clover has already freed herself. He tries to carry their bags to the train but they'll have none of it. "It's only a few steps!" laughs Mrs. Cutter. She boards with a toss of her head and turns to wave. Dr. Clover stands with him for a moment. He is unsure what is required of him and starts to say something, but she puts a hand on his wrist. "We solved the mystery, Mr. Schellbach, but we may not have warded off the scandal. Who knows? If revenue goes up, those in charge of the coffers may plant a skeleton in someone else's garage. Maybe yours," she says with a smile.

She climbs aboard the train and he watches until the last car rumbles out of sight. She's right, of course. He'll have to be on the lookout for such a thing.

Limax Maximus

Euell packs with great care, as if it were a month of travel and not just a picnic. He tries to imagine what foods she likes. All he can come up with is liverwurst. But does she like liverwurst? He can't remember. His mind travels back to the day they met in Babbitt's, quite by accident. They spoke at some length about liverwurst, but she never revealed her position on it. Suddenly he worries about this. Her guarded nature troubles him. But it attracts him as well. Those glimpses of her bodily hunger. Those are blissful moments for Ranger Wigglesworth. He decides not to risk the liverwurst and instead buys a loaf of sliced white bread, two tomatoes, and a roasted chicken. For dessert, a pound cake and a sack of oranges in case Jane is secretive about eating sweets. He hopes she's not.

What to wear is his next dilemma. He would like to look neat and clean, yet a little wanton. A little chafed and weather beaten. A devil-may-care man at home in the outdoors. He wants, at all costs, to avoid looking official, yet he'd like to exude the confidence and competence he feels when he's in uniform. He settles on a pair of faded dungarees and a rust-colored short-sleeved shirt with black buttons. He's given a good deal of thought to buttons since his last encounter with Jane, and he hopes she's thought along the same lines and reached the same conclusions.

At a quarter to eight in the morning he stands in the shade outside his house, waiting for her. The day is already hot, and the sweat gathers at the small of his back. He finds it hard to stay still and walks around in a circle, kicking at pinecones. He stretches his arms above his head, trying in vain to relieve the pressure in his chest and throat. At eight o'clock he goes inside and sits at the kitchen table and tries to drink a cup of cold coffee left over from breakfast. He checks his pack to make sure he hasn't forgotten anything—knives and forks, a clean sheet that will have to serve as a tablecloth, a pillow for afterward, and the book, of course, Pilsbry's *Land Mollusca of North America*. He hears a car and goes outside again, but it isn't Jane. At eight thirty he realizes she isn't coming.

At first the thought frees him in a sudden, surprising way. What a fool he's been! What was he thinking, asking a married woman to come away with him in her brother-in-law's car, the day after she sent her husband home on the train? He retreats inside and hasn't the heart to unpack the food and put it away. He flops on the bed, feeling agitated and exhausted, and something else he can't quite put a name to. Finally it comes to him: he's lonely. A great cavern has opened up inside him. He

closes his eyes and sees a line of dwarves. He hears them sing-
ing a dreary tune. The beams of their lanterns cut the cavern's
darkness in a sharp, unpleasant way. Finally they stop on a high
ledge and one by one turn to the wall and start swinging their
picks. He feels the blows—stinging bursts of pain, as if he's
drunk too much lemonade, then a dull ache around his heart
as the dwarves resort to sledgehammers, crushing the wall and
rolling the rubble aside. What are they after, for God's sake?
Gems? Crystals? Euell can't imagine. They throw away their
hammers and beat at the rock with their bare hands, their great,
ugly bodies lifting off the ground with the effort. Their leader, a
fellow with long, coarse orange hair and beard, wearing a grimy
tunic, calls out something in dwarf language and one by one
they line up again. One by one, starting at the back of the line
and using their picks as anchors, they throw themselves off
the ledge. Soundlessly. There is no thump as they hit bottom.
Their leader goes last, and he carries his lantern with him as
he falls. Its light grows dimmer and dimmer until finally Euell
can only make out a yellow glow, followed by a faint shattering
sound, then a burst of flame rises from below, and a buffet of
warm air.

He wakes with a start. Jane is covering him with a blanket.
She smiles in a distant, distracted way. He feels strangely calm
and moves his legs to make room for her. She sits down and the
bed creaks noisily, which seems to embarrass her.

"You were shivering and talking in your sleep."

"I'm too hot now."

"I wonder if you have a fever."

He takes her hand and puts it on his forehead. She laughs nervously and closes her eyes. She turns her palm up and presses the back of her hand to his temple. Her knuckles feel cool and hard. "Normal," she tells him, and gets up and moves about the room, resting her hands on the back of the chair, trailing her fingers across the kitchen table, touching each object, each surface in his house, as if she is there to rent or buy. She stands in the doorway, her back to the bed. Her blouse is pale blue. She's wearing a white skirt. "You know, I was here once before. You were away, but Hugh was here." A jolt of jealousy runs through his limbs. Is this what she intends? But she turns and smiles at him. "He isn't very tidy, Hugh."

"No," says Euell. "No, he's a pig. My friend, but a pig."

"I'm sorry for being late. And out of sorts. And . . . nervous. I've been . . . I've so looked forward to our outing. Do you still want to go? If you don't, I can—"

"Of course," says Euell, leaping out of bed. "Of course I do. I'm ready to go. I didn't mean to fall asleep. I had everything packed and I waited outside . . ." He takes a breath. "I guess I just gave up. I had the strangest dream, Jane. About dwarves."

"Dwarves? How horrible."

"A lot of people like dwarves."

"Like them? How could they? They're short and burly and they scowl a lot."

Euell laughs. He scoops up his pack with the picnic things, and without thinking, he takes her arm. He leads her out of the house to the car, Oliver Hedquist's giant Chevrolet, which makes him feel like a dwarf himself. A tiny skull—*Peromyscus eremicus*, a cactus mouse—hangs on a string from the rearview mirror. He opens the door on the passenger side and waits for her to climb in, but she is of another mind. "Oh, I think I'd better drive. It's Oliver's car and . . . I think I'll drive. You can tell me where to go," she adds cheerily, as if he's a little boy in need of entertainment.

To his surprise she starts off in the wrong direction. "It's the other way," he says, as lightly as he can. She nods, but continues on, and he realizes she has her route picked out. She has given some thought to her journey out of town, and her thought is to avoid the village altogether. This chastens young Ranger Wigglesworth. He sits awkwardly, his hands pressed together between his knees, leaning slightly forward as if straining to see the future, if only the future of this day. And there at the other end of the world sits Jane, sharing nothing with him but the wide front seat.

"I'm sorry," he says suddenly.

Jane keeps her gaze straight ahead. Over her left shoulder the canyon falls away. "Whatever for?"

"For me it's just a picnic. I mean it's not *just* a picnic, but it's not much more than a picnic, if you see what I mean."

"Don't be silly."

"*Silly* isn't a word I would ever use to describe myself."

"Well, I'm using it. You're being silly. Ridiculous, in fact."

"Ridiculous! Now where do you get that? I don't think you know me very well, Jane Merkle. I don't think you know me at all. I've been many things in my life, but not ridiculous."

"Add that to the list."

They drive in silence past Grandview Point, then Lipan, past Desert View Watchtower. All the places, the overlooks where Euell imagined he would stop this day with Jane and point out features of the canyon, folds of rock that always, embarrassingly—and thrillingly—reminded him of a woman's body. His tongue sits heavily in his mouth, like a skinned pack rat. He can summon neither words nor thoughts, though his intent, some miles back, was to apologize for not understanding what she risked this day and to thank her for risking it, though *risk* was a more serious word than he wanted. He couldn't find the right word, and now he can't find any words. Oh, miserable, miserable day. He turns to the window but sees only a wall of trees. He wants a spacious view, a view of the canyon, but to see it he'll have to turn his head toward her. And not wanting to turn toward her *is* ridiculous, so he does—and sees she's crying.

He moves close to her, across the seat, which feels like a journey of many miles. He puts his arm around her shoulder, expecting she may frown and shrug him off, which he is prepared for. But instead, to his surprise, she cries harder, making soft, wet hiccuping noises. Her nose runs; tears drip from her chin. Everything about her is transformed from glacial chilliness to summer rain in the desert. "Jane," he says. "Jane, Jane."

"No one's ever called me that," she sobs. "No one, until you."

"But it's your name."

"Not when you're somebody's wife," she sputters. "All those other things—*my dear, my beloved, my darling*—they impersonalize love. They're factory words. Anyone can say *my love*. They can say it to anyone else without even knowing their name. I'm tired of endearments, Euell. I'm Jane. My name is Jane."

He strokes the back of her neck and she shivers. He starts to pull his hand away, but she shakes her head, "I like it." He's afraid her eyes are closing. But suddenly it seems worth any price to have her relax at his touch.

Down off the rim they drive, leaving the pines behind. Ahead of them the long view of Cedar Mountain and the deep canyon of the Little Colorado River. To Euell, in a sort of trance, it's a landscape made of flesh and skin, miles and miles of warm soft skin—Jane's. His hand rests on her bare shoulder, beneath her blouse. He can't imagine ever speaking again, ever moving again. Ambition and worldly accomplishments are the farthest thing from his mind. He turns to her and says, "My father called my mother Mousie. Sometimes he called her Miss Mouse."

At Cameron, Jane asks him to drive. All the way up to Lee's Ferry she sleeps with her head in his lap. He strokes her hair. It's short and shiny brown. He imagines it long, running his hands through it, great, smooth fistfuls of hair. But it's short now, and he can look inside her ear. He's never looked inside a woman's ear. It's dark and tunnelish, and he can imagine the old endearments, like a line of rusty cars, pushing their way in, filling the tight, closed space with noise and smoke. He looks up from her ear as a passing car honks its horn, warning him he's drifting across the road.

He parks beside the river, and the quieting of the engine wakes Jane. "Good afternoon," he says.

She sits up slowly, stretching her arms behind her head. The hem of her blouse trembles, exposing a narrow band of pale skin. She looks around. "Where are we? Oh, Euell, this must be . . . !"

He nods. "El Rio Colorado."

"It's so *red*!"

"That's where it gets its name. Colorado. 'Red' in Spanish."

"It's the color of the canyon."

"It *is* the canyon. A river of liquid rock, too thick to drink, too thin to plow. That's what they say about her."

"Her? Why is it a she?"

"Rivers are."

She shakes her head. "This one's a he."

He feels a maddening shyness creep back into his body. "Are you hungry?"

"Famished."

"I know a place upstream. A flat rock and a place to swim."

"In here, you mean? You swim in the river?"

"There's an eddy."

"Wouldn't you be swept away?"

"It's a place along the shore where the current goes upstream."

"We'd be swept away just the same, only upstream, not down."

"You're right," he says, irritated by her logic. "But it doesn't go upstream forever. It's circular. An eddy circles up and back, so all you have to do is relax and trust it, and it'll bring you home again."

"Right to your door?"

"Something like that."

"Oh," she says brightly, then bites her top lip. "But I didn't bring a suit."

"It doesn't matter," he says quickly, and gets out of the car. "We'll try to have a good time anyway."

She climbs out behind him. "Euell. Don't be angry with me." She catches his arm and looks up at him. Her eyelids are puffy from her nap. Her hair is mashed on one side. He'd like to take hold of her and slip off her clothes and bury his face in her flesh. He takes a deep breath and says, "I like you too much, Jane."

"No," she looks directly at him, her eyes bright and green. "No, you don't. You like me just the right amount, Ranger Wigglesworth. And I like you, too. Now let's go find that rock of yours before I faint from hunger. Give me something to carry. I'm used to carrying things. Oh, look! A cloudless sulphur, I'm sure of it. Oh, how stupid of me! I should have brought a net."

"Looks like you did," says Euell, retrieving a net from the back of the car.

"Oliver," laughs Jane. "It's his doing. He knew my mind was on other things, and yours was too. Do you know, he once said to me . . ." she trails off. "He calls this our adventure."

She runs away after *Phoebis sennae*, and Ranger Wigglesworth shoulders the pack. He likes to watch her with a net. She's quick and athletic and doesn't give up. She has a habit of rushing her swing, but that will come. She misses the sulphur but brings in a many-tailed swallowtail and a pygmy blue, beautiful specimens both. It's past midday and hot as hinges, but the afternoon clouds are forming. They sit on a rock by the river, eating chicken sandwiches with sliced tomatoes and drinking cold water from a canteen.

"Last time I was here I saw *Anax junius*," he says.

"What's that?"

"A green darner."

"Oh." She wrinkles her brow. "An aeshnid, isn't it?"

"That's right. Caught it in my hands."

"You didn't."

"Luck," he admits.

"Pure luck."

"Well, I don't know about that. I've been catching for a good long while."

"Not with your hands. That has to be luck."

"Your luck now," he says, grinning, "to be with a lucky fellow. Come here." He pats the rock beside him.

"I'm too hot," says Jane. "I want to swim, then climb out on this rock and lie down."

"While I read you a story."

"A story! You've thought of everything."

"Oliver thought of the net."

"Oh, pish. You don't need a net anyway. You catch things with your bare hands."

He would like to swim with her but she wants to swim alone. He shows her the eddy and tells her to stay close to the shore, and that's enough. She isn't afraid. She trusts him, she says. She takes off her clothes and slips quickly into the water. A flash of her naked body is all he sees. She circles up and back a few times. It seems to please her, the way the water takes her on a swirling journey, then delivers her to her rock each time. She climbs out and dresses, and then he swims. He doesn't hide his nakedness the way she did, and when he comes out of the river, he leaves his clothes off because he feels comfortable with her, and the feel of the hot air on his skin is delicious, and he wants her to be comfortable with him in this way. He lies flat on his back on the rock and wonders if she'll look at him. He feels her gaze and cracks one eye open and watches her. She takes in his body for a long time.

Finally he sits up. "Is this all right?" She nods, and he says, "This is how I am when I'm alone. But I can cover myself."

"No. I'm . . . " She smiles. "No."

"What I like about this rock is that the shade hits it."

"Just when you think you can't stand another minute of sun."

"I want it to rain today."

"Not on our picnic."

"After our picnic."

"After our picnic," she agrees.

"Would you like to hear a story now?"

"Yes. I've been waiting for the story."

"You haven't been waiting idly, I hope."

"Idly? Heavens no! I've had a great deal to do since you emerged from the river. I've been very busy, Ranger Wigglesworth, don't you worry." She looks at him with an odd smile.

He pulls the Pilsbry from the pack and leans back on his elbows. "This is a love story, Jane."

"A love story? What is that great heavy book?"

"*Land Mollusca of North America*. You haven't read it, I hope." She shakes her head. "Good. This is a story about the mating habits of *Limax maximus*, one of the most impressive Romeos you'll ever find."

"And who is he?"

"A giant slug."

"Ah. Of course."

"Settle in here next to me," says Euell, reaching out to her. "I want you close." He lies back, his head propped on the pack. She lies down beside him and puts her hand on his chest. It feels warm and cool at the same time. "First I'll describe our hero. Yellowish-gray with black spots, about a hundred millimeters long."

"How long is that?"

"The length of a breakfast sausage."

"Goodness. He's a behemoth."

"He's a behemoth all right, but he's not exactly a he. He's more of a we." He feels her hand slide to his belly. "That's part of his irresistible charm."

"Why don't you read it," she says.

"If you're ready." He opens the book and begins: "'When the pursuer overtakes the pursued, each touches with its tentacles the tentacles of the other after the manner of ants. Then begins a circular procession, each with its mouth at the other's tail, and this procession lasts from half an hour to two hours and a half. Careful observation leads me to suppose that during this performance each is eating the external mucus from the other, for a purpose which will presently appear. The circle now grows more contracted, the slugs overlapping and showing evident excitement, the mantles flapping before and behind. Then suddenly the slugs intertwine fiercely and launch themselves into space, heads downwards, but suspended by a thick strand of mucus, for the distance of 15–18 inches. The fall is generally as rapid as if there were no support, but it is gently checked at the finish. On one occasion, however, the fall was very gradual, and during the descent the couple were busily eating more mucus from each other's bodies. The thread appears to come from their mouths, and runs along the center of the footsole of each, joining into a single thread where their tails intertwine. I have seen a couple suspended from a projecting beam in an outhouse, and also from the leaves of a currant bush, and also from the branch of a yew tree, and once from a glass pane of a greenhouse; but a perpendicular wall or tree trunk is the usual situation.'"

"Oh," says Jane. She laughs and turns her face into the side of his body. He feels her lips and hair against his rib cage. Her hand is on his belly. He moves his arm around her back and shoulder, tucking his hand under her blouse. "Shall we take this off?"

"I don't want you to move."

"Does it unbutton?"

She nods, and he reaches his free hand across and starts to unbutton her blouse.

"Who invented buttons?" she says.

"The Chinese."

"It can't be the Chinese."

"Why not? They had all those concubines."

"How do you know so much about Chinese concubines?"

"Doesn't everyone?"

The last button falls away. He peels off the blouse like an offending layer of skin and sees she left off her underwear after swimming. She lies beside him, not helping, not hindering. She's given up in a way, and he reminds himself to be good to her, and slow. He'd like to take her breasts in his hands. They're small and plump. He's never seen them by daylight. But she nestles close against him and he lies back again, his arm supporting her head. He remembers he brought a pillow. Would she like a pillow? It's harder and harder to think. She runs her hand in slow circles around his belly, dipping lower and lower until his groin aches and his penis starts to rise. He reaches for something to cover it with. She gives him her blouse.

"I can't use your shirt, Jane."

"Of course you can. But why do you want to hide it?"

"I'm . . . I don't want to embarrass you."

"I'm not embarrassed," she laughs. "If I were embarrassed, I'd keep my hand to myself. Read me more about *Limax maximus*. That's what I'd like. The story's not over, is it?"

"Far from over."

"You've left us hanging."

He smiles, and she feels him relax, and his own *L. maximus* rises in response to her slow, intentional touch. "'Directly the descent is accomplished, an organ is protruded from the genital orifice of each. This organ, cylindrical at first, quickly assumes a club shape of from 1½–1¾ inches in length, but presently a frilled edge appears along one side as if unrolled, and in a second or two the unrolling is complete.'"

She takes hold of him and he gasps, but reads on. "'The unrolled organs now commence to intertwine, finally closing round each other so as to form a knot of which it is easy to count the whorls. The two upper whorls of the knot thus formed now spread out in the form of a mushroom or umbrella. During 5–10 minutes the slugs hang motionless with the tentacles contracted and flabby, while the two upper outspread whorls keep revolving upon one another; and in this extraordinary manner the mutual act is consummated.'"

"'Consummated,'" whispers Jane. "The author has a gentleman's sensibility."

"He does," Euell manages to say.

"Do you like this?"

"What you're doing there?"

"Yes."

"I've never liked anything so much in my life."

"I don't believe it."

He turns to her. His face is flushed. "I want to make you feel nice, too."

"In a little while."

"I don't know if I can wait."

He's a young man, she remembers. Morris was an old man. *Is.* She doesn't want to think about Morris now, and she puts him out of her mind. Her hand moves on its own, hers and not hers, and very soon there comes the magnificent spasm and a soft throaty cry. Then a prolonged, almost deathly human stillness, which prompts her to raise her head and look out at the only moving thing—the river, pushing its great load of red silt seaward.

Afterword

"'In Xanadu,'" says Morris Merkle to the young springer spaniel at his feet, "'did Kubla Khan a stately pleasure-dome decree, where Alph the sacred river ran, through caverns measureless to man, down to the . . . ,' down to the what? It has to rhyme with *decree. Sea!* That's it." He reaches out and strokes the dog's ear. "It's the predictability, Martine, the order in rhythm and rhyme. That's what we like. Well, like? I don't know. But it's the reason it sits on our brains and pops out at unexpected moments when we're not concerned with Kubla Khan or poetry or anything out of the ordinary. We were thinking about steak, weren't we? And another splash of libation." He gets up and refreshes his glass, then goes to the Frigidaire and removes two identical packages. One for him and one for his pup. He'll grill them outside. It's June and good grilling weather.

There's no art to crumpling newspaper. A tight twist is all it takes. But in Morris's experience, while many are in possession of this information, just as many lack the conviction to follow through. They roll loosely and toss a flaccid ball of dampish newsprint into the barbecue and expect a decent fire to come of it, a conflagration worthy of Joan of Arc. Pah! When a mess of smoke and floating ash is all they get, they blame it on the news itself, not even the paper it's printed on. And certainly terrible things are happening in the world, but the war in Korea hardly has the power to prevent a man from grilling his dinner—*if* the man is willing to twist his paper well. It's a bit like cleaning a gun, thinks Morris, though he has no firsthand experience in such matters, having missed both world wars and never having seen the point of hunting, except to exercise a dog. A clean gun and a well-laid fire can go to work for a man, especially if he's hungry and surrounded by enemies.

It's a warm evening. The air is infused with the smell of honeysuckle, but Morris Merkle, sitting by the barbecue, smells only cooking steak. Martine looks up at him with dewy eyes. She's small, undoubtedly still growing, but she'll end up smaller than her predecessor. She has an easygoing nature, and she's not in love with squirrels or garbage, as Martin was. She seems, instead, in love with her master. And New York sirloin. She likes hers rare. Morris is happy to oblige, but tonight something occurs that leads him to forget the sizzling meat, even when the dog violates etiquette and whines and nudges his hand. Not until she barks, a soft, chesty sound closer to a human cough, does he look up and see the meat aflame.

He rises slowly to his feet. In his hand is a letter from Jane, written and sent a year ago but unopened until this moment. It's a jolly letter, full of gossip and unimportant things, something about the loss and recovery of a purse. The content is unremarkable on every level, but his dear wife's determination to involve him in her daily life from afar touches him deeply and makes him long for her company now. Now, when she is less apt to include him, no longer so willing to share herself with him, though they passed the winter hours with apparent affection and, he would say, a modicum of happiness. But her heart is in Arizona, and for the summer, at least, her fair body has traveled to meet it.

"What was I thinking?" he says to Martine. He removes the charred steaks from the grill and proceeds to cut them in strips. He can think of no motive, no reason for not having opened her letters, and now to find them in a pile of old newspapers— he has only himself to blame. He was cross at her, perhaps. It seems unlikely, even absurd, but maybe it's so.

He must be honest with himself. His mind travels back to his engagement to Eleanor. It was in her untidy cursive on a piece of heavy stationery that he received the blow, the severing of their tie. (He can still feel the weight of the paper in his hand in the last moments of his ignorance.) The memory disturbs him. How is it that a man cannot see his own blindness? Eleanor is not Jane, and Jane is not Eleanor. Eleanor in her letter cut him away, and Jane in hers wished to include him. Yet a man who acts out of blindness draws to himself the very thing that blinded him. In his case, a withdrawing of affection. He knows, of course, Jane has placed her heart elsewhere. Had he read and responded to her letters, might she have placed it all the more with him? He thinks not. He has progressed in his understanding of the female need. His love for his wife is not love for something won or possessed. He is experienced in many ways she is not, and understands her desire for romantic exploration. It saddens him, but makes them more equal.

Whatever it is, or was, he sees no point in prolonging his regret or reinforcing his culpability. He puts the steak knife down, reaches into the basket of newspapers, and pulls out the letters. The dog looks at him in astonishment as one by one he feeds them to the coals and they catch fire.

He fixes himself a plate of eggs and serves the ruined meat to Martine. First he apologizes to her. It's not cooked the way she likes it. But something happened that will never, ever happen again. She needn't worry. It has nothing to do with her. She's still the best dog, the very best. It's human business.

A Note from the Author

This novel arose from a need to express my appreciation for the incredible landscape of Grand Canyon. I found my original inspiration in Mrs. Merkle's name, which I borrowed from a tag affixed to a pin on the underside of a butterfly in the museum at Grand Canyon National Park. Tags of this sort are sources of information. They measure only one centimeter by two-and-a-half, yet there in the lepidopterist's handwriting, a print so small it can only be deciphered with a magnifying lens, we are given genus and species of the specimen, the date and place of its capture, the taxonomist who classified it, and the person who collected it—collection being the term used for capture and death. Thus we can piece together the where and when, and of course the what in the form of the butterfly, and from this a picture grows, a story. Mrs. Merkle, on the seventeenth of July, 1951, brings down a wood nymph or two at Point Sublime on the North Rim of Grand Canyon. E. Wigglesworth captures a red admiral in the same place at the same time. There is no mention of Mr. Merkle, though there's evidence of his collecting the day before at Grand Canyon Village on the South Rim, which to the North Rim is a far distant place. There, in the company of H. C. Bryant, superintendent of Grand Canyon National Park, he chases down a single painted lady while the tireless Bryant captures fifteen field crescents, three sisters, thirty-four painted ladies, and an acmon blue. These are the facts. From here it is no great leap to fiction, and I have leapt.

Fictional too are the motives and meditations of several historical characters who populate this book. Elzada Clover was indeed a botanist, but only in my imagination a gumshoe. Her associate, Lois Jotter Cutter, did not return with her to Grand Canyon to solve a mystery. Louis Schellbach and his family lived for many years at the South Rim where he was Chief Park Naturalist. His boss, H. C. Bryant, was an ardent lepidopterist as well as superintendent of Grand Canyon National Park. Brothers Ellsworth and Emery Kolb photographed the canyon for decades, and the skeleton in Emery's garage, for years the subject of speculation, has recently been identified as that of an unfortunate victim of suicide. Brief mention is made of Norm Nevills, Bill Gibson, Neez Charlie, and Supai Mary, all of whom lived and breathed. Mrs. Merkle is entirely a product of my imagination, though her name is real enough, and her collector's skill and spirit. However modest her contribution to science may have been, she certainly inspired a world of fiction.